Waking Lucy

Waking Lucy

AMERICAN HOMESPUN 1

LORIN GRACE

CURRANT
CREEK PRESS

Cover Design: LJP Creative © 2023, images iStock, Midjourny

Bible quotes from the King James Version

Formatting © 2017 LJP Creative
Edits by Eschler Editing

Published by Currant Creek Press
Utah, United States of America

Waking Lucy © 2016 by Lorin Grace

Fifth printing: October 2023

ISBN: 9780998411002

For Marie Lindsley Rinard—
"that one teacher."
Thank you for the pen.

One

SAMUEL DODGED THE PITCHFORK FULL of falling straw as laughter sounded from the hayloft. Another waterfall of the golden fodder poured down to join the pile on the barn floor, forcing Samuel to leap out of the way to avoid the new deluge. Water sloshed out of the bucket he carried, soaking his left pant leg.

He set down the dripping bucket, wrung off his hands, and peered up into the loft. "Daniel George Wilson!" He threatened his younger brother with a shake of his fist.

More straw spilled from above, hitting Samuel in the face. Sputtering dust, he shook himself off, then stomped his feet and slapped at his clothes until he dislodged most of the stalks. The remaining fragments stuck out at rakish angles from his dark-blond hair, making him appear more scarecrow than scary. His blue eyes narrowed. "So help me, if you drop another piece of straw on my head, you'll find yourself in with Ma, peeling potatoes!"

"Aw, don't be such a grump. I was just trying to have some fun." Daniel's blond head peeked over the edge of the loft, sprinkling more straw on the barn floor. The youngster's grin faded at the scowl on his older brother's face.

"Yeah, Samuel. Don't be such a grump." The twins joined in from the stalls, where they were milking the cows.

"When I was little you were fun. What did they drink in Boston, grumpy tea?" Daniel jumped off the bottom rung of the ladder, giving the straw pile a kick. He took a step back, well out of his older brother's reach. At nine, Daniel wasn't tall enough to see over the high stalls but was wise enough to stay out of reach of any older brother he had teased.

"Yeah, Sam, what's wrong with ya?" Samuel didn't know which one of the twins had asked him the question. To him, John's voice was identical to Joe's, just as Joe's appearance was indistinguishable from John's. The twins left him guessing which brother he addressed more times than Samuel would ever admit. He suspected they knew his dilemma and often exploited it.

The singsong voice of the other twin followed close behind. "Samuel has girl problems. Samuel has girl problems. Poor, poor Samuel." The final words came with a melodramatic tune. Samuel winced, knowing what came next—a Wilson-twin tune, guaranteed to torment.

"Oh, poor Samuel," they sang in unison. "Can't he catch a girl? No, no, oh, so, no. Oh, oh, poor Samuel!" Daniel clapped and danced to the twins' theatrics. "Bring her flowers, bring her sweets, and give a kiss so bold. But poor, poor Samuel, will still be left in the cold!"

Ha. I haven't taken her a thing. And I have yet to kiss her. I doubt you even know how much I wish I could even speak with her. An exasperated sigh escaped Samuel's lips. He hefted the bucket over the stall to fill the trough. Old Brown snorted in response. Rubbing his horse's nose, Samuel muttered about the injustice of having younger brothers. Old Brown nodded, turned to the fresh water, and drank, unaffected by the boys' banter.

"No, no, oh, so, no. Oh, oh, poor Samuel." The false bass on his name pained his ears, even if the tune was catchy. How the two made up these little songs mystified the family. Samuel moaned. He knew the chorus would get stuck in his head and haunt him for weeks. Poor Samuel, indeed!

He made no comment. Anything he said would prolong the teasing, guaranteeing the song would be repeated until everyone in the house was humming the tune.

"Running from the pretty girls' taunts. He can't catch one he wants. No, no, oh, so, no. Oh, oh, poor Samuel!"

The words made him think about Elizabeth Garrett's brazen flirtations. Did that girl not understand the word *no*?

"Moping around the house, he will never get a spouse. No, no, oh, so, no. Oh, oh, poor Samuel!"

With each verse, the singing became more exaggerated. Though he couldn't see them from where he worked, Samuel imagined wild hand gestures and facial expressions being added to the repertoire. They would have a future on the stage. If only they would go. Now.

Samuel found himself longing for the lecture halls of Harvard where he spent the last three years. Even memorizing all 206 bones in the body was less torturous than listening to his brothers.

"No, no, oh, so, no. Oh, oh, poor Samuel. Oh, oh, poor Samuel!" The song ended with a high screech provided by Daniel. Snort, oink, moo, stomp—several of the animals joined in or protested by making as much racket as they could.

"Back to work, boys. Ma won't wait dinner on you." Samuel moved to the next horse stall. "And, John, if any milk is spilled or goes sour with Joe's singing, I won't defend you to Ma."

All three brothers laughed in response, but Samuel heard enough shuffling and bucket clanging to know they'd returned to work.

A muttered "old grump" reached his ears.

He tried to blame his foul mood on the early winter blizzard. Even his cheerful youngest brother, Mark, was snappy from being cooped up in the house.

But Samuel knew his real problem was the girl. The one he wanted to catch. *Oh, poor Samuel.* It was unlikely he would catch her after the letter he'd written indefinitely postponing their wedding.

He'd talked with more than one girl since he'd returned home, but not her. Busybody mothers anxious for their daughters to catch his eye and hopeful maidens had continually buzzed around him, waiting for him to choose a queen bee. They flitted and floated about, saving their honey-coated stings for each other. The brazen ones clung to his arm, eyelashes fluttering. "Oh, I hope my boys grow up as strong and tall as you." Did other men fall for such bold flirtations? He shook his head in disgust, unwilling to admit that their charms had nearly worked.

Samuel dumped a scoop of oats in each of the horses' mangers. Old Brown pressed him for more. "You don't care what I think, Old Brown, just as long as I give you what you want. You should spend some time with Elizabeth. You two have much in common." He patted the horse and added an extra handful of oats to his trough.

Old Brown and Elizabeth did have too much in common—they were both vain, selfish, and conceited. At least Old Brown was honest with his affections.

Elizabeth was more akin to a spider than a bee. Mesmerized by her beauty, Samuel had stepped into her web. A shiver ran up his back. He wouldn't have noticed her if he hadn't been trying to avoid the one girl he always planned on calling his wife.

His plan had been perfect—attend medical school, come home to take over for old Doctor Page, and marry Lucy. He was not executing that plan well. In fact, he'd been dismissed from medical school. He had managed the "come home" part of the plan, albeit it in shame.

He needed a new plan. The plan he'd followed for the past five weeks had turned into a disaster. He heard a squish and sighed. Yes, that plan was a disaster resembling the stinky muck that now encased his boot—the price paid for not paying attention when entering Maple's stall. He scraped the offensive mass off his boot as best he could, then searched for a pitchfork to scrape off the remains. If only the mess he'd made of his life could be fixed so easily. The corners of his mouth twitched up. Two weeks ago he'd metaphorically pitchforked Elizabeth out of his life. It was a start.

John—or maybe Joe?—smirked as Samuel retrieved the pitchfork. Joe whistled the notes to their impromptu ditty, and when Samuel glowered, John's smile widened—or was it Joe who'd smirked?

"Get working," Samuel snapped, though he knew he would regret being harsh.

Maple, heavy with foal, snorted her resentment of his intrusion into her domain, even to clean it. Women. With a single glance they could cut you down to nothing.

He'd deserved the glare he received at church three weeks ago. The censure in Lucy's eyes left no doubt as to how she felt about his playing with the spider and the bees—all because he didn't want to answer the hard question.

"*What happened to becoming a doctor?*" She had asked, those warm-brown eyes boring into him as she'd waited for his answer. He'd promised himself he would recount every last embarrassing detail. Not once in sixteen years had he resisted her requests. She deserved an answer. If not for the blizzard, he would have given her the answer already. Well…he actually could have gone Saturday. The day had started out clear. The Sabbath was not a good excuse to not go. And today? Well, he'd just kept busy.

If he were to repair things properly, he would also need to speak with Lucy's stepfather, James Marden. But he didn't have an answer for James Marden, either. How would he support Lucy? Farming wasn't as bad as he remembered, and he enjoyed woodworking with his father, but neither seemed as important as the work of a doctor. However, he'd proven he was more likely to endanger lives than save them.

James Marden would most likely grant him leave to court Lucy while Samuel found a way to support her. But how would Samuel apologize to her for his foolishness and convince her his pursuit was in earnest?

He rehearsed his apology several times each day, but words failed to express what he felt in his heart.

When he finished with Maple's stall, he patted the horse. The mare inspected him, searching him for a treat. Finding no reward, she tossed her head and turned away. Would Lucy turn away too?

They were supposed to wed in a month. The intentions had been posted. He probably should cancel them with the magistrate as it was unlikely the intentions would be concluded within the prescribed year.

Coming out of his thoughts, he suddenly realized how silent the barn had gone, aside from the usual animal noises. Where were his brothers? Silence and younger brothers was never a good combination.

The straw piles he'd dodged earlier now lined the contented animals' stalls. The milk buckets were cleaned and put away. The loudest sound came from the cows chewing their cud.

Samuel scratched where a bit of straw still clung to and tickled his head.

Had Ma rung the bell for supper? Being late would mean going without until morning, another hazard of four younger brothers. Grabbing the coat he'd shed earlier, he sprinted out of the barn and into—

A snowball.

Or ten.

From all sides.

One hit him in the back of the head and left a freezing trail into his shirt collar. Samuel instantly regretted not putting his coat and scarf on in his hurry to get to supper. Dropping both items where he stood, Samuel scooped up a handful of snow for his counterattack.

A battle cry came from all sides, then laughter filled the air as a second barrage flew toward him. The well-planned three-sided attack blocked his way to the house, and he fell as the icy missiles pelted him one after another.

Before he knew it, one of the twins had jumped on his chest and was filling his face with snow.

Above the din, Ma's dinner bell rang, and the enemy troops fled, leaving the dogs to lick the snow off Samuel's face with their slobbery tongues. He pushed them away and rolled to his feet, dislodging the mountain of snow covering him in the process. Gathering his coat and scarf, he started plotting his revenge as he ran toward supper.

Two

HUMPH! LUCY SIMMS LANDED ON her backside in a snowdrift, her hand having slipped off the rope once more. Blinking, she glanced up at the setting sun and waited for her lungs to refill with air. It wasn't the first time she'd fallen into the snow today. As she rolled out of the drift, one of her gloves shifted, allowing some snow to slip inside. She shook her hand to dislodge the ice crystals before they could melt and slapped the snow off her backside the best she could. Not that it helped. Beneath Papa Marden's greatcoat, the hem of her dress was frozen stiff. Tiny icicles dangled from the strands of brown hair escaping her head scarf. Just a few yards away, the warmth of the kitchen fire called to her.

Determined, she turned her back to the front door. If she stopped to warm up again, she feared she would not be able to force herself to finish all the chores waiting to be done.

Mercifully, the rope that had slipped from her hands remained within reach and now dangled over the porch roof. Running the rope over the roof and hauling up her precious cargo had taken more than two hours. Each time the rope had fallen back to the ground, something inside Lucy had fallen too. All that remained was to tie a knot securing the rope to the porch post.

A sudden gust of wind tossed the snow from the eaves overhead, dusting flakes across her face—a grim reminder of the early winter blizzard. The wind then whipped the snow around the house with an unearthly howling, obscuring even the closest trees and battering the house until its walls quivered. It had ripped branches off the stoutest of trees and then buried them deep under the snow, where they lay in wait to trip her.

It was not the worst blizzard she'd witnessed growing up on the north shore, but it would be the one she would never forget.

Everything was wrong.

Massive blizzards didn't come in November. They waited until December or even February.

What would the rest of winter bring?

Papa Marden would have known if more snow was coming or if it would thaw next week. Lucy longed to hear his voice reassuring her all would be well. He would tell her that tomorrow was in God's hands and not to worry herself. But Papa Marden was in God's hands now.

And all was not well.

Lucy sneezed. *It is just the cold,* she told herself. *I'm not ill.* She ignored the rawness in her throat. *It's just the effects of spending hours out in the bitter cold.*

Grabbing the dangling rope, she wrapped the end of it around the support post and the two ropes already tied there, but her cold fingers were as ineffective as tying the knot with soup ladles. She clapped her hands together to warm them enough to try again, but her fingers slipped, and she had to start again.

Stupid, stupid girl. Her father's voice, now silent these past nine years, filled her mind, chastising her for her foolishness. She should have gone to the Wilson's for help today, but the thought of being around Samuel hurt too much. He would insist on helping her. He always did. But if Elizabeth Garrett found out, Lucy would pay for every moment of his help. This morning, no amount of aid seemed worth Elizabeth's wrath if she thought Lucy were trying to steal Samuel.

In school, Elizabeth had exacted revenge behind the teachers' backs and hid behind her innocent eyes. If Lucy hadn't loved learning so much, the five years of Elizabeth's torture would not have been worth it. Many times she sat down to her lunch only to find her bread devoured by ants or surrounded by a snake in retribution for getting higher marks. All the girls knew better than to tattle for fear of further retribution. In recent years, Lucy heard tales from girls who'd crossed Elizabeth where men were concerned. Her vengeance was worse than what they endured in school. The stories of ruined dresses, tresses, and reputations had Elizabeth's scorn written all over them. Now Elizabeth had set her sights on Samuel, and Lucy stayed far away.

Besides, Samuel didn't want her anymore. The words in his last letter—all thirteen words—still stung. *I'm a failure. I can't support you. Sorry. No winter wedding. Respectfully, Samuel.*

Respectfully? After all the endearments he had written over the last several months, he'd signed his note, "Respectfully"? She'd tied the note up with the rest of his letters and buried them in the bottom of her trunk. One day she would burn them.

She wondered if her pride was worth the difficulties she faced today. Even Elizabeth would understand helping a neighbor in need. Wouldn't she?

Nope. Nor would she understand the hug Lucy would get when Samuel learned of her plight. A hug that would further break Lucy's heart.

A smattering of clouds hovered in the darkening sky. She hoped it wouldn't snow again. More snow meant she would need to wait longer before anyone could come to the farm or she could leave to seek the help she needed. She would go in the morning. By morning she would cry out all her tears and wouldn't be so desperate for comfort. It would be safe to get help then.

She offered up a quick prayer, asking that it not snow again. Would this prayer also remain unanswered? Lucy had prayed for the lives of Ben, Papa, and Mama, for strength, for wisdom, and finally just for help, any help.

But nothing had come.

She continued to pray anyway, as Papa Marden would have done.

On her third attempt, she was finally able to secure the rope to the post. The not-quite-sailor-worthy knot joined the two others there—the one tied by Papa, the other by Mama. She hoped her knot would hold through the night.

The cow's mournful lowing from the barn echoed the sound of Lucy's heart. At least she could fix the cow's complaints with a bit of care.

Trudging across the yard, she thought of all the chores still waiting. The animals would need food and water. At least the milking didn't need to be done as Bessie, large with calf, had dried up weeks ago. And the nanny goat needed milking only in the morning. Had she managed to get this morning's milk into the lean-to, or was it now sitting somewhere spoiling or freezing? She couldn't remember at first, but then it came to her. Sarah, her little sister, had put some on her pease porridge this morning. She must have put it in the lean-to. What else was she forgetting? Her mind felt like it was moving as slowly as an ice-clogged stream.

As Lucy entered the barn and unwound the scarf from her head, great lumps of snow fell onto the floor and her hair stuck to the multicolored wool like strings of molasses to a spoon. Lucy ran her hand over her hair, breaking its magnetic hold on the scarf. She batted several errant strands out of her face and wished she'd taken the time to rebraid her hair this morning. She stifled a yawn.

The hair fell in her face as she picked up a bucket, so she momentarily set it down and pushed her hair back with one hand. Boring brown. Even their plow horse was blessed with prettier hair than she was. Once, Samuel had pulled her hair, asking if it felt sticky, like syrup. Lucy hadn't realized he was teasing, and she'd blistered his ears. No wonder he was kissing Elizabeth now. Better a flirt than a shrew.

Who needs him anyway? He didn't even check on us after the storm. Though he'd checked on them after every storm since the winter she'd turned six. So what if he couldn't afford to marry her? He could still care. Or had that ceased along with his ambition?

"Don't you ever come and check on me again, you worthless ... worthless ..." she said out loud, but she couldn't think of a word to call him. Putting a voice to her thoughts didn't help. She still wanted him here to hold her and let her cry out all the emotions that bubbled inside like a pot of burning stew. Lucy sighed. She was beyond tired and being a silly ninny.

Bart's snort brought Lucy's attention back to what the hungry horse considered weightier matters. She rubbed the ill-tempered animal's nose, then gave him his ration of oats. Barney nickered, asking for his share. She moved to the stall and emptied some oats into his trough, then set the bucket down. The odor of the stall made Lucy gag.

She patted Barney's neck. "Sorry, old boy. I just can't clean it tonight. I promise I will tomorrow." Barney tossed his head.

Lucy was so tired even the thought of lifting a full pitchfork overwhelmed her. Climbing into the hayloft would be inviting another fall, this time without a snowdrift to catch her. The mucking would have to wait.

Hay, oats, and water she could handle. A full night's sleep would give her the strength to complete the barn chores that had been neglected since Papa Marden…Lucy blinked back tears. Tomorrow. She could do the rest tomorrow.

"I know I promised the same last night," she said, even though the animals probably didn't understand. The poor animals. She should have gone for help. Her fear of interacting with Samuel wasn't a reason they should suffer.

She rested her head against the stall, stifled a sob, and grabbed the bucket. A good cry, along with everything else, would save for later. More work awaited her in the house. Sarah would no doubt be straining at the window, watching for her. Her little half-sister had been so good all day. Tomorrow Lucy would need to make some special time for her. Perhaps they could make some gingerbread letters or practice reading from one of the old primers.

Tomorrow would be better. It had to be.

The nanny goat bleated, tired of waiting her turn. Lucy counted herself fortunate the ornery goat had stayed in her stall. There wasn't a jail in the entire country that could hold the animal once she decided to escape.

Nanny's and the bossy cow's stalls were bordering on unhealthy. Lucy's arms shook as she struggled to move some of the larger flops into the corner of the stall with the pitchfork.

Hopefully, Papa Marden was too busy welcoming Mama and the baby to heaven to look down and worry about the barn. She knew he would be disappointed with her care of it, but he would understand. Papa Marden always understood.

The face of Mr. Simms with its usual sneer of contempt filled her mind as vividly as if he still lived. He would have been quick to condemn and punish her for the state of his beautiful barn. She didn't know what he would be doing now, but it wouldn't be welcoming Mama. People speculated that he'd gone to the other place.

Her eyes strayed unbidden to the far corner of the barn and the tack room. Lucy's heart raced, and her breathing became ragged. She closed her eyes and tried to calm herself. She took in a deep breath, then held it and began counting the way Papa Marden had taught her. Gradually the unpleasant thoughts of her natural father began to fade.

Releasing the memories as she exhaled, she added a bucketful of water to the pig trough, then set the bucket down, glad to be finished. Before securing the barn door, she checked to make sure the cats were inside.

Wind-tossed snowflakes danced around the yard. Lucy reached for the rope that usually guided them from the barn to the house in the snow but caught only air, her arm flopping uselessly to her side. She glanced at the roof, where the rope now held its precious cargo secure, and she sighed. There was no other rope. She could see light flickering from the cabin window and used the path she'd forged during the blizzard to guide her tonight, but she'd need a new guide line before the next big storm.

Sarah and supper waited.

Lucy shut the heavy door behind her. The stone fireplace her grandfather had built radiated warmth. Her nose began to thaw before she could take off her scarf. Light reflected off the plastered, painted walls. Stew simmered over the fire, its aroma mingling with the ever-present scent of woodsmoke. The smell alone should have been enough to warm any soul, yet it could not penetrate the cold, empty place inside Lucy.

Sarah jumped up from the braided rug where she was playing with a rag doll. "I waited like a good girl. I didn't leave the rug. Even to use the necessary. And I need to!" The five-year-old hopped from one foot to the other, her chestnut curls bouncing beneath her cap.

Lucy managed a weak smile. "I am sorry I took so long. Let me move the stew, and we can run out together. Grab your cloak."

A quick check reassured her supper had not burned despite her taking longer than she had anticipated. Using her still-mittened hand, she removed the pot from the crane and set it on the hearth to cool.

"Ready." Sarah stood by the lean-to door, continuing her impatient dance under her brown, patched cloak.

Sarah dragged Lucy down the well-worn path to the privy. The waist-high stone garden wall made a guide rope unnecessary.

When they got there, Lucy lifted the lantern high and searched for fresh animal tracks. Finding none, she opened the door, and Sarah rushed in.

They returned to the house at a more leisurely pace, Sarah stopping to make mitten prints and doodles in the snow on the top of the wall. Pausing, she squinted at the roof.

"Is heaven on our roof, Lucy?"

"No, sweetheart. Heaven is way up with the stars, past the clouds." Lucy swung her arm wide to include the expanse of the darkening sky.

"But you said this morning that Mama went to heaven." Sarah pointed to the three quilt-covered bundles on the main cabin roof. "If she is in heaven, why did you put her on top of the house with Papa and Ben?"

"Oh, Sarah." Lucy knelt down on the snowy path and set the lantern at her side. She turned Sarah to face her, pulling the little mittened hands into her own. "They are all in heaven. Those are just their bodies. I put Mama's body up there to keep it safe from the animals, just like we did with Papa's and Ben's. Just until we can get help digging graves." *If the ground doesn't freeze through first.*

"Remember, we talked about Ben's and Papa's spirits going to heaven even though their bodies stay here?"

"Like Jane?" Sarah tilted her head.

"Yes, Sarah, like Jane." Lucy thought of their two-year-old sister, buried last spring on the hill behind the house near her grandparents.

"Can I take Mama flowers like I do Jane?"

"Yes, sweetheart, as soon as there are flowers." Blinking back tears, Lucy drew Sarah in for a quick hug.

"Good!" Sarah pulled away. "I will take the yellow ones to Mama and the pink ones to Jane." She paused, her brow furrowed. "What about Papa and Ben? They don't like flowers."

Lucy struggled to grasp where Sarah's five-year-old mind had wandered. "I am sure they will like flowers if you bring them."

"No, Ben won't!" Sarah's foot stomped a hole in the snow, then her face brightened. "I will bring him pinecones. He likes those, but not to throw at me." Sarah waved her finger, scolding her absent brother. "Maybe Papa would like a rock. Like the ones he always puts in piles. He likes collecting rocks." Sarah spun around and danced down the path.

Lucy raised her eyes heavenward. Papa Marden made rock piles by the fields, but not because he loved the rocks. He hated them. The confounded things were always jumping up to bend his plow, he claimed. Papa Marden would have laughed to hear his rock pile called a prize collection. For a second, Lucy thought she could hear his deep chuckle, the sound warming her more than the fire had.

A wind gust swept the snow off the rock wall—a warning that their conversation would be better finished inside. Collecting the lantern, they hurried back into the warmth of the house.

"Will Mama stay on the roof all winter?" Sarah wiggled out of her cloak and mittens.

"I am not sure." Lucy tried to extract her long braid from her greatcoat. "When this clears and we go to town, maybe we can hire someone to dig the graves. Or maybe get some of the Wilson boys to come." The hair was tangled around a button. She added rebraiding her hair before bedtime to her growing list of must-dos.

"Oh, like maybe Samuel." Sarah batted her eyes. "You'd love for Samuel to come. Oh, Samuel, help me. You are so strong." She teased in a high, false voice. "That is what Elizabeth told him."

Trying to ignore her sister's words, Lucy yanked hard on her hair, ripping the braid loose from the coat. Several long brown strands remained caught on the button. "Ouch!"

"Lucy loves Samuel. Lucy loves Samuel," Sarah sang as she skipped around the table. Lucy regretted every word she'd ever said to her mother with her sister nearby.

"But Samuel Wilson doesn't love me or even know I am alive anymore," Lucy muttered under her breath as she rubbed the tender spot on her head. If only she could rub her heart—maybe the ache of that statement would lessen as well.

With a sigh, Lucy watched Sarah continue her dance. Stopping the dance would add fuel to the teasing or end in pouting.

A sharp cough, strong enough to double her over and force her to catch her breath, changed the direction of her thoughts. Lucy straightened. She refused to think of getting ill, or of Samuel Wilson. "Sarah, set the table please."

Sarah collected a stack of pewter bowls from the cupboard.

"Lucy?" she said as the bowls wobbled in her hands. "What do I do with these?" Lucy turned toward Sarah. Two of the bowls now sat at their places on the table. In her hands, she held three more. She stared at the table, tears beginning to stream down her face. The pewter dishes clattered to the floor with a hollow clang. Sarah covered her face with her hands, and her little body began to shake with sobs.

Gathering Sarah in her arms, Lucy sat down in Mama's rocker, not able to answer through her own tears. They simply held each other close.

How can a five-year-old understand? Lucy rocked her sister, at a loss to know how to help. At almost nineteen, she found she could not comprehend the permanent changes in their lives. What had started as a nasty cold with Sarah had spread to the rest of the family, in days becoming fatal to the others. Somehow Lucy had escaped it.

When Sarah had come downstairs this morning, Lucy delivered the news that Mama had died too. Sarah had taken the news stoically. Lucy hadn't told her about the baby born during the night. She'd wrapped both bodies in the colorful medallion quilt—a wedding gift from Mrs. Wilson and her mother's favorite. Sarah asked why Lucy used the best quilt rather than an older one like they'd used for Papa and Ben. Lucy told her how much Mama had loved the beautiful blanket. The truth—that she had not dressed Mama fittingly for burial—was not for a child's ears.

The creaking of the rocker was the loudest sound in the cabin.

When both girls had cried themselves out, Sarah put her hands on Lucy's cheeks, bringing her back to the present, and peered deep into her big sister's eyes. "Is Mama happy with Papa and Jesus?"

Unable to speak, Lucy nodded.

"And Ben and Jane too?"

Lucy wiped her face with the back of her hand. "Yes, she is happy with Ben and Jane too." *And the baby.*

"Good." Sarah scrambled out of Lucy's lap and picked up the scattered bowls. "Let's eat. Papa would tell us we should eat and go to bed so morrow can come and the sun can shine, because problems always seem bigger in the dark."

Lucy half smiled. Papa Marden had said, "Go to sleep little one. On the morrow, your problems will look smaller in the sunshine. Problems, like shadows, are always bigger in the dark."

For the first time in her life, Lucy doubted Papa Marden's wisdom.

Sarah readied herself for bed as Lucy washed the bowls and banked the fire. She scooped the hottest embers under the copper curfew so they would last until morning. Then she pushed the curfew into the back corner of the stone fireplace where the coals would stay the warmest. The other fire might die in the night, but there would be no need to use one of their precious matches to start the morning cook fire.

"May I sleep with you?"

Lucy thought of her narrow bed and shook her head. Sarah often kicked, and Lucy needed rest tonight. And Sarah's bed upstairs was far too small for both of them. "No, sweetheart, my bed isn't big enough."

Sarah's crestfallen expression garnered a hasty afterthought. Lucy promised, "But when it is sunny and I can wash Mama and Papa's bedding, we can both sleep in the big bed."

"For certain?"

"Absolutely."

Sarah clapped her hands in delight. "Tomorrow?"

"No, but soon. It must be a sunny, warm day first." Lucy closed the curtain on the window and bolted the door. Her bed seemed to draw her to it like a current sucking a stick into the rapids. She could not wait to get Sarah settled in.

Sarah pointed to the big Bible on the shelf. "Will you read and pray with me since Papa—" The rest of the sentence hung heavy in the air. Papa Marden had read to them from the big family Bible and listened to the little ones' prayers every night. Like Sarah, Lucy missed the nightly ritual.

Last night, as with the night before, neither she nor Mama had read from the large Bible that had been Papa's domain. Instead, they'd read a Psalm from the small Aitken Bible Lucy kept on the shelf above her bed. The smaller Bible was a gift to Lucy from Papa Marden on the day he married Mama. The little Bible was the first version printed in the United States and approved by Congress. Papa said it would be a family heirloom her grandchildren would brag about to their grandchildren. It was one of Lucy's prized possessions.

Lucy stumbled over her feet as she reached for the large, British, printed family Bible, her lack of sleep threatening to topple her on the spot. She paused to regain her equilibrium.

Lucy's arms shook from the strain as she lifted the heavy book. Dropping it onto the table, she sat on the long bench. Sarah squeezed in next to her. Lucy opened it randomly and hoped tonight's verse would not be a "Thou shalt" or a "begat."

Her finger landed on a verse from the Gospel of John. "Peace I leave with you, my peace I give unto you: not as the world giveth, give I unto you. Let not your heart be troubled, neither let it be afraid."

Peace. What would peace feel like? Papa Marden's hug? Mama's humming? She needed that now. Lucy could have pondered on the verse longer, but Sarah began to wiggle, anxious to pray and go to bed.

Sarah hurried up the stairs to her bed while Lucy wrapped a hot brick in flannel to keep Sarah's feet warm.

Listening to Sarah's simple prayers gave Lucy pause. Could hers be as simple? She sighed. Sarah did not have to worry about what to do with the farm or how they would live. Trusting her parents to God and that He would help her be a good girl seemed easy for a child.

As she began to descend the narrow stairway, Lucy's legs gave out on her. Only her tight grip on the banister kept her from tumbling headfirst down the last four steps. Pulling herself upright, she noticed the Bible where it lay open on the table. One more chore before she could crawl into bed.

Retrieving Mama's writing desk from its shelf, Lucy opened the Bible to the back, where her Grandfather Stickney had recorded the names of his parents, wife, and children. Under her mother's name below the date her grandfather had penned thirty-six years ago on the occasion of Mama's birth, she wrote the word *died* and the date. Then she turned to the page after her mother's marriage to Mr. Simms and his death date, to the marriage of Mama to Papa Marden eight years ago, which was written in Mama's beautiful script. Mama had added the dates of Ben's and Papa Marden's deaths to the book. Below little Jane's name and death date, Lucy poised her pen to write "Baby boy."

Tears blurred the page before her. How sad that her tiny brother had come into the world and then out without even a name. She was the only person alive to have ever seen him or hold him. He'd breathed but a little, but he deserved a name—Papa's name.

Wiping her eyes with her sleeve lest a tear fall and smudge the ink, she wrote in her neatest script:

James Marden Jr., Born and died the 27th
day of November in the year of our Lord, 1797.

The words ran together, and Lucy straightened to protect the wet ink from her tears. The room spun. She steadied herself. At the top of the page, she noticed her name written in an unknown hand. The words didn't make sense...maybe it was her tears or the dim light from the lantern playing tricks on her eyes.

Extinguishing the lamp, she vowed to read the entry again by daylight. Her limbs felt as stiff as deadwood as she stood. For a moment she doubted she could manage the ten short steps to her room.

Finally reaching the bed, she sat on the end to remove her boots, her hands shaking, and the dim light of the fire casting macabre shadows on the floor and walls as it filtered through the door to her room. Lucy rubbed her eyes and sighed. Then, grabbing her quilt, she turned into her pillow and sobbed.

Three

EMMA WILSON BRUSHED OUT HER hair, not daring to guess at the number of gray strands weaving their way through its length. She refused to believe they represented the majority. With ten children, seven of whom were living, it was a wonder any hint of color remained. This fall sprouted more gray hairs than could be attributed to little Mark's illness or the early blizzard. She blamed them on the return of her second son from Boston. Samuel, who had always been of a cheery disposition, had returned silent and moody. In the past two months, he had been the cause of more silvering than the twins in a year. Too bad hair powdering was falling out of fashion. Her hair would soon be white.

She'd cornered Samuel again this morning to learn of his plans, to no avail. Every question was met with a shrug of his shoulder or grunt, his unwillingness to speak turning the conversation into a lecture.

Her brush caught on a tangle.

In the mirror, she watched her husband, Thomas, cross their bedroom toward her. He reached over her shoulder, removed the brush from her hand, and started brushing her hair. Though he did not count aloud, Emma knew he would brush exactly 126 strokes.

After having her hair up all day, it felt like a bit of heaven to feel someone brushing her tresses out. Emma closed her eyes and relaxed. Thomas never seemed to tire of the nightly ritual he'd initiated the first night they were together. On that night, tucked in the sleigh, he'd used his fingers for a comb after pulling out all her hairpins and tucking them in his pocket. And he'd spoken of his love with each pin. "One hundred strokes for beauty," he whispered in her ear as he finished. He would whisper the same tonight, adding, "Plus twenty-six for the years of my love."

On nights when he felt particularly amorous, he would forgo the brush for his fingers, returning them both to the days before her blonde hair had darkened and started to gray. On four occasions, he'd even come into the bedroom while she'd labored in childbirth and brushed her hair, much to the annoyance of the midwife.

Emma pictured the younger versions of themselves at this same spot in the days when their cares and worries had been so different. Discussions of harvesting, war, and weather had peppered their conversations. Diapering and midnight feedings had been exchanged for talk of grandchildren. Thomas Jr. and his wife were to present them with a second come early spring. Yesterday at church, she'd learned her Carrie would birth her first sometime in the summer.

Thomas held her hair in one hand, lowered his head, and nuzzled the spot behind Emma's ear. The gesture almost guaranteed she would be awake for a while longer.

She bent her neck, allowing him better access.

"So what is bothering my wife this night?" Thomas bowed low to wrap her in his arms. She leaned into the curve of his shoulder and let his strength soak into her.

She started to braid her hair, and Thomas released her.

When she'd secured her braid with a length of ribbon, she stood and turned into her husband's arms.

"It is your Samuel who vexes me. What is he thinking?"

"I take it my wife does not agree with the girls he spends his time with." Thomas tugged her to the edge of the bed.

Emma nodded as she allowed herself to settle onto her husband's lap. "I am too old and too fat for this, you know. After ten children, I am not as thin as I used to be." Emma batted at her husband's shoulder.

"Ah, but the blizzard has set me in mind of a sleigh ride and a good snuggle." Thomas captured his wife's lips to prove his point.

Emma couldn't help but giggle. "Mr. Wilson, you are a naughty man." She punctuated her statement with a kiss and soon forgot all about the gray hairs her son was giving her.

Much later, in the warmth of her husband's arms, Emma again pondered Samuel's actions. Without warning, he'd returned from Boston declaring that doctoring was not for him. In the weeks since, there had been no further explanation.

"Why does Samuel seem determined to take up with one of the empty-headed girls from town, especially after posting intentions with Lucy?" Gloomy enough when she thought he might fall for Margaret Drabble, but Elizabeth Garrett?

Thomas gave her a little squeeze but didn't comment.

"She is a mother-in-law's worst nightmare, if ever one existed." The conniving girl would make every family gathering miserable with her complaints and airs. Elizabeth had learned from the best because her mother was ten times worse. As wife of the magistrate, Mrs. Garrett considered herself the grande dame and demanded to be treated as such. If Samuel ever married Elizabeth, Emma would need to resort to kidnapping her grandchildren in order to see them. Emma couldn't stand the thought of such spoiled grandchildren.

"I think what the children saw is being blown out of proportion. I don't believe Samuel had anything to do with it."

"Really, nothing to do with a kiss?"

"Mm-hmm." Thomas nuzzled her shoulder, a sign he wanted to sleep.

Why can't he just marry Lucy? He'd proposed to Lucy by letter late last spring. They'd posted intentions during the summer, hoping to wed when he came back from medical school this December. Afterward, they would both return to Boston. If any of her children had the opportunity to be as happily married as she and Thomas were, it was Samuel with Lucy.

On the verge of falling asleep, she realized the Mardens had been absent from church again yesterday. With all the excitement of Carrie's announcement of their newest grandchild, she'd noticed little else. By the time she searched for Anna to share the news, most of the congregants had left. Now that she thought about it, the Marden pew had been empty. Guilt flooded her. Becoming a grandmother was no excuse for forgetting her dearest friend. Snuggling deeper into Thomas's side, her last coherent thought was that she must check on Anna in the morning.

Emma watched a figure emerge in the gloom. The woman's cloak was pulled tight around her body. As she stumbled in the snow, the wind howled all about her, tangling her cloak and making it difficult to walk through the high snowdrifts it created. The woman fell into a drift but made no attempt to rise. Her unbound hair shrouded her face like a veil. Emma drew near and pulled the hair aside. It was Lucy who lay dying in the snow, just as Anna had twenty years ago. But unlike her mother's, Lucy's pale face was not covered with blood.

Heart racing, Emma sat up in bed, relieved to find she'd only dreamed the frightening scene. Emma often dreamed of that terrible night with Anna but never had Lucy taken her place. The setting was different too—not in the woods but on Hill Road, near their house. Emma's breathing slowed. A dream. Not a memory but a warning. She was sure of it.

Thomas, disturbed by her movement, pulled her back into his embrace. Although comforted by her husband's closeness, she slept little the rest of the night.

Samuel, his father, and his brothers all waited eagerly for Ma to place the platter of biscuits on the table and sit with them so they could say grace and eat.

But Ma did not sit down. "I dreamed about Anna Marden. Someone must check in on them today."

Samuel watched as his father closely studied each of his brothers. Oblivious to their father's scrutiny, his brothers eyed the biscuits and ham on the table. Who could be spared today? Whoever Father sent would be gone most of the day. James Marden would no doubt need a hand after the blizzard. Thomas let his gaze rest on the twins for a moment. They were of an age where they could be a great help, or a great bother. Since the younger boys were not yet big enough to help any more than the young Marden boy, that left—

"Samuel, you will go to the Marden's. Help James with whatever he needs. I expected Ben to come by now to sled with Daniel and Mark." Thomas tousled the hair of his youngest son, who despite being gravely ill not two weeks ago seemed none the worse for it.

"Can I go too, Pa?" Mark reached for an unusually fluffy biscuit. The action did not go unnoticed.

"Grace has not been said yet." Emma moved the biscuits to the opposite side of the table, then she answered for her husband. "No, Mark. Sarah was ill two weeks ago when Lucy and Ben brought the molasses, remember? It was the day before you became ill. Until we know they are all well, you need to stay here."

Mark bobbed his head, still focused on the fluffy biscuits now beyond his reach.

Samuel forced himself to answer. "I'll go."

The Marden's. The last place he wanted to go but the one place his heart wanted to be. *Ready or not, today is the day I stop avoiding Lucy.*

All the things he needed to apologize for pelted his mind like last night's snowballs. He hoped his apology would convince Lucy to rekindle their relationship. Being whitewashed by his brothers was more comfortable than Lucy's cold shoulder. Didn't she realize it was half her fault Elizabeth had thrown herself at him because she was jealous? *Another poor excuse.*

He could justify all he wanted, but he was a louse.

Samuel looked up when amens echoed around the table. He'd missed hearing morning grace, but no one seemed to notice. His four brothers were focused on getting their share of the food before starting the day's work. Doubtless, more than one had eyed the biscuits during their father's talk with God. He grabbed the fluffy one and plunked it down on his plate. Across the table, Mark's shoulders slumped.

Emma handed the butter crock to Samuel. "I'll send a small basket of food with you."

Samuel took the boiled eggs from Daniel. No one reacted to Ma's announcement. With the expectation of another Marden after Christmas, it would have been odd if Ma didn't send something.

His stomach churned. He hoped he could keep his breakfast down. Childbirth was another of his failures as a doctor's apprentice. Thankfully, Ma and Widow Potting handled most of the birthing around here. He'd shared his failures with old Dr. Page, who had counted on Samuel's help in the growing community. *How did I ever think I could be a doctor?* The thought filled him with shame and made swallowing difficult.

Ma finished her meal and bustled around the large kitchen, adding more than bread and butter to the Marden's basket. Crocks of this and slabs of that were wrapped and nestled inside of the third largest of the baskets Ma kept in the kitchen. Samuel cringed. Riding a horse and balancing one of mother's not-so-little baskets would be harder still in the snow. A cloth sack would be simpler to maneuver, but it would be useless to suggest it, as cloth sacks allowed the bread to become smashed and the jellies to tip. He could walk the mile and a half to the Marden farm, but with the snow, he would rather take his horse.

Emma set the basket next to Samuel. "Stop playing with your biscuit and get moving. I feel as if the Mardens need our help now."

Samuel stuffed the last bite into his mouth. No one ever argued with Ma's feelings. More often than not, they proved to be like Biblical Joseph's gift from God, telling of a future only he could see. Perhaps that was why his mother's intense gaze made him wonder what she didn't tell them.

four

No smoke curled up from the chimney silhouetted against the ice-blue sky. No fresh footprints in the dusting of snow that had fallen last night.

The bellowing, mooing, and bleating coming from the barn sounded to Samuel like a protest of neglect.

What Samuel didn't see or smell as he rode Old Brown into the Marden's yard worried him more than what he did. The animals would keep.

Ma was right. Something was wrong at the Marden's.

Vowing to check on the animals as soon as he checked on the family, he secured Old Brown to the porch rail. Bound to the nearby post, three ropes ran up and over the roof. He fingered the intricate knots, wondering why James Marden had tied them there. He jerked his hand away as a reason came to mind. He hoped he was mistaken. There were few reasons to lash anything to a roof during a winter storm.

He knocked on the door. Thud. Something fell just beyond the door, but no one answered.

"Hello in the house."

Bang. Scrape. Bam. The door vibrated as someone attempted to open it.

Impatient, Samuel set the basket down. He stepped to the window and tried to peer inside. The curtain parted, revealing a small, chestnut-brown head of hair and a pair of tear-filled hazel eyes.

"Samuel!" the child shouted with relief.

He tried the door. Bolted. "Can you open the door?"

The child shook her head. Her attempts must account for the noises he'd heard through the door. Wasn't there someone else to open the heavy door? There was no way he could lift the crossbar from outside. Should he break the window?

The little face disappeared. More scraping and banging echoed from within the house. Samuel stood perplexed. A slam from the back of the house solved the mystery. The lean-to door. Of course. Why hadn't he thought of it? Years ago Lucy had shown him the loose stone in the garden wall where James Marden had hidden a key.

"Samuel! Samuel, you came!" The shout crescendoed as the child raced around the corner. Her ill-attached cloak flew behind her, and her stockinged feet left little footprints in the snow. She launched herself into Samuel's arms. "You camed! You camed! I knew you would."

What on earth? The little girl was half dressed. Breadcrumbs stuck to her face, which smelled of apple preserves. How long had things been in such a condition to leave a child of five years fending for herself? He dreaded the answer.

"I prayed and prayed you would come!" She hugged him, transferring the crumbs and apple preserves to his shirt.

"Thank you, God!" she said and raised her arms to the sky.

Samuel struggled to place a name for the girl—*Jane? Sarah?* He wasn't sure which of the girls had passed while he was in Boston. The impatient child squirmed out of his arms.

"Hurry, Samuel!" She grabbed his hand and tried to drag him off the porch. He scooped her up and carried her around the house over the half-cleared path.

As they reached the back of the cabin, Samuel's heart sank. Strapped to the roof were three quilt-wrapped bundles—frozen corpses awaiting burial. From the sizes, one must be Ben, the other two adults.

Please, not Lucy. Still carrying the child, Samuel ducked inside the lean-to's squatty door. No fire blazed in the massive stone fireplace, and his breath hung visible in the air. The dim light coming through the curtains showed the large gathering room was clean and tidy. The little girl must not have been left to her own devices for long. Where there were three bundles on the roof, someone besides the child in his arms was still alive.

Or they lay in the house with no one to add their body to those on the roof.

The girl wiggled out of Samuel's arms and dashed through the door near the stairs, her cloak falling to the floor as she ran. He noticed the tracks made by her wet stockings. Samuel shed his heavy coat and hung it on a peg by the door. Picking up the girl's cloak, he did the same for her. As cold as it was, he would have kept the coat on, but it hindered his movements.

"Lucy, wake up! He is here. I told you he would come. I prayed. Please, Lucy." The girl's words changed to sobs, and Samuel's heart stopped. Lucy was not one of those on the cabin roof, but neither was she conscious. He froze. The young one might not recognize death.

The little girl peeked around the doorframe. "Samuel?"

Samuel didn't need to see more tears or to be asked twice.

In two strides, he entered Lucy's little room. Frost coated the partially curtained window panes, casting misshapen shadows that reached out like fingers to strangle what little life was left in the room.

Lucy lay in her work dress on the narrow bed with one boot still on. Her unbound hair framed her pale face. Her tangled clothes and quilt told the story of a restless night. She moaned and attempted to move in her sleep.

She lived. Samuel's heart began to beat once again. He pulled back the curtain to illuminate the room, and the shadows retreated into the corners.

A cloth lay askew on Lucy's forehead, evidence of the five-year-old's nursing skills. He was impressed. She must have observed Lucy doing the same with the other members of the household.

"How long has Lucy been ill?"

Sarah wiped at her eyes with the back of her hand. "Lucy t-tucked me in l-last night. I try-tried to w-wake her up, but she won't w-wake up. She is h-hot just l-like Ben."

Kneeling next to the bed, Samuel removed the cloth from Lucy's forehead and replaced it with his hand. Her forehead was hotter than a full warming pan in January. "Did you put this on her head?" he asked, the limp cloth now hanging from his hand.

The little girl nodded.

"What a good nurse you are." Samuel stood and patted her awkwardly on the head, laying the cloth over his shoulder.

"I helped Lucy." A smile grew on her face.

"Yes, bright eyes, you helped Lucy. Can you help some more?" *Like tell me your name, ride for the doctor, or be years older so I don't need to worry about leaving you here?* While he wished for the impossible, there were things she could do to help. She could fetch water and sit with her older sister while he attended to other matters. Her ability in finding her breakfast and in trying to cool Lucy's fever testified that this little Miss Marden who stood before him was smart. Just like Lucy.

He shivered. Warming up the house needed to come first, for everyone's sake. He picked up a quilt from the floor where it lay in a heap. "Help me get Lucy under this quilt, and then I will start the fire."

"But Lucy is still dressed."

Samuel laid the quilt at the end of the bed and looked at Lucy's clothing. Surely the set of stays in her work dress made breathing difficult. He hoped her sister could help remove them. He had helped undress unconscious women once or twice as an apprentice, but this was Lucy. He could feel the slap he would receive if he even touched her bodice. Removing the garment could mean a rolling pin to the head. But this was necessary. This was professional, not personal.

"She can't go to bed in her dress," the child protested again and gave him a look, letting him know she thought him daft for thinking of tucking Lucy into bed in such a manner. Definitely Lucy's sister—the raised chin and crossed arms a shared trait.

"She will be warmer this way until I get the fire going." Samuel pulled the quilt over Lucy despite the child's protests. Then he took in the half-dressed state of the little girl in front of him. "Don't you need more clothes on?"

"Will you button me?"

Samuel nodded. "Get some dry stockings."

He wasn't sure the little girl heard him as she scampered up the stairs. Samuel rubbed the back of his neck. He was doomed to help all the Marden maidens with their clothing this day.

Leaving the door open, Samuel went to tend the fire. He surveyed the clean room for other clues as to what might have occurred the past two weeks. A chair blocked the front door. The girl must have stood on it to try to remove the latch. James had never replaced the old-fashioned bar for a lock and key like on the lean-to's entrance. A writing desk, inkwell, quill pen, and family Bible lay at one end of the kitchen table. The Bible belonged on its shelf. The writing desk and ink should be someplace a child could not reach. The other end of the table held a crock of apple preserves and a quarter loaf of bread, and the crumbs scattered about matched those on the little girl's face. He began to get a good idea of what had happened here. Maybe the Bible would contain the information he sought for confirmation, but right now he needed to start a fire more than quench his curiosity.

The wood box sat empty, but he found a pile of wood left to dry in the lean-to. The fuel might be an adequate supply for a day's fire.

How long since James had passed?

Sarah! The little girl who'd taken ill before Mark had a fortnight ago—Ma had called her Sarah. Had the Marden's and Mark experienced the same illness? Both he and Sarah had survived; the others had not. The rest of Samuel's family remained well. He rubbed the back of his neck. If only he had completed his apprenticeships, he would have recognized the diseases from the books he'd studied and the lectures he'd attended.

How long had Lucy cared for everything alone? Shame at his reluctance to talk to her flooded over him. He'd once promised Lucy he would always be there for her—a promise he was destined to break, just as with the other promises he had broken.

Carrying an armful of wood from the lean-to, he knelt by the large fireplace and lifted the copper curfew to discover a handful of hot embers. Samuel breathed a deep sigh of relief. Starting a fire from flint and steel would have taken much longer, provided he could even find James's set or a match.

Despite the distress of the morning, Sarah had not touched the fireplace. At least she had not become desperate enough to break one of the first rules every child learned from the cradle.

In moments, a small fire burned.

Sarah tiptoed down the narrow stairs. In her arms were her leather stays and a yellow overdress. She held them out to Samuel.

Bewildered, he turned the stays one way, then another. Sarah blew out an exasperated sigh. She stilled his hands and threaded her arms through what were most obviously armholes. She turned her back to him and lifted her hair, and he buttoned the three carved wooden buttons.

Sarah then slipped on her pinafore. As she raised her arms, he noticed she'd changed her stockings. "Don't forget to bring your wet stockings down to dry by the fire."

He needed no prompting on what to do with the sash. Hundreds of times when Lucy was this age, she'd asked him to tie her sash. The confounded length of cloth was forever getting caught on a branch or winding around a bush as she'd traipsed after him in the woods. Once, after he'd rescued her three times in only an hour as the sash caught on brambles, he had become so frustrated he'd threatened to tie her to a tree and leave her there. He hadn't been serious, of course, but Lucy had begged him not to, promising never to ask him to tie her dangling sash again. For the next several months, the sash was tied in any number of creative ways, and Lucy had never troubled him about it again.

Sarah held out her cap, which he settled over her head, then tied the strings under her chin. Her hair sprung out in all directions from under the edges. A good brushing could wait until later.

Once the fire started to roar and crackle, Samuel found a clean pot in which to boil water. He stepped out of the lean-to door and filled the pot with snow, then he hung the pot on the crane and swung the arm over flames. Inside the lean-to, he found a half-full bucket of water, a thin sheet of broken ice floating on its surface. Sarah must have used this water to cool Lucy's brow.

He took the cloth from his shoulder and dipped it into the bucket, then moved back to Lucy's side. Her breathing had become labored. There was no putting the task off. The stays needed to be removed.

Laying the cloth at the head of the bed, he turned to Sarah. "Can you help me? We need to get Lucy out of her...dress." The heat rose in his face as he thought of all the clothing he'd need to remove.

He started to recite the Lord's Prayer as a way of distancing himself from the task before him.

Please let her be wearing a thick winter shift so I don't—Samuel added and stopped. Somehow his words were more than the regular "Lead me not into temptation" he'd quoted all his life. In Lucy's condition, seeing her shift would not exactly be a temptation, but not proper, either. Studying for the past three years to become a doctor, even if he would never be one, should cover any objections his mother might voice at his undressing Lucy.

Nevertheless, he failed to vanquish the blush that stole across his face. This was the one woman he'd dreamed of having the right to undress someday. In those dreams, they were married. But after the stupid letter he'd sent, he doubted he would ever get the chance. Undressing her was not going to help one bit.

I saw you in your shift. Please marry me. It would undoubtedly elicit a slap.

To his relief, under her homespun skirt and bodice and linsey-woolsey petticoats and leather stays, Lucy wore a heavy winter shift. One prayer answered. The tightly woven linen shift rose to her neck and fell well past her knees. He gently lifted Lucy and instructed Sarah to unbutton the skirt and untie the petticoats and pockets. A corner of Samuel's brain registered disappointment as Sarah untied the stays outlining Lucy's curves, leaving Lucy's beautiful, feminine shape hidden beneath the heavy shift.

Muttering under his breath, he began repeating the Lord's Prayer again.

Freed of her confines, Lucy took a deep breath that ended in a coarse, barking cough. For a moment, her eyes fluttered, her fever-glazed eyes meeting his, her lips parting. Samuel thought she would speak, but another cough cut off anything she might have said. Her eyes closed again, but her parched lips remained open as she drew in several ragged breaths.

He did his best to avert his eyes while Sarah struggled with the long woolen stockings and garters. He could offer to help. Lucy would never know. How many times would he need to repeat the Lord's Prayer before he received an answer today? He tried to not stare at her exposed knees.

He may have failed at his apprenticeship, but he felt like he'd learned to see his female patients as people rather than objects. Dr. Warren, one of the lecturers, was adamant about treating people with dignity. "*Think of the patient as a member of your family,*" echoed through his mind as he covered her now-bare legs with the quilt. *Sister* was not one of the ways he caught his mind referring to Lucy. *Wife, friend, darling, his*—but never could he call her sister.

Lead me not into temptation! She is burning up, and here I am wondering what the curve of her calf feels like.

"Sarah, fetch me a cup of water, please." *Or some snow to dump over my head.*

She ran and grabbed a tin cup from the cupboard and dipped it in the bucket. The water sloshed about as she hurried across the room, leaving a trail of droplets.

Samuel cradled Lucy's head in his hand and attempted to force a few drops of water between her parched lips. He hoped more had slipped inside than the amount that now dribbled down her chin.

A distant memory of another time he'd tried to help Lucy with a drink filled his mind.

"No, Swamuel. Lucy do by self. No help!" three-year-old Lucy had yelled moments before she'd managed to drench both of them with fresh milk from the tin cup she'd succeeded in wrenching from his hands. As a seven-year-old boy, he'd learned the fastest way to cross

Lucy was to do something for her when she didn't want help. Heaven help him if she woke up while he tried to aid her now.

He knelt by the bed and placed the cool cloth over Lucy's forehead. He had not felt so inept at helping a patient since fainting during Dr. Warren's surgery. What to do? He owned no leeches, and he would not bleed Lucy without them. If he passed out after using a knife, he could bleed Lucy too long. It could be a fatal mistake. He shook his head in self-loathing. A small but growing group of doctors had begun to argue against bloodletting as a cure. He hoped they were right.

He could do little for Lucy but try to cool the fever and get some tea or broth in her. Though water, often the source of illness, could be dangerous, but until he could prepare something better, it would have to do. Better to get some liquids in her to help quench the fire burning inside. Samuel could not think of Lucy joining the bodies on the roof.

He rubbed his knees. He needed a chair, but his choices were limited. The strait-backed chair Sarah had climbed on in her attempt to open the door looked uninviting. He returned the chair to its place at the end of the table. He settled on the rocking chair. It was comfortable enough to sit in for a period of time and small enough to maneuver around Lucy's room. He set the rocker near the head of the bed, then looked at Sarah.

"I need to feed the animals. Can you sit with Lucy?"

Sarah scrambled into the rocking chair and nodded earnestly. She clutched a rag doll to her chest, her eyes wide. He could think of naught to say to calm her. It was too soon to tell her that all would be well.

Samuel shrugged on his coat and lifted the latch bar from the door. "Stand on the porch and yell for me if anything changes." Stepping onto the porch, he tripped over the basket he'd brought with him. Grateful for his mother's foresight in packing so much food, he brought the basket into the house and set it on the table.

"When I return, we will see what my ma packed. I think I smell gingerbread."

Sarah nodded, the curls escaping her cap bouncing around her face.

Old Brown snorted his approval when Samuel untied him from the rail and led him to the shelter of the barn. This visit would last too long to leave his mount saddled in the cold. James had never filled all the stalls in the barn Mr. Simms had built, which guaranteed Samuel would find an empty one to settle Old Brown in for the day.

The sun, now directly overhead, made a valiant effort to melt the snow. The sounds of a small riot carried from beyond the barn doors, the goat's angry bleating egging the others on. The noise grew as he entered. The cow and one of the horses still had water, but the pig trough stood empty. The stench of the barn made him wonder how long it had been since James had cared for things. The stalls needed a good mucking. He didn't dare take the time to do a thorough job now, though. He wouldn't leave Sarah alone longer than necessary. It would take more than a day to set things to rights. Perhaps one of his brothers could help. Help would come. Ma was bound to send someone when he didn't come home in time for supper.

Samuel unsaddled his horse and settled him in an empty stall, then he found a milk pail and sat down to take care of the nanny goat. As he milked, another thought entered his mind. Would he ruin Lucy's reputation by being here? Little Sarah could not be considered an adequate chaperone. Not that there was anything to chaperone. He was a doctor caring for a patient.

But Samuel would never be the doctor he'd studied to be.

The gossips in town loved to make more of the story than they should. A recently spurned Elizabeth would delight in such tales—anything to hurt him for refusing her affections.

Samuel exited the barn less than an hour later. The sun glinted off the iron ring next to the barn door. Where was the guide rope? Surely James had tied one up before the blizzard was in full force. There wasn't a man in the area who would neglect to string up the lifesaving rope. The knee-deep path through the snow showed that the same route had been followed to the barn since the storm had commenced. The path was in line with the angle the rope should follow.

Where was it? Samuel searched the barnyard and the path to the cabin, assuming the rope must have been secured poorly and come loose in the storm. He found his answer tied to the porch column. The three ropes. Lucy had run out of rope and used the guide rope to secure the last body to the roof to keep it away from wild animals. She'd had to trust the worn path to guide her.

He closed his eyes and took a deep breath. *How did she find the strength to do it? Why didn't she ask for help?*

Getting the rope over the roof was difficult even with the lean-to to aid in roof access. His admiration for her grew. Unlike some of the women he met in Boston, she was not some simpering flower hoping for a good match. Again, he regretted his choice to consider Elizabeth, even for a day. He should have followed his mother's hints to go see Lucy at her cousins in Gloucester when he'd first returned from Boston. Justifying not taking the five-hour ride had been easy, but deep down he feared Lucy's reaction to his last letter more than he feared the sight of blood.

Five

SAMUEL SHUT THE CABIN DOOR, careful to not make a sound. He removed his muddied boots. No point in making a mess to clean up later. The house was much warmer, but the floor was still cold. He wished for his regular shoes. He wondered if he could find a pair of Mr. Marden's later. He crossed the room to Lucy's door.

Lucy slept peacefully, her quilts still smoothed over her prone body. Curled up in the rocker, Sarah clutched her doll, her tiny snores making a lilting, whistling sound. As Samuel leaned on the doorjamb and stared at the two Marden girls, a heavy weight settled around his heart. So much loss and so much sadness for one home in so short a time. It was not uncommon for entire villages to be depopulated by one form of illness or another. But these were not nameless faces in a newspaper article.

He had known this family as long as he could remember. He even had memories of Grandfather Stickney, who'd died before Lucy was born. His emotions swirled about like a dense coastal fog. Responsibility, sorrow, and love mingled with every breath he took.

What would Lucy do when she recovered? If the barn was any indication, the farm was too much for her to run alone. She could rent out the land. She might sell. Did she even legally own it? Would the farm go to some relative he'd never heard of? She couldn't leave. Not until he'd courted her properly.

If I court her now, will she think I am trying to rescue her or secure a farm since I have no funds?

It was going to be difficult to convince Lucy to marry him after breaking their engagement. Now that she'd become head of the Marden household, it might be impossible. This changed everything. Lack of a chaperone and the responsibility of raising her sister would provide ready excuses for Lucy to thwart his efforts. As if his stupid letter wasn't enough.

Samuel slipped closer to his sleeping charges. Sarah was going to wake feeling stiff and sore from sleeping in the rocker. He needed to be able to sit near Lucy to force more liquid down her throat anyway. Scooping Sarah into his arms, he went in search of a more comfortable bed. Contemplating the narrow stairway, he decided moving Sarah to her parents' bedroom would be simpler, so he pushed open the bedroom door with his back.

The smell of blood and death assaulted him, and he gagged.

The bed was unmade, its bare straw tick lumpy and stained. Samuel backed out before the odor overwhelmed him. He should have guessed. Lucy would not have had time to put the room to rights.

Upstairs, he tucked Sarah into the bed in the smaller room. He placed the rag doll next to her and covered her with a quilt. He glanced into the other room, relieved to find Ben's old bed neatly made, as if waiting for Ben to come home and tumble in after a day of sledding. At least he would not need to sleep in the barn during his stay. The pegs on the wall no longer held Ben's clothing. A slingshot lay on the top of a closed chest, homage to the little boy who had lived there. Samuel's heart ached. He knew how hard it was to lose a beloved sibling.

After changing the cooling cloth on Lucy's head for the hundredth time and coaxing some tepid ginger tea down her throat, he decided to take care of his dinner. Ma's basket contained fresh bread and cheese as well as a good-sized chunk of ham. He toasted the cheese and warmed the meat over the fire with a long fork.

As he ate, he read the entries in the back of the family Bible. A few recently penned entries told the story he did not dare ask little Sarah. Ben had died as the blizzard started. James Marden had passed five days later, on Saturday. Both entries were written in the same hand that had recorded Benjamin's birth. He assumed from the feminine flourish that Anna had written them.

If only I had come when the storm ended. Guilt threatened to choke him as he tried to swallow a bite of bread. Saturday morning had dawned clear. By afternoon, a light snow was falling, but visibility had been good until the full force of the next storm had hit after dark. On Sunday, only half the congregation had attended church, and no more snow had fallen. Old Brown could have easily navigated the few drifts that blocked the mile and half journey.

Unblinking, he stared at the writing at the bottom of the family list in disbelief. Lucy had written the next entry. After dozens of letters, he could not fail to recognize it. A baby had been born and died sometime yesterday. Sarah had not mentioned a baby. Perhaps Lucy had spared her the knowledge. He hadn't asked Sarah much about the family, partially because he was unsure of what to do with her tears, which had fallen more than once since his arrival.

Lucy must have delivered her baby brother before Anna Marden had died. No wonder the large bedroom was in such a state. Between his mother's birthings and medical school, he knew childbirth was not a clean process. And there was blood. Samuel put down food, unable to eat another bite, his stomach churning as he recalled the pungent odor and appearance of the bedroom.

It was a wonder Lucy had not taken ill sooner. She could not have slept much, if any, since Saturday morning. Then she'd managed to hoist the bodies onto the roof. Had Anna tried to help? Given her condition, hauling her husband's body onto the roof could have triggered early labor even without the addition of illness. *Why didn't I come?* He called himself every foul name he'd ever heard for the lowly coward he was. A few of them might earn a fine for swearing if said in the wrong company.

He pictured Lucy cradling the tiny infant. Had he cried? Had she? If he'd been there, would he have been able to hold her, or would he have absented himself? Lucy would have cleaned her mother and laid her out, placing the babe in her still arms before wrapping them both in a quilt. He tried not to picture what she must have had to clean.

It was no use. He raced to the privy, where he lost his dinner. Great, he thought sarcastically, now just imagining blood was enough to make him ill. Samuel didn't understand this new aversion to blood. Until this past spring, seeing blood had caused him to flinch—a reaction he considered perfectly normal. But then his reactions had become stronger—nausea, shaking, and then fainting. He tried not to think of what would happen when his future wife struggled to present him with a child. He would be worse than useless.

Walking back to the house, he pondered the bundles on the roof. They could not remain there long as all around him the trees were shedding their snowy coverings. The sun had started to warm the earth. The bodies lay on the east-facing roof, which was fortunate, but if they got a full thaw, being out of the afternoon sun would not preserve them for long.

Samuel dumped the remains of his dinner in the slop bucket and returned the family Bible to the shelf near the fireplace. He doubted Sarah could read well enough yet, but he rather she not accidentally find out about her baby brother. He was at a loss for where to store the ornate writing desk. He decided to place it in the large bedroom. Taking a deep breath, he hurried into the room, setting the desk on the couch, then he threw open two windows in hopes the room would air out. He drew in a breath at the window before retreating from the room. He could not leave them open for long lest the entire house cool down, but he hoped it would be long enough to air the room sufficiently.

An hour or so later as he sat rocking in the chair next to Lucy, Samuel looked up to see a disheveled and blurry-eyed Sarah slip into the room. She climbed onto his lap. Clutching her doll in one arm, she stuffed her thumb in her mouth and settled into the crook of

Samuel's arm. He wasn't quite sure how to react, so he kept rocking. His younger brothers had never curled up in his arms. Vague memories of his younger sister Beth cuddling with him nudged at his memory, but she had not yet been four when she'd died.

Creak, creak, the rocker sang. Samuel's leg began to fall asleep, but he continued to rock.

Sarah pulled her thumb out of her mouth and placed her hands on Samuel's cheeks. He tried to ignore the moisture there. She stared him in the eye and pronounced, "I like you too, Samuel Wilson." Sarah hopped off his lap and ran to inspect the basket on the table.

Too? What did she mean? He rubbed his leg and flexed his foot before standing to supervise the gingerbread distribution, then he rubbed the back of his neck. *Too* could mean he had more of a chance with Lucy than he dreamed.

All afternoon he waited for one of his brothers or Pa to come riding into the yard. He needed Ma's wisdom and more help in the barn. Perhaps they could fetch Widow Potting from town to stay the night with Lucy. Or the doctor might know which malady she was facing. He didn't want Ma here. He could not risk exposing her to whatever had killed the Mardens. She was still tired from late nights caring for Mark and seemed to tire more easily since he'd returned home.

Lucy tossed and turned, winding the covers around her body, and her fever climbed. Samuel wished for his mother's herb box. The herbs hanging from the ceiling here at the Mardens were useless to him as he was not sure what many of them were without labels. He remembered the Mardens owned a box, but the shelf where it had once sat was now empty. He'd only succeeded in finding the ginger tea. Using a teaspoon, he managed to get Lucy to take most of the cooled liquid. The laborious process of caring for the ill surprised him. Doctors diagnosed but rarely stayed for the duration.

The sun was setting when Samuel returned to the barn. Why had no one come to see why he'd not returned home? As he fed the animals, he contemplated taking Old Brown and running home for help. Lucy was sleeping soundly now, and the trip would take less than a half hour, even allowing time for Ma to make a new basket. He could make it in fifteen minutes if he asked for help and returned without waiting. By the time he'd fed and watered the last of the animals, he decided the fifteen-minute option was his best. He would leave after checking on Lucy and Sarah. But as he stepped out of the barn, icy raindrops pelted his face and the wind caught his hat, tossing it into a snow drift. Samuel reconsidered his plans. Retrieving his hat, he ran for the house.

He was not leaving tonight.

Six

THOMAS WILSON BOWED HIS HEAD, ready to say grace, and paused. He glanced around the long table. "Where is Samuel?"

"He hasn't returned." Emma worried her lip.

Thomas scowled and began the prayer.

When dinner was over, Emma made a show of fussing over the uneaten food. "Perhaps you should get the sleigh out and we can take this over to Marden's. There must be something wrong to cause your son to miss supper." She'd wanted to ask Thomas to go all afternoon and had cooked almost twice what they could eat in preparation for such a trip. Samuel's prolonged stay had heightened the anxiety she'd already been feeling for one of her best friends and family.

"Sorry, my Emma." Thomas took her hand. "The wind is picking up, and it has started to sleet. I don't dare travel on a night like this. Our Samuel will be fine. He has a good head on his shoulders. James must have seen the danger too. No doubt that's why he didn't come home."

Later, when Thomas was brushing Emma's hair, they listened as the last of the sleet pelted their window and silence replaced the roaring wind. Their eyes met in the mirror, and they silently resolved to head for the Marden's as soon as possible.

At first light, Emma and Thomas were gliding over the ice-frosted road toward the Marden farm, the snow-covered world sparkling around them. Sunlight danced and twinkled off every surface. Emma recalled the morning after her first sleigh ride with Thomas twenty-six years ago and wondered if he were thinking of it as well. He'd alluded to the sleigh ride the other night. She tightened her hold on his arm. The glance he gave her sent heat to her cheeks. He remembered. He moved the reins to one hand and placed the other on her knee. The horses slowed.

"Woman, if we are going to get this food to Marden's while it is still warm, I think you'd better not look at me like that again. As I recall, there are lots of ways to stay warm in a sleigh mired in a snowbank." Thomas winked and squeezed her knee before taking the reins in both hands again, speeding the horses back up. Emma stifled a giggle. She would arrange for a midnight sleigh ride soon to see if he could keep her as warm as he claimed.

Sarah danced around. "Company!"

She heard the sleigh bells before Samuel, who was trying to coax more tepid tea past Lucy's parched lips.

"Sarah, don't open the door," Samuel cautioned, crossing the room. "Sit with Lucy."

Samuel grabbed his coat and stepped out onto the porch just as his father reined the horses to a stop.

Emma stood, ready to jump down from the sleigh.

Samuel raised his hands. "Stop, Ma. Stay in the sleigh."

She sat down, looking alarmed, her eyes raking over him. He knew how disheveled he must look. He imagined his hair stood on end and wondered if dark circles rimmed his eyes. Under the open coat, his shirt was rumpled and half tucked in.

"What is going on here, son?" Thomas shifted in his seat.

Samuel rubbed the back of his neck and glanced heavenward before answering. "James, Anna, and Ben are dead."

Emma gasped.

Samuel winced. He should have softened the news. He continued before his parents could ask any questions. "From the dates in the family Bible, it appears that Anna died, along with a baby boy, Monday, before Sarah woke up. She hasn't mentioned a baby, so I don't think she knows. James passed Saturday, and Ben the Monday prior."

"Sarah? Lucy?" Emma squeaked, her hand over her heart.

"Sarah seems well enough. From what she told me, she was the first one to take ill. Lucy succumbed sometime the night before last after putting Sarah to bed. When I arrived, she was fevered. It is bad. She alternates between fever and chills. She has been moaning and coughing all night and has yet to be fully conscious."

"Well, then, I will stay and take care of her." Emma stood to take herself out of the sleigh again.

Samuel held up his hands. "No, Ma. She is contagious. I can't risk you getting it too." He looked pleadingly at his father. Anna Marden had been his mother's closest confidante; he knew convincing her to return home would be difficult.

"But, son, you can't—" Emma waved her hands helplessly. Samuel guessed she was thinking of how his being a single man would prevent him from properly nursing a sick, unmarried woman in all the necessary ways. Bathing, chamber pots, changing…

"I trained to be a doctor. I may not be one, but I can take care of Lucy."

"No, it's not that…" His mother's voice trailed off again as she turned to Thomas for help.

"Son, what your mother is trying to say is it isn't proper for you to care for Lucy alone."

Samuel rubbed the back of his neck. He'd thought about this dilemma as he cared for Lucy throughout the wee hours. He hoped that almost being a doctor would be good enough, but he could not picture the Reverend Woods accepting it as an excuse.

"Surely people would understand," he said. "I am not going to take advantage of a sick girl. And she is in no condition to throw herself at me. Sarah is here. That should be enough to keep tongues from wagging." But his arguments sounded hollow even to his own ears. They had been more convincing in the predawn hours when he'd first made them. Elizabeth's mother would waste no time creating a sordid tale for any who would listen if she got even a hint of his presence here. The gaggle of gossips who met under the guise of quilting for the poor would condemn Lucy before finishing their first square. He wouldn't be shocked if a couple of the older women didn't make Lucy a scarlet letter *A* as their Puritan grandfathers would have. Piety overruled charity far too often for his taste.

His mother lowered her head as if praying. When she looked up, she gave Samuel the expression he knew would compel him to do whatever she wanted.

"Samuel," she began in the quiet pleading tone mothers used when they wanted their children to see reason. "You stayed the night without a chaperone. Most will forgive you due to the weather and her dire need. But if you choose to stay another night, there are some who will forgive you, but most will hold it against Lucy. She has always been a faithful young lady. She doesn't deserve you ruining her reputation. I am going to stay." Emma slipped out of the sleigh and came to stand before him, determination burning in her eyes. Samuel cast another glance at his father, who chose not to weigh in.

"No, Mother, you can't. It could kill you, too." Samuel was torn. He knew by staying he was risking Lucy's reputation, which was already fragile because of her father, the notorious Mr. Simms. But Ma was not healthy. She had not been for some time. She tired easier than she had before he left for Harvard three years ago. His father might not see it, but to him his mother was not as vibrant as she had been in years past.

"Son, you are right. It could kill your mother, or it could even kill you. It might kill Lucy, but it might not. Only God knows. I appreciate you trying to spare your mother, but this is bigger than being ill. If you stay, what will it mean in two weeks?" Thomas paused, and Samuel hung his head. "If your ma remains here, no one will question Lucy's character."

Samuel rubbed the back of his head. "What can I do? I can't leave her with Sarah to care for her. And, Ma, I can't let you expose yourself to this...this..." Samuel waved his arms wide. "I don't even know what it is. Couldn't Widow Potting come?"

"No, she is at a lying-in, and we have at least two more in the coming week to attend."

"There is another solution, son. Marry her." Thomas delivered the sentence with a quiet air of finality.

"What?" Samuel dropped both arms and stared into his father's face. Had he mistaken his father's words?

"Marry her. If you care at all for Lucy or her reputation, it is the best way," Emma agreed. "I don't know what happened before you came home, but you were engaged. The reverend announced your intentions."

Doubt filled Samuel's mind. He couldn't ask the question he wanted to. *What if she despises me?* So he asked the other difficult question. "What if she dies?"

"If she dies, you'll be a widower with an instant family. Sarah will be your responsibility, as will this farm."

Samuel grew uncomfortable under his father's scrutiny. It had not occurred to him marrying Lucy would be a way to save her reputation. He'd thought if he could get the reverend to make some statement or something, then all would be well. Samuel opened his mouth, then shut it. *Sarah, my responsibility? The Marden farm? I can't!*

Samuel swung his arm wide to encompass the barn and fields beyond, his frustration mounting. "People will say I married her to get the farm. It seems so mercenary. Marry a sick girl to gain a farm." But now that he had no prospects, gaining the farm was the only way he could afford to marry.

"Then, son, you'd better be the doctor you were trained to be and make sure Lucy lives." Thomas's stare became sterner, if that were possible.

"Will you send for Dr. Page?"

His father shook his head. "We passed him on our way here. He was pushing that old horse of his south as fast as he could go. I doubt he could get here before tomorrow. What can he do that you can't?"

Save her, he thought to himself. But, starting to realize that what his parents were suggesting might be the only answer, he asked, "How soon should we wed?"

"As soon as it can be arranged."

Samuel reeled at the answer. They'd planned to wed near Christmas time, before he'd called off the engagement, but the thought of wedding the pale woman who lay inside was so unethical. Whoever heard of marrying a woman in such a state? Shouldn't she recover first? "Shouldn't Lucy get some say in this? I don't think she knows I am even in the house. Who would believe we spoke our spousal vows?" Samuel hedged.

"Unfortunately, you cannot do as we did, exchanging vows *verba de praesenti*. It is illegal in Massachusetts. The Reverend Woods frowns on unsanctioned marriages. He'll insist on officiating. Or the magistrate can come."

Elizabeth's father? Never! Better the stoic reverend than the pompous magistrate. At least Reverend Woods was discreet.

Emma squeezed Thomas's hand. "You know the reverend would insist. Remember the fuss he caused when he found out we'd married under a snow-filled sky with no witnesses?"

Thomas smiled. "We listened to an entire month of sermons condemning the practice of common-law marriage and were forced to appear before the magistrate to pay a long-overdue fine. The expression on his face when your ma told him we went for a long sleigh ride and thought we might be in New York was priceless." Thomas and Emma shared a smile.

Samuel cleared his throat. The idea had disaster written all over it. The silence around them lengthened.

His father broke it. "Son, either marry her or come home. I can't have you ruining Lucy's reputation or your own."

"We could wait until she is better. Who would know?" Desperation marked Samuel's words.

"*We* would, and all it would take is one word from your little brothers before every gossip from here to the coast is talking about it." Emma shook her head.

"The magistrate could charge you with fornication if his wife and daughter pressed him."

Father would think of that. Magistrate Garrett was quick to fine those who broke the tiniest of laws.

"You love me enough that you don't want me to go in there and possibly die." His mother seemed to be choosing her words carefully. "The question your father is asking is—do you feel enough for Lucy that you want her to live and do so without a shadow over her for the rest of her life?"

"I haven't…We haven't…I should have," Samuel mumbled, realizing he didn't sound much different than his five-year-old brother when he wanted a sweet.

Thomas raised a brow. "What did you say, son?"

"I will marry her."

"Good, I will discuss this with the Reverend Woods. Since your intentions were posted three months ago, there should be no problem performing the ceremony tomorrow." His father did not mention contacting the magistrate.

Samuel's mouth hung open. "T-tomorrow? Lucy is quarantined! She isn't even conscious!"

He assumed his acquiescence now would be enough as they would be engaged. He wasn't sure Lucy even liked him anymore. Marriage to an unwilling wife would be a nightmare. Lucy hated to be compelled to do anything. More than once he had been the recipient of her defiant chin when he hadn't been his best self. Once, he'd ordered her to let him fish in peace. She'd left only after tossing rocks into the pond. She would make his life miserable. He could taste the burned and undercooked meals he would endure as penance while he waited for forgiveness.

He needed more time. Maybe she would wake long enough to be coherent and they could discuss the matter. Inspiration struck. "Where can we wed? No one should come in the house."

"Just bundle her up and carry her out to the porch. The reverend will need to see you together for a moment."

"But if she is still unconscious, even the minister can't call it a marriage."

"Then Sarah will be her proxy," Emma quickly answered back.

"Sarah can't be a proxy. She is five." Samuel rolled his eyes. "The little chatterbox could say anything."

His mother bit her lip as if she might laugh. "True, she is young, and when asked if Lucy favors you, she will speak the truth. And I am confident Sarah will repeat enough to convince everyone that Lucy favors you."

In embarrassing detail.

If Lucy had any feelings for him still, Sarah would make them much larger than they were, just like she and Matthew had embellished their story when they reported Elizabeth's kiss. His mother seemed sure Lucy did still care for him. But Ma had not seen Lucy's face when Elizabeth had sidled up to him in church last month, possessively claiming his arm.

Disaster? No, it would be worse than a catastrophe. Was it even possible to endure the silence as long as he knew Lucy could inflict it? She hadn't spoken a word to him for over two years the last time she was upset with him, far surpassing her record of three weeks when she was seven. Once, she had resorted to the trick of speaking through another. *"Joe, will you please tell your older brother to stop staring at me? His attentions are not welcome."* Had it not been out of desperation, he doubted she would have ever spoken to him. She'd come upon him first when sent to fetch his mother when Sarah was born. By the time she'd remembered she wasn't talking to him, Sarah was a week old. Reluctantly, she continued to speak to him when he promised to never tease her again. He teased her a million times in his mind, but never once had he acted upon his imaginings.

Samuel put both hands behind his neck and bent his head forward. *Oh, God, what is the right thing to do? I can't let Lucy die, but to force her into a marriage without her consent...* He waited for an answer. The snort of his father's horse broke the silence. *Please stop this insanity if it be wrong.*

He raised his head and dropped his hands to his side. "Bring Reverend Woods in the morning, and we will be ready. But first, we must take care of the graves." It seemed disrespectful to wed under the bodies of Lucy's mother, stepfather, and younger brother. "Will you bring my brothers also? I don't think the ground is frozen, but there will be quite a bit of digging."

Thomas nodded and gave Samuel a look of approval, the look Samuel had desired since returning to Boston. Odd that he would get his father's approval for doing the right thing in the wrong way.

Emma broke the silence, gesturing to a hefty basket. "It is enough to feed you and Sarah for a day or two. The small crock is beef broth. I will bring more as long as Lucy is ill."

Samuel took the basket. "Father, can you send John and Joe this afternoon or early tomorrow?" Samuel asked. "Lucy has been unable to tend to everything in the barn since—" The sentence faded away as Samuel gestured toward the roof. "Anyway, the stalls need a good mucking, and I don't want to leave Sarah alone with Lucy for the time it will take to do it."

"I'll bring all the boys. Mark can help in the stable, and the others can help with the digging of the graves. Anything else?"

"I can't locate the herb box. I am sure Mrs. Marden owned one."

"She owned a nice carved one," Emma confirmed.

"I found some ginger tea. Could you send over some peppermint, willow bark, and anything you think might help?"

"Is that what they taught you in school? Home remedies?" asked Thomas.

"No, Pa, but they did teach us that sometimes herbs can work as well as bleeding a patient."

Emma harrumphed. As a midwife, she often voiced her disdain about how doctors thought removing blood could cure anything.

"And, Ma, will you pray Lucy lives and forgives me?"

Samuel turned back into the house, his shoulders burdened by more than his mother's heavy basket.

Seven

Sarah rocked in the chair next to Lucy. Samuel stared at her. How was he going to explain the wedding to Sarah?

Setting the basket on the table, Samuel reached up to rub his head again. Mother always said if he worried too much he would rub the hair clean off. For a moment, he wondered if he might be bald before his wedding.

Sarah came to inspect the basket.

Her smile widened as Samuel unloaded ham and baked beans, potatoes kept warm in a towel, a crusty loaf of bread, and slices of shortening bread. There was also a fresh shirt for him.

Sarah clapped her hands and hurried to set the table.

Samuel poured the broth into a small pot and set it on the coals to heat; he would try to feed it to Lucy after giving Sarah supper.

He was tempted to tell Sarah about tomorrow's wedding now, but Lucy deserved to be told first, even if she could not hear him.

The day dragged on with Lucy shivering, then burning up, Sarah napping, Sarah needing to visit the privy again, and Lucy shivering again.

Samuel developed a new empathy for his mother.

Only the barn improved. Pa sent the twins over, and they spent the afternoon mucking and cleaning out the rancid structure. Although the barn needed more work, the stalls no longer reeked of neglect.

Supper was brightened by Sarah's chatter. He hadn't realized there was going to be a momma barn cat soon. Sarah insisted Samuel read the Bible before tucking her in with a warm brick and listening to her prayers.

Samuel choked up as Sarah blessed "Mama and Papa and Ben in heaven" and continued, "Thank thee for sending Samuel to take care of me and Lucy." He wondered if Lucy would be thanking God for sending him to her when she realized she would be stuck with him the rest of her life.

"Where are you going to sleep?"

"I'm going to stay up with Lucy the same as I did last night. I don't think I'll sleep, but if I do, I'll sleep in the rocking chair."

"That's what Mama and Lucy did when Papa and Ben were sick." Sarah raised her arms for a hug. He was amazed by the trust she showed in him. From the moment she'd seen him through the window yesterday morning, she'd accepted his being there and never doubted his help. Lucy had once trusted him—when she was five.

Once Sarah was tucked in bed and had drifted off, he stepped gingerly down the stairs lest a creak disturb either of the sleeping ladies. Lucy moaned and muttered something unintelligible as he reached the last step. By the time he entered her room, she'd stilled.

Samuel poured a bit of broth into a bowl and spooned the liquid between Lucy's lips. He was rewarded with a cough. When he tried to straighten the quilt, she attempted to toss it off. If her eyes had opened, he would have thought she was trying to be disagreeable.

Samuel realized he was rubbing his head again and stilled his hand. There was enough to be teased about without rubbing himself bald by morning.

"Lucy, just a little bit more." He held the spoon to her lips. "I am not sure if you can even hear me, but I've got a whole lot to say to you. Maybe if I say it now, you'll remember when you wake up and won't be too upset with me." *Or at least not so irate that you chase me home.*

"I'm not going to be a doctor, so people are not going to be too happy I am here tending to you. I know everyone expected me to be a doctor, but I faint at the sight of blood. Hard to imagine, but

I do. Didn't bother me all until about a year ago when we lost a young ...so I was dismissed from my apprenticeship. I promise you, tonight I'm going to be the best doctor I can be. You must live." *For so many reasons I can't even try to explain.*

"I have a surprise for you." *Not exactly like your favorite maple candy.*

"We are getting married in the morning." To his ears, he sounded falsely cheerful, like his ma did when he was in trouble. He rolled his eyes. *Worst proposal ever.*

The one by letter was eloquent, even if he never gave her that first promised kiss.

"I am still getting over the shock myself. I know I haven't even asked if you still want to be my wife. If you live till morning, you're not going to have much choice anyway, no matter how sick you are. Reverend Woods is not going to be pleased I spent two nights here without a proper chaperone. And neither are the old gossips." Heat rose to the tips of his ears. Lucy was not a lecture cadaver. Nor was she a backstreet doxy seeking free medical care from carefully supervised students.

Samuel slipped another sip of broth between Lucy's lips. He knew he was rambling, but this might be the only chance he could ever say everything at once. Telling her now would be good practice for when he explained later.

"I made a choice. I know I've been exposed to whatever illness you and your family have suffered. Ma offered to stay, but I wouldn't let her. They say I can only stay if I marry you."

"This isn't how I planned it." He set the empty bowl on the floor and took one of her limp hands in his.

"I've wanted to marry you for years. I was trying to get my nerve up to call on you and explain the letter and everything that happened. And I hoped maybe by next Christmas you would be willing to be my wife if I could afford it by then."

I'm trying to explain myself to an unconscious woman, and I still can't get up the nerve to say what I must. Samuel went to refill the bowl. He paced the cabin while he waited for it to cool.

It cooled faster than he expected. He coaxed another sip of broth down Lucy's throat. A faint moan escaped her parched lips. Samuel was sure she was completely unaware of his presence.

"I know it sounds like I've been forced to marry you, but it is not like that. I never wanted to call things off. But you deserve better than a failure, but ...I really like you." *More than like. Adore? Admire? Love?* He'd written better lines in his letters.

"Remember when I pulled your braid? You were wearing the blue dress Mr. Marden bought for your birthday. I pulled it because I didn't know what to say. You looked so much like a girl. That sounds stupid. I always knew you were a girl, but more like my sister sort of girl. My little shadow, but in the blue dress you looked more like a woman type of girl." Samuel trailed off, lost in the moment, when he realized Lucy was more the girl he wanted to steal kisses from rather than take fishing for trout. Or perhaps steal kisses while fishing.

"I didn't mean to make you mad. You were happy and so different than you used to be. I thought I could tease you like the other girls. I wasn't trying to be mean."

"I know I explained that in our letters, but I feel the same now as I did then. I am so unsure of what to do."

He could not recall a time when he couldn't remember having Lucy around. She had been his little shadow for years. He knew her better than he did his sister Carrie. The day he realized Lucy could be more than a friend was a shock sweeter than finding forgotten candy in a pocket. At age twelve she'd stopped being his shadow and became his light.

Then there was the day the friendship had ended with a single tug of a braid. He had not anticipated her reaction. "Samuel Taylor Wilson, you've grown up just like the rest of those mean old boys." Radiant in her anger, she'd stomped her foot. He had been dumbfounded. "You promised you would never be mean to me. You lied. I'm never going to like you again." Then she'd turned and run. Almost two years passed before she'd spoken to him again. Thankfully, the letters they'd posted back and forth the past three years, especially those after his sister's wedding, had restored the easy camaraderie they'd enjoyed as children, sharing their hopes and dreams.

Dreams he shattered.

"I'm pretty sure you hate me after the note and Elizabeth. I hope you change your mind, because if you never like me again, this is going to be one long marriage. If I could do it all over, I would have ridden to Gloucester the second I realized you were visiting there when I returned home. I would have run from Elizabeth's flirting so the children would not have carried tales that were not true."

He gently washed her face.

"I saw the slap when George Laurier tried to get you under the mistletoe at the Christmas ball three years ago. I should have done the same with Elizabeth, even if she was a lady."

Barely.

"I wanted to maneuver you under the mistletoe too." *Caring for you is going to be ever so much worse than stealing a kiss under the mistletoe.*

Samuel envied George the slap and wished he had been bold enough to say something to her then. Maybe they would have married last year.

Samuel filled the silence of the next hours by talking about Cambridge and the grand ships in the Boston harbor. Some of them reminded him of the stories of pirates, or privateers, as Lucy preferred to call them. During the summers, they'd play on the raft Thomas Jr. had built. While Junior wanted to act out stories of ruthless Barbados pirates, Lucy would insist they pretend to be the brave privateers who'd hoodwinked the British during the war. Samuel had found himself trapped between his older brother and best friend and suggested they be both.

He took the empty bowl and set it in the dry sink. Rewetting the cloth, he returned to her side. "I know we haven't officially courted because of our plan to marry and return to Cambridge before I graduated. We've never even kissed." He placed the cloth across her brow. "I owe you an apology for even glancing at Elizabeth. It was stupid to think if I ignored you that my problems would disappear. I didn't feel worthy of you when I got back. Since you were not here—No, none of it was your fault. You probably thought I'd lost every bit of sense I ever had to allow Miss Garrett within ten feet of me. Carrie declined to tell me about how horrid Elizabeth had been in school until after the children told the tale of us kissing in the orchard. How did I not know about the ants or the ink in your desk? I guess until that last year you were at the dame school, so I didn't witness her behavior."

"She has new tricks now. No wonder you avoided me. For the record, the kiss they saw—I didn't initiate it. I never thought a woman could be so brazen. I pushed her away, but by then they'd left. I think she kissed me because she knew Sarah and Matthew were spying."

Lucy shivered again. He pulled up the blankets.

"There is no way to apologize for this, is there? And I am going to have to repeat all of it when you awaken." Samuel wished for the thousandth time that he had not come up with the stupid idea of avoiding Lucy. It hadn't made anything better.

"I wish you would wake up. Even if you don't want to be married, it would be ever so much better if you did." He found himself praying that God would see fit to heal Lucy and that his poor doctoring skills would be enough.

"Remember when we could talk about everything? That's why I knew you would be the only one I could ever tell about the blood. I am so ashamed. I thought I would get over it. Instead it got worse. A man can't be a doctor and not deal with blood. I tried. Honest, I tried. We need a doctor, and I thought after helping you with all your scrapes that I could be one."

Lucy moaned and started to thrash. Samuel laid his hand on her head. She was hotter than ever. He pulled off the quilts and rinsed her arms and face.

"Don't you dare die on me. I promise I will be a good husband and you won't regret living. Please wake up."

For the next hour or so Samuel prayed as he worked to cool Lucy off as she writhed and moaned. Finally she calmed down. For a moment Samuel thought she might have died. He thought of listening for a heartbeat, but putting his head to her breast seemed a bit too intimate. After what seemed like minutes but was just a few seconds, Lucy sighed.

Samuel released the breath he'd been holding, then covered her with a single blanket against the chill of the room and rose to check the fire.

The wood box was almost empty. There was enough dry wood to last the night, but tomorrow morning he would ask his brothers to bring more wood into the lean-to.

Samuel yawned. He needed sleep. He stood in the doorway of the large bedroom. The room had lost most of its stench. Still, whiffs of death lingered in the shadows. The oversized four-poster mocked him. He knew better than to sleep on the straw tick without bedclothes, especially one that needed fresh straw and washing. Lucy must have removed the soiled linens and hid them from view, intending to wash them on the first sunny day. He hadn't seen them about the house. She must have placed them where Sarah could not find them. His mind wandered about the house and barn, finally settling on the basket in the corner on the far side of the bed in her parents' room.

He needed to find the outdoor kettle and wash the linens in the morning before his family arrived. After they were boiled in hot water, they could be ironed dry. He hoped he could get away without scrubbing them. Passing out while scrubbing sheets was not acceptable. His wedding day would not be the day to test his strength.

The faster the large bedroom could be back in order, the fewer questions Sarah could ask. Apparently Lucy had planned to put the room to rights and let Sarah sleep in the big bed with her soon. Sarah mentioned the promise every time she had the chance.

Samuel started to blush. This would be his bed—his and Lucy's. Best not to let his mind wander in too far. It might tuck itself in and curl up for the night.

He backed out of the room. He didn't belong there yet.

First Lucy needed to get well. Then she might forgive him for marrying her while she couldn't even protest. Sarah and Lucy would share the bed for a long time while he slept in Ben's bed. Or the barn.

Pulling the quilt from Ben's recently freshened bed across his shoulders, he thought about the quilt-wrapped bodies on the roof. He'd recognized the quilt his mother had made for James and Anna's wedding because he had been cajoled into helping with it. He was surprised she'd chosen the quilt as her mother's shroud, yet, considering what the quilt represented, the gesture was fitting. He wondered if Lucy had made a special quilt for her marriage bed.

Samuel caught himself rubbing his head again. Yup. Bald by morning, or at least well before Lucy ever let him in the big bedroom.

Lucy moaned and started to thrash about once again.

Samuel leaned over her, attempting to calm her, his hand on her shoulder.

"No, no! Not Mama! I'm the bad girl. I'm the bad girl."

A nightmare.

"Hush, Lucy. You're safe." Samuel brushed the hair from her forehead.

"No! No! No barn!" Lucy shouted and tried to rise.

Samuel restrained her by the shoulders. "Lucy, it's Samuel. You're safe. Hush, now. Hush."

Lucy's eyes fluttered open. "Samuel?" She gazed at him for a moment before taking a deep breath, then her face relaxed, and her eyes closed as the dream left her.

Well, at least in her nightmares she must not hate me. Hope filled Samuel with the thought that his presence had calmed her. At the same time, he worried about a nightmare so vivid it gave Lucy the strength to fight him and try to rise.

The mantel clock announced the time—three in the morning. Before the small hand of the clock completed a full rotation, he would be married. Then he would write his name next to hers in the Bible: *Samuel Taylor Wilson married Lucy Simms, November 30, 1797.* He hoped it would be the last entry he would pen for a while.

"Lucy, I know you are sleeping, but I still have much to tell you, or ask you." Unbidden, his hand reached up to rub the back of his head. He jerked it back. He would not be bald for his wedding. "Elizabeth was a mistake. I kept hoping she could be more…more like you. Be my friend. She seemed so eager. I don't know what all she seemed. Since you can't agree with me at the moment, let's just say I was an idiot to see anything in her at all. Ma tried to get me to see you first, but I was so ashamed. I didn't want you to pity me. You had such faith in me being a doctor. I'll make a much better farmer. And I still have woodworking." He knew he was repeating himself, but if Lucy could hear him in her dreams, it might help later.

"People will say I married you for this farm. It's not true, Lucy. I would marry you without the farm because, well, you are you. I am not doing this very well. Maybe it's good you can't hear me ramble on."

For a while, Samuel rocked silently. Eventually he dozed, until Lucy stirred. He woke enough to adjust her quilts.

He still needed to ask her one question.

"I know you will never believe me later, but I am going to ask." He unfolded himself from the chair and set his quilt aside, then knelt at her side and brushed the hair from her face. Gently, as if picking up a crystal vase in a Boston store, he cradled her hand in his. He ran his thumb back and forth over it, wishing she could feel the connection, and asked the most important question of his life.

"Lucy Simms, will you do me the honor of being my wife? You don't need to answer right away, but I will take your living through the ceremony as a good sign." He brought her fingers to his lips and pressed a kiss to their tips, bowed his head, and prayed.

Eight

SAMUEL AWOKE TO A LITTLE hand trying to pry open his eyes. When he did open them, he was greeted by a hug.

"You stayed. Is Lucy dead yet? Are you going to put her on the roof of heaven too?" Samuel had seen a glimpse of how talkative the little girl could be last night, but it had not prepared him for the onslaught of questions she had for him so early this morning. He opened his arms, and Sarah climbed into his lap. "Lucy is still very much alive. See, you can see her breathing, and she isn't as hot as she was last night.

"Is that good?"

"Yes, little one. That is very good."

They rocked for a moment. Samuel contemplated how to tell Sarah about the day's plans and not create more questions than he could answer.

"I have something important to tell you. After we eat, my ma and pa are going to come with Reverend Woods and my brothers. We are going to go out on the porch, but we can't touch or hug any of them because we are under quarantine."

"Qu-or-in-tine?" Sarah's mouth struggled around the new word.

"Yes. That means there is sickness in the house and healthy people must stay away."

"But you came."

"Yes, I came to take care of you and Lucy."

"Then why is Reverend Woods coming? To bury Papa and Mama and Ben?"

"Partly for a funeral, but they are also coming so I can marry Lucy."

"But you don't want to marry her. I heard her tell Mama."

"I do want to marry her."

"But Lucy is sick. Sick people don't get married." Sarah gave him a knowing look.

"In this case, sick people do marry."

Sarah scowled at him. Samuel raised his eyes heavenward. *God? I could use a little help here if I can't convince a five-year-old I should get married.*

"But Lucy doesn't have flowers. She needs flowers to get married. Your sister had lots and lots and let me hold some." Sarah delivered this statement with all the authority of a mother of five eligible daughters.

Samuel remembered the little girl dancing about with her miniature bouquet. He had been more interested in her older sister, who'd stood up with Carrie. Lucy had radiated such beauty the morning of the wedding in his parents' parlor. He'd envisioned himself saying his vows to her as he let his mind wander during the ceremony. Lucy had little flowers woven into her hair. Lavender. He had been tempted to propose on the spot. Instead, he'd proposed by post a month later.

"And she needs a dress. She was going to go get fabric, but you wrote her and made her cry. So she didn't sew a new one." Sarah's brow furrowed a perfect imitation of his ma when she scolded him. Were women born knowing that pose?

"And she has to talk and say yes. Lucy is sleeping and can't say anything," Sarah continued, seemingly not needing to breathe between sentences.

"You may need to say yes for her. If Lucy was awake, do you think she would marry me?" He wasn't sure he wanted to hear the answer, but better now than in front of witnesses.

Sarah studied Samuel.

"Do you know she is alive?"

"Of course she is alive. I helped her stay alive all night." What inane questions five-year-olds asked.

Sarah shook her head. "I thought Lucy said you didn't know.. ."—her face scrunched up—"Why would she say you thought she was dead?" she asked.

It suddenly dawned on Samuel that Sarah was referring to a past conversation. One centered on his lack of attention. He could almost hear Lucy complain. "*Samuel doesn't even know I am alive.*" His sister had expressed similar sentiments about more than one young man. He swallowed. "I think she meant I hadn't been properly courting her."

"Do you like Lucy? And will you be nice to her? No more making her cry?"

"I made her cry?"

Sarah held up her hand and counted on her fingers. "When you sent her that last letter. When you kissed Elizabeth at the cider pressing."

"I did not ki—"

"When you didn't come when the storm was done. You make her cry lots. That's not very nice." A scolding finger wagged in his face.

Samuel nodded. If he opened his mouth, he would blurt out the truth, and Lucy should hear it before her little sister did. He loved Lucy.

"Then you can marry my big sister, but only if you are very nice. My papa was nice. But Lucy's first papa wasn't. He yelled all the time and never smiled." Samuel thought it peculiar she would know about Mr. Simms.

"I promise to be very nice to Lucy."

"Forever and ever?"

"Forever and ever." Tension flowed out of Samuel's shoulders as he gave Sarah a broad smile.

"Where will you live?"

"Right here."

"Where will I live?"

"You will live with us.'

"Will you sleep in Ben's room?

"For now I will."

"Lucy promised we could sleep in the big bed. When she gets well, I get to sleep with her. Do you want to sleep in the big bed too? It is the bestest in the whole house. Maybe you could sleep with Lucy too."

Samuel nearly choked. A five-year-old had just given him permission to share a bed with her older sister. Oblivious to his dilemma, Sarah continued her questioning.

"Will you be my new papa?"

"No, I will be your brother-in-law. That is almost the same as being your brother."

Sarah's brow furrowed as she pondered this.

"Should I call you Brother Samuel?"

"No, you can just call me Samuel."

"Will there be a cake? I like cake."

Samuel laughed and tugged at the hair sticking out from under her cap.

Sarah hopped off his lap. "I better get dressed. Can I wear my church dress?"

Samuel nodded.

"And, Samuel? Will you brush out my hair all pretty? Mama's brush is on the table in her room. It is the prettiest brush in the whole house."

"You get your clothes, and I will get the brush."

As he brushed the fine chestnut hair, he noticed his hands were shaking. Thankfully Sarah didn't want any braids, just a ribbon.

Samuel sliced some bread and smothered it with butter. He gave it to Sarah and asked her to sit in the chair next to Lucy. He hurried to take care of the animals. In the barn, he found a large cauldron and hung it over the outdoor pit. After filling the pot with snow, he started a fire. Once it melted, he would add the bedclothes and let them boil clean. He hoped it would be done before everyone arrived.

After a more substantial breakfast, Samuel washed in the lean-to and changed into the fresh shirt his mother had sent.

"Lucy can't get married in her shift," Sarah announced when Samuel reentered the room.

"I am going to wrap her up in her quilts, so no one will see her shift."

Sarah furrowed her brow, a sign Samuel now recognized as an expression of deep thought.

"Then we must brush out her hair. When girls marry, they don't have braids. They have pretty hair. Can you put it up?"

"I don't know how."

Sarah's brow furrowed. "Well, brushed out it is pretty. Lucy has very long hair. If you can't pin it up, better let it down."

Samuel nodded. He untied the ribbon on Lucy's braid, careful not to pull her hair. Sarah helped him unravel it. He brushed it, careful of any snarls, giving extra care to every rat's nest he found, not wanting to hurt her. Then he arranged it around Lucy's head. Samuel thought she appeared even paler against the contrast of her dark hair. He'd always loved her hair. It reminded him of making maple syrup in the big cauldron when the sun shone on it, with hints of red and the darkest of browns. The one time he'd teased her about it, he asked if it were sticky. It was not. It was silky, like a baby kitten's fur. Under different circumstances, he would have liked to play with it much longer.

"She still needs flowers, like in her hair at Carrie's wedding." Sarah's face twisted in concentration. Samuel bit his cheek to prevent him from laughing out loud. The little girl's eyes popped open wide as inspiration came. "There is some lavender hanging on the ceiling. You can get some." Sarah tugged Samuel out of the room and pointed to the cluster of lavender among the dried herbs and vegetables hanging from the rafters. He reached up and broke off a stem. The dried lavender was as delicate as it was fragrant. Samuel set it on the table. "Let's leave it here until just before we go outside. That way it won't break."

Sarah smiled at his choice.

Then he went back into the bedroom and stared at his bride. There was no blush to color her cheeks as at Carrie's wedding. No sparkle in her eyes. Today he would not look into her eyes and be met with a shy smile as they said their vows. Her lashes wouldn't lower demurely when he was given leave to kiss her, though he doubted that part would be said. If there were any color staining her cheeks, it would be from fever. Any color would worry his heart, not cause it to beat faster.

If Lucy would open her eyes, even looking at him in anger would be better than this deep slumber.

As if she heard his wish, Lucy's eyes opened but focused on Sarah. "Sarah?"

"Oh, Lucy, you waked up! Now you can marry Samuel. We fixed your hair."

"Sarah, I told you Samuel doesn't love me; I can't mar—" Lucy slurred her words as her eyes slid closed once more.

"But he does, Lucy, he does." Sarah's pleas did no good as Lucy slept on.

Samuel led Sarah away from her sister's side. "Did Lucy ever tell you she couldn't marry me?"

"Yes, she said you didn't know she was alive. Which is silly, because you see she is not on the heaven roof." Sarah rolled her eyes at him. "She said you loved someone else. That is silly because Mama and Mrs. Wilson say she loves you and you love her but you are both fools." Sarah added a nod of agreement to her statement.

Samuel rubbed his neck. The old saying was true—little pitchers did have big ears. He pondered what she'd said. "*Samuel doesn't love me*," not "*I don't love Samuel*." Did he dare quiz Sarah? Maybe, just maybe, Lucy would forgive him someday and come to see how he loved her.

"Hello in the house!" Samuel recognized the shout from one of the twins.

"Stay with Lucy." The command was unnecessary. Samuel grabbed his coat and hurried out.

Both boys stood several yards from the house.

"Ma and Pa said to expect them about noon," John yelled, his hands cupped around his mouth.

"Ma sent some food in the basket there." Joe pointed to a basket Samuel hadn't noticed on the porch. "Also your go-to-meeting clothes."

"Samuel's getting married today! No, no, oh, so, no. Oh, oh, poor Samuel. Ooooo!" they sang in unison. Samuel groaned. He thought he'd erased the tune from his head.

"No, John, we got it wrong! No, no, oh, so, no. Oh, oh, poor Lucy!" The teens' laughter filled the air as they disappeared between the barn doors.

Noticing the steaming caldron, Samuel retrieved the bundle of soiled bedding from behind the house. He tried not to examine the bundle too closely as he used the long paddle to stir the laundry. The Mardens, like most neighbors, had built an outside fire pit with a windbreak where laundry could be boiled, soap made, and lard rendered, along with all the other smelly jobs he'd detested helping with as a youth. Before returning to the cabin, he yelled at Joe, or possibly John, to give the vat an occasional stir and to let the hot water do most of the work.

Inside, he hung his coat and glanced at the mantel clock. Ten. Two more hours and he would be a married man. Shaking his head in disbelief, he watched at his sleeping bride-to-be. *No, no, oh, so, no. Oh, oh, poor Lucy.* Indeed.

"Samuel? Lucy is really hot." Sarah's worried face turned up at him expectantly.

Samuel placed his hand on Lucy's brow. Her fever had returned.

He retrieved a bucket of snow, which he used to cool Lucy's face and arms.

"You should do her legs too. That's what Lucy did to Ben," Sarah shared.

Samuel nodded. Even though he had done the same during the night by the dim light of the fire, to do so in the light of day with Sarah watching made him squirm uncomfortably. "Forgive me, Lucy …it must be done." He tried to concentrate on the benefits of the cooling snow. By daylight, he couldn't help but acknowledge the magnificent curve of Lucy's calf and delicate ankles.

"Think like a doctor," he muttered under his breath, trying to banish such thoughts. He concentrated on bathing Lucy's face and her arms, cursing the part of his brain that again filled with thoughts of how nice it would be to fully take Lucy as his bride. Doctors didn't think like that, but, then, doctors generally didn't marry their patients either.

As she had last night, Lucy started to mutter and moan in indecipherable sentences.

"Oh, it is one of Lucy's bad dreams," piped Sarah.

Samuel raised one eyebrow as Sarah explained.

"Sometimes Lucy has bad dreams and she yells. Mama would sing to her. Should I sing to her?"

Samuel nodded.

Sarah began to sing, her sweet voice filling the room. "'Lavender's blue, diddle diddle, Lavender's green, When I am king, diddle diddle, You shall be queen. Lavender's green, diddle diddle, Lavender's blue, You must love me, diddle diddle, 'Cause I love you.'"

Samuel choked on his own breath. A love song with several bawdy verses, and lavender—the fragrance he'd always associated with Lucy. Even mingled with the smells of the sickroom he could still make out its sweet fragrance. Sarah didn't seem to know the racier verses, a small mercy in Samuel's mind. He imagined sharing kisses and more with Lucy in the shade of a tree. The thoughts made his heart race. He'd often heard the drinking song sung in Boston's taverns, and though Sarah wasn't aware of the fabled lovers' tryst, he was. Now he pictured Lucy as his queen. Valiantly he tried to not imagine acting out the song with his soon-to-be wife. But he couldn't help himself as he thought about how there was a perfect little vale near the stream on the Marden property where wild lavender grew. He attempted to cool his thoughts as he used more snow to cool the fever.

"Down in the vale, diddle diddle, Where flowers grow, And the birds sing, diddle diddle, All in a row. Lavender's green, diddle diddle, Lavender's blue, You must love me, diddle diddle, 'Cause I love you." Sarah's voice faltered on notes.

As his agitation over the song grew, Lucy began to calm with Sarah's singing. Her muttering stilled. Mercifully, Sarah stopped singing.

Samuel dipped the cloth again and noticed Lucy was starting to shiver. Quickly he pulled the quilt over her. Had he cooled her too much?

Please, God, let her live ... at least long enough to ... to what? In his mind he pictured Lucy singing to her own daughter, Sarah helping her. Yes, he wanted Lucy to live long enough to have a family and long enough to love him. Would that God grant him such a boon?

Voices drifted in through the closed windows, and he glanced at the clock. Both hands stood at attention. Noon. They'd worked for more than an hour to bring Lucy's fever down. He rubbed the back of his neck. How would this work? Could he risk wrapping Lucy in a blanket and taking her to the doorway? Ma had said something about Sarah being a proxy. Samuel dismissed the idea. Better to let everyone know Lucy was alive. A quilt should suffice to keep her warm and covered if they were quick. For once, would Reverend Woods be succinct?

"Company is here," announced Sarah.

Nine

"Remember what I said about not hugging my ma?"

Sarah nodded and took her cloak from Samuel's outstretched hand.

As he expected, his parents, younger brothers Daniel and Mark, and Reverend Woods were in the wagon-turned-sleigh, its wheels replaced by runners. He nodded to each and noticed there were more men on horseback behind the sleigh, among them his older brother Thomas Jr. and his sister Carrie's husband, Paul. Since both lived east of town, he knew Ma had been busy spreading the word. He recognized four other men from church. One was Elizabeth's older brother, and two were the husbands of notorious gossips. He was sure they were sent as informants. He was surprised to see George Laurier. Once Lucy's friend, the two had not spoken since she had slapped him for trying to steal a kiss. Samuel suspected he'd come for Lucy's sake.

"How is Lucy?" Emma asked.

"Still holding her own," Samuel said nonchalantly. He didn't want to share the details with the entire group.

"She scared me." Sarah piped up from beside him. Samuel rolled his eyes. So much for avoiding details. "She got all hot and then cold, just like Ben did. It took us forever to cool her off. And she ruined her pretty hair that Samuel brushed out for the wedding." Samuel placed his hand on Sarah's shoulder, hoping she would stop speaking. Emma smiled and nodded her acknowledgment. That nod seemed to be enough to stop Sarah. Samuel filed that bit of parenting wisdom away for future use. Maybe showing he was listening was all the little chatterbox needed to end her prattle.

The family climbed out of the wagon, and Emma herded the boys off to the barn.

Reverend Woods, dressed from hat to shoes in black, was as grim as ever. He addressed Samuel from the wagon bed, where he remained sitting ramrod straight, as if he were one of the several shovels lying next to him. "Samuel, your parents told me of your choice to care for Miss Simms despite the lack of a proper chaperone."

Sarah stood on her toes, making herself as tall as possible, and cleared her throat several times. "Thank you, Miss Sarah, for doing your best to help too," the reverend kindly noted. "I agree with your father. The proper step is to wed so both your reputations remain spotless. Since your intentions were posted several months ago, I can officiate. However, the lack of ... shall I say, progress ... in your relationship these past few weeks has made me wonder if matrimony is right for you. My other option is to allow the magistrate to fine you for fornication...so a marriage it will be."

Samuel glanced at the rest of the men. All seemed preoccupied with tying their horses, but he knew they were hanging on every word, filing it all away to be reported verbatim later.

"Since today is a fair day and the snow is melting, these good men volunteered to come and dig the graves." The reverend gestured to the eavesdropping men.

That is not why they volunteered, and you know it. Samuel did not let the sarcastic words cross his lips. He didn't need to. His crossed arms and let his glower say it for him.

"If you don't mind, we will take care of the burial first. Funerals before weddings, I always say." The minister turned and directed the men to the hill where the Marden's family plot lay.

Emma took a step forward. "Samuel, I brought some more things for you. I'll have the boys put them on the porch. And, Miss Sarah, I brought a little cake for after the wedding, for you and your new brother Samuel to share." Emma placed particular emphasis on the word *after*, but not so much on *share*.

Sarah clapped her mittened hands for joy. Samuel's gentle hand on her shoulder restrained her from running to Mrs. Wilson. "I wanna hug you, but I will save it for when the quart-er-tine is gone and Samuel says I can." There was no mistaking the sincerity of the promise.

"Samuel, may I speak with you privately?" Emma nodded her head in Sarah's direction.

Samuel bent to look Sarah in the eye. "I need you to watch Lucy for a moment."

"I'll yell if I need you again." Sarah rushed back into the cabin, her hair bouncing with her excitement.

Samuel gestured toward the side of the house, where the laundry still soaked in the cauldron.

"Are you ready to do this, son?"

Samuel rubbed his neck, shook his head, nodded, and finally shrugged. "Ma, I am sure I want to marry her, but I am worried about Lucy's reaction."

Momentarily distracted, Emma peered into the huge pot. "What is this?" Steam still curled from the top, though the fire had burned down to just embers.

Samuel groaned. He had not been able to get back out to move the bedding. Not something he wanted others to witness.

"Oh, it's the bedding to Mrs. Marden's bed. Lucy hid it in the bedroom. I figured I'd better wash it up."

"Samuel, you are not—?" Emma didn't finish the question, but the blush on her cheeks let him know the direction of her thoughts.

"No, Ma! Not—not until Lucy agrees." The heat rising in his face was not from the steaming linens. "Anna delivered a baby boy before she died. I didn't want the bedclothes sitting around." *The odor of blood was going to cause me to faint.*

Emma nodded.

He picked up the paddle to stir the linens. There was no real way to express his thoughts about what Lucy had endured.

Emma reached for the paddle. "I'll finish these. They will need to be hung and ironed." Emma stirred the cooling laundry, lifting it and inspecting the sheets. She clucked her tongue. "You were never any good helping with laundry, never scrubbed long enough. I'll ask your father to bring over a bale of sweet straw I was saving. The ticking on James and Anna's bed probably needs changing too."

"I'll get the ticking and empty it."

Emma put up her hand.

"Not today, son." She nodded toward the hill. "We don't need those men going and telling their wives any more tales. In fact, I am better off bundling these up in one of the baskets and finishing them at home. Most of the men here wouldn't think bedsheets hanging out on the sunniest day in weeks as unusual. But if childbirth left a stain that hadn't washed out—" The uncompleted thought hung uncomfortably in the air.

"Oy." Samuel reddened again. There was no use adding imagined problems to those already existing.

Thump! The boys dropped a crate on the porch. Emma winced at the sound. "Your brothers put everything on the porch. I sent your good clothes over earlier. Go on and hurry now. I won't have one of my boys getting married in his everyday work clothes." Emma clucked at him.

Samuel wondered if she thought the greatest travesty of the day was his clothing. Lucy would not know what he wore. She was in her shift! But he supposed he should make the effort to dress as presentable as he would were she able to stand beside him.

Samuel gathered several items in his arms, including a new yellow-and-blue star quilt. He fingered the corner. When had she made it? He knew the pattern's name because he'd admired the one she'd made for Thomas Jr.'s wedding and received a discourse on the name and pattern for his comment.

"Samuel," Emma called. "Save the quilt till—well, until you are married." This time Emma blushed a bit.

A few things? His mother needed a new definition of "a few," thought Samuel as he made his fourth trip into the house. There was his trunk, a smaller one he didn't recognize, a crate of linens, and the new quilt. Not to mention the daily basket of food. The little frosted cake promised Sarah sat on top, wedged in between several small loaves of bread.

He set the coveted dessert in the center of the table. Sarah left Lucy's side to inspect it. She gave Samuel a hopeful smile. When he shook his head, she returned to Lucy.

He hoisted his trunk up the stairs, intent on using Ben's room as his for the time being. He placed the new linens and quilt in the corner of the big bedroom. He thought it best to let Lucy decide when to use them. The little trunk was tagged with Lucy's name. He put it in her parents' room too.

Lucy slept peacefully as Sarah rocked next to her whispering to her doll about the cake. She promised the doll her very own piece. Samuel wondered if he should indulge her this one time. Two pieces of cake shouldn't give her a tummy ache if he sliced them both thin. He smiled. Sarah's joy was contagious.

Samuel left her in the rocking chair and took the opportunity to run up to Ben's room to change into his Sunday clothes.

He was just straightening his collar when someone knocked on the door below.

Samuel rushed down and opened it to find his father and Reverend Woods standing at the edge of the porch.

"The grave is dug. We are going to get them off the roof now." His father's gaze drifted to the ropes tied to the post.

"Your mother thinks it best if you and Sarah come up while I say a few words." From his tone, it was clear the minister did not agree. While he encouraged children to attend church, he didn't approve of children at funerals.

"Ma knows you don't want to leave Lucy. She asked Joe to stand here by the window. If he hears anything, he will send John running." Thomas indicated the bench near the door.

Samuel considered for a moment "What of the quarantine?"

"Just stay on the downhill side, and we should be far enough away."

Samuel nodded. Sarah should see the blankets holding her family in the ground and not just disappear from the roof.

"I'll get Sarah ready."

Thomas nodded. "We will get them down now." He stepped to the ropes. Samuel shut the door but quickly opened it again.

"Pa, one of those ropes was the guide rope to the barn. Will you make sure Joe puts it back up? The ring is to the left of the barn door."

Thomas nodded and continued to work on the knotted ropes.

Samuel closed the door. He knelt on one knee in front of Sarah and did his best to block out the sounds coming from the roof above them.

"The men finished digging the grave on the hill. Reverend Woods is going to give your folks and Ben a proper burial. You are a big girl now, and the minister says you can come. We won't stand near the rest of the people. Let's get your cloak and scarf and walk up together."

Sarah nodded and glanced at Lucy. "Lucy?"

"Joe will stay outside listening for her. We won't be gone long."

Sarah slipped into her sister's room and patted Lucy on the arm before disappearing upstairs.

Samuel sat in the rocker Sarah had vacated.

"Lucy, we are going to do the funeral before we have our wedding. I won't be long. If you were awake, I would carry you up the hill so you could be there too. I am so sorry, sweetheart." As he brushed the hair away from her face, it tangled around his fingers. They'd brushed it out too soon. He wasn't sure there would be time to do it again between the funeral and the wedding. His finger caught in a tangle. He vowed he would make time even if the wedding party stood in the yard waiting. It was the one thing he could do for Lucy on her wedding day.

Sarah reappeared with a small round river rock, a pinecone, and a bit of flowered cloth cupped in her hands. Samuel raised his brow.

Sarah gave him one of her long-suffering looks, telling him it should be obvious what she was doing. "For their graves. Flowers for Mama—but I don't have real flower so I took dolly's blanket—a rock for Papa's collection, and a pinecone for Ben."

Once she explained, he knew she was right. It should have been obvious.

Another knock. "It's time, son!" echoed through the door.

Samuel buttoned Sarah's cloak, wrapped a scarf around her neck, and poured her treasures into her mittened hands.

Halfway up the hill, he swung Sarah into his arms as much to help Sarah over the snow as to give him something to hold. His heart ached for the woman lying in the cabin.

Reverend Woods kept his remarks brief as he stood over the single grave holding the three quilted cocoons. There had not been time for coffins. The quilts would be the final shrouds for the four Mardens. Either Reverend Woods was unaware or had been warned by Emma as the sole mention of the baby was a reference to "James, Anna, and their sons." The plural was probably missed by others, who didn't know of the baby's birth.

In the spring, Samuel would order a proper headstone with all four names. By the time Sarah could read it, Lucy would be able to tell the story of their baby brother.

As soon as he'd finished his prayer, Reverend Woods asked Sarah to toss a bit of soil into the deep hole.

Sarah looked at the quilts, then at the minister. "They are not really there. They are in heaven."

Reverend Woods gave the child a patronizing smile and turned to Samuel. "We will be down in a moment to handle the other matter. These men can finish the work." Several of the men he'd indicated gave slight scowls. They'd come to report on the wedding and had been outsmarted by the clergyman. "Your brother and brother-in-law can witness. It would be best if you could bring Lucy outside. Just wrap her up. I will keep it short. I don't want to make her worse, but I want to do this right."

Elizabeth's brother stifled a smirk, then he looked at the house and his grin faded. The porch was not visible from the hill. There would be nothing to report beyond the minister's words.

Samuel picked up Sarah and waded through the snow back to the cabin. *How can the minister claim to "do it right" when Lucy is sleeping?*

Sarah's singing drowned out his thoughts. "Samuel is marrying Lucy! Samuel is marrying Lucy!"

Joe stepped off the porch as they approached. "I didn't hear a sound, Sam."

"Thanks, Joe." Samuel set Sarah down and went into the house.

Joe was right. Lucy was sleeping in the same position she'd been in when he'd left.

Samuel took the brush and tried to smooth her tangled hair. He winced for her when he caught a bad snarl, but Lucy didn't even flinch.

"Sweetheart, this is your last chance to back out. I am going to wrap you up and carry you outside. When we come in, you are going to be Mrs. Samuel Wilson." His efforts with the brush this time around did not match the results he'd produced earlier. No one but Sarah and he would see Lucy's beautiful maple-syrup hair, but he sensed the need to make Lucy as presentable as possible. Or as presentable as an oblivious bride being wed in her shift could be. He knew his father brushed his mother's hair one hundred strokes every night. *What would Lucy think if I told her that on her wedding day I brushed twice that?*

Lucy was going to toss a fit when she learned of her wedding and her state of undress. It would have been better had they said their vows *verba de praesenti*. But heaven knew a multitude of brides and grooms had wed in a less-respectable state of dress, married by unwitnessed vows through the ages, than Lucy was right now. At least there were no affronted fathers or firearms involved here.

Samuel wrapped a quilt around Lucy, making sure her feet were well covered. He hoped she would approve of his choice. The blue flowered print and green squares put him in mind of her song. Lucy's face peeked through the gap in the quilt. He left another quilt over a chair near the fire to warm her when they returned.

"Don't forget this." Sarah held out the sprig of dried lavender they'd set aside. Samuel tucked it into Lucy's hair.

Despite the bulkiness of the quilt, Lucy was still much easier to carry than he expected. Sarah held open the door for them to pass through.

Reverend Woods stood with Samuel's parents flanking him, his younger brothers smirking. Thomas Jr. and Paul kept their faces schooled so as not to show their thoughts.

"You will need to take her hand."

Using the porch rail, Samuel balanced Lucy while he fished out her hand. He tried not to let her shift show.

"Adjust the blanket so I can see her face, too, please." Satisfied, Reverend Woods opened his book and started. "Being now assembled in the...Samuel Taylor Wilson the woman you now have by the hand , you take to be your wedded wife and you promise by Divine assistance to love and honor her..." The familiar words flowed around Samuel until the reverend paused.

"Yes." His answer was more of a squeak than the decisive 'yes' he planned to utter.

Reverend Woods continued addressing Lucy. Her inert form in Samuel's arms grew heavier the longer the minister spoke, and he found it necessary to adjust Lucy a bit. As he did so, she moaned, and her eyes fluttered.

"Sa—?"

"Darling, Reverend Woods wants to know if you will marry me," Samuel whispered as the reverend spoke.

"...you will cleave unto him only, so lo—"

"—es" Lucy turned her head into his shoulder and closed her eyes. The sounds she made were not much different than some spoken in delirium only an hour ago. Samuel doubted their validity even as he watched his ma dab her eyes.

Reverend Woods took Lucy's mumbling as an affirmative answer to the question he'd posed and continued with the next section. "I then pronounce you to be Husband and Wife; married according to the laws of this Commonwealth..." He looked up from his book and around to each member of the small gathering. "Ordinarily I would tell you kiss the bride, but considering..." Reverend Woods said, faltering. This had to be the most unusual ceremony of his career.

Samuel nodded and placed a kiss on her brow. Or at least he meant to. His mouth caught the corner of the quilt and a wisp of her hair, causing him to gag and cough. Chuckles sounded around him.

"Congratulations, son!" Emma cheered. "Now get her back inside."

Sarah followed him. "Now we can eat cake, right, Samuel?"

"Of course. Dolly should eat a piece too, don't you think?"

She flung her arms around his legs, nearly causing him to topple and drop Lucy onto the bed.

"Sarah, will you get the quilt from the chair?"

Sarah laid her cheek on it. "Warm," she purred.

Samuel unwrapped Lucy, taking care not to wake her, and covered her with the warmed quilt. Checking over his shoulder, he found Sarah more interested in the cake than in him. He placed a kiss on Lucy's brow. One day he would wake Lucy with a proper kiss, but for now he let her sleep.

Ten

WHEN ASKED LATER, SAMUEL COULD recall only generalities of the three days following the "wedding." Bringing down Lucy's fever. Guiding Sarah to the necessary. Chasing a raccoon from the necessary. He did remember that, but not which evening. It was hard to forget opening the door to a critter who'd decided to defend its territory. Sarah's scream didn't help. After banging on the back of the little building, Samuel had persuaded the raccoon to leave, but it had heartily chastised him from a nearby tree.

Too late, he found the Marden's herb box, where it had slid under the couch in her parents' room, nearly empty. The mortar and pestle were also there, but the mortar had been crushed by a misstep or perhaps a fall to the floor as Lucy had rushed about, caring for her mother. Each afternoon his mother or brothers came to exchange the emptied crocks for another one of his mother's dinners. His brothers spent time in the barn as evidenced by the growing compost heap.

On the third night, Joe, or maybe John—Samuel was too tired to even attempt to guess which brother it was—brought the food basket over with notes for Samuel and Sarah. Emma asked Samuel to check his flour and sugar supplies and make a list for the next day's trip to the mercantile. The portion addressed to Sarah caused Samuel to panic. "*And, Miss Sarah, when the quarantine is over, I want you to help me with all of my Christmas baking. It should take three or four days, and you can sleep on our guest cot …*"

Samuel choked. Did his mother think getting Sarah out of the house for three days would . . . Samuel was not ready to be alone with Lucy. The problem was, he thought about it way too much. Every time it was necessary to cool Lucy down, he had to squelch his errant thoughts. When she shivered, he thought about warming her. When her dreams overcame her, ideas of protecting and soothing her filled his mind, which he did follow through on for the most part. He didn't need those thoughts while staring at his mother's handwriting.

Near midnight, Lucy's fever burned hotter than ever before. Samuel hoped this would be the final crisis as he ran cooling cloths over Lucy's face and arms. Her lips cracked despite his efforts to administer sips of broth often, and her face took on a hollowness.

"Come on, Lucy. Let's fight it one more time. You need to wake up. You owe me a big slap across the face because what I did is worse than George under the mistletoe. I maneuvered you into matrimony."

As he ran the cloth over Lucy's feet, he admitted something he'd refused to acknowledge all day. The shift must be changed. There was a clean shift in the laundry his mother had returned. If Lucy wasn't going to be angry enough at finding herself married, just wait until she learned he'd changed her shift. Sighing, he inched the shift up past her knees so he could pack snow around her legs.

"I'm her husband. There is nothing wrong with a husband changing his sick wife's shift." No matter how many times he repeated it, it sounded false. There was everything wrong with it if the wife didn't know she was married. He would wait until after the fever broke. Maybe she would wake up. Or maybe Sarah would grow enough in her sleep to be able to do it herself. Doubtful. He'd learned to his embarrassment that Sarah couldn't tie the strings to her own shift. She would be of no help.

Lucy's fever continued to climb. Samuel needed to remove the shift she was wearing to cool her better. "If I don't take this off, sweetheart, you could die," he apologized. "Of course, if I do, you will kill me, so either way . . ." He slipped the shift over her head, careful not to snag her hair.

Again and again he covered her with handfuls of snow, but each snowball melted as fast on her fevered skin as if it had been set on the hearth. *Please, God, let her live. I promise to not be a foolish husband.* He made several rash promises he knew he would break in time with the melting snow as his witness. How could he not admire her ankles?

"Lucy, I promise not to make you sad ever again." Samuel followed that with even more unkeepable promises. Had Lucy heard any of his promises, she would hold him to them, at least until they drove her crazy. The one where he promised to do all the laundry for a year would result in all the whites turning pink and her red shawl shrinking to fit Sarah. Fortunately, that promise wouldn't last the week.

As for his promises to God, some he would keep. Others he was probably forgiven for breaking even as he made them. Try as he might, part of his brain refused to see Lucy as a patient, even though his concern was to preserve her life by cooling her. Later he found images of her cooling skin burned into his memory.

After what seemed hours, though by the clock was not more than one, Lucy's temperature finally dropped. Her breathing became less labored, and her face relaxed. As Samuel covered her with a blanket, he realized the damp and soiled linens must also be changed.

He stretched and pondered how best to complete his task. Moving her to the big bed wasn't an option since the emptied tick still required filling. There was Ben's bed upstairs, but carrying Lucy up the narrow staircase could easily result in him bumping her head or, worse, waking her. As much as he prayed for her to awaken, there were certain moments he was glad she wasn't conscious as she would never allow his ministrations.

As he rubbed his head, the solution came to him. Samuel was pleased with this flash of inspiration. Perhaps baldness had its purpose. He dropped his palm from the back of his head.

Leaving the blanket over Lucy, he first rolled her toward himself, then removed the soiled bedclothes from the far corners and as much of the bed as he could. He worked as fast as he could to put on the fresh ones lest Lucy roll off the edge. He stood like an awkward marsh bird doing his best to try to block her in while reaching to tuck in the corners. He was thankful for his height. A shorter person would not have been able to reach the back corner and still keep hold of a sleeping body.

Samuel rolled Lucy onto her side so she faced the wall. Her hand came to rest on the wall. He'd finished removing the damp bedclothes when Lucy began pounding on the wood and screaming frantically.

"I'll be good! I'll be good! Let me out!"

Worried she would hurt herself, Samuel reached around and grabbed her wrist, hugging her to him as he whispered in her ear. "Lucy, it is all right. You are safe."

He alternately sang the lavender song and murmured soothing comments, proclaiming his love and protection for her as she struggled, until each struggle became less violent than the last and she finally relaxed. Then he rocked her. He didn't recall placing her in his lap as he'd sat on her narrow bed. He wasn't sure how their struggles had brought them to this position, but there was something right about it. As she relaxed, her hand came to rest on his chest. He couldn't resist kissing her brow, wishing for Lucy's permission to kiss more.

To his horror, Lucy chose that moment to open her eyes.

"Samuel?" she questioned with a dazed expression.

"Hush, Lucy, you are very sick. Sleep now." He brushed his fingers across her brow. The proximity of his palm forced her eyes to close. *Please sleep. I am not ready to explain why you are in my arms in the middle of the night in nothing more than a quilt!*

Lucy's hand slid up from where it rested to cup his chin.

"Samuel?" she asked again.

"Sweetheart, I'll explain everything in the morning." He stroked her brow again. *Please, please sleep.* He was tempted to make more rash promises if she wouldn't fully wake. Holding her in his arms and kissing her had broken at least one made that night. He had not waited for her to give her permission for such behavior. He doubted any new bargains would be believed or honored. Hadn't the others all been begging her to wake up? He should have been more specific about the timing.

Lucy sighed and closed her eyes, snuggling into him. He froze, hoping she would slip deeper into slumber.

He was seven and she just three the first time he'd held her in his arms. Lucy had stayed with his family when her arm was broken. Hadn't he held her almost this same way one night when she'd cried in pain as they waited for his mother to make some tea? Well, not quite the same way. He hadn't wanted to kiss her then. He hadn't even wanted to hold her. But the same feeling of protection and warmth he'd experienced as a seven-year-old boy swelled within him now. Lucy trusted him. Would she when she woke up? He leaned back against the wall and held her as she slept. He also dozed, dreaming a sweet dream not unlike what he was doing now but with a happy and willing Lucy in his arms.

After he was sure she was sleeping, he eased himself off the bed. The light from the fire cast a golden glow on the white cloth of the shift he'd placed over the chair to warm.

The shift! Samuel rubbed his neck. Could it wait? He glanced at the stairs. There was at least an hour before Sarah would wake up. Wife or not, changing Lucy was going to be embarrassing enough without an audience. Samuel shook himself awake. Best to do this now. And quickly. He poured some hot water in the bucket that held the melted snow he used earlier. If he was going to dress her in a clean shift, he ought to at least wash around her neck…

Oh, Father, please let me do this without thinking about Lucy in the way I am thinking. Help me to think like a husband—no, I mean a doctor. A doctor!

He rolled Lucy onto her side, facing the wall, careful to keep her from touching it lest it trigger another nightmare. Then he dipped the cloth into the bucket of warm water and cleansed her neck and upper back where the broth and sweat had accumulated. As a doctor, he'd never appreciated the human back the way he appreciated it now. *No. I am a doctor*, he reminded himself half a dozen times. The doctor in his brain noticed the crisscross pattern on her back. The bumps felt a bit like those he'd gotten on his face after falling asleep on his arm while studying. He traced them, trying to smooth them. With so little light, he wasn't sure, but they felt like scars. Why would Lucy have dozens of scars on her back?

He and his brothers sported a few ragged scars, but they were straight and even. He'd seen scars similar to this once—on a horse— the horse that had thrown and killed Mr. Simms nine years ago. Mr. Simms had whipped his horse every time he raced down Hill Road. Had he done the same to his daughter? Why hadn't Lucy told him?

The clean shift did not slip on as easily as the other had peeled off. Hearing stirring upstairs did not help Samuel's nervousness. He found himself muttering an apology as he wrestled with the stubborn garment. Lucy, it is all right. I am your husband. *Think doctor, not husband.* It was a pointless exercise to continue to pretend the night's events had not stirred him, but he continued to try.

When at last he wrestled the shift down around Lucy's knees and covered her with a warm quilt, he sank into the chair. Embarrassed by the direction his thought had taken, he felt the heat in his face. He would well deserve more than a slap from Lucy for some of the thoughts occupying his mind. More like an entire week in the barn. Samuel ran his hands over his face. Lucy was going to be livid. He smiled. An angry Lucy would be welcome after this Lucy. Well, as long as she could forgive him.

With a kiss.

Eleven

A JABBING PAIN IN HIS arm woke him. Sarah stood next to the rocker, finger poised to poke him again. She'd caught him dozing in the rocker—again.

"Samuel, you need a nap!" she announced, planting her fists on her hips, seemingly oblivious to the fact that she'd just woken him from one.

Samuel pulled his hand down his face, trying to clear his mind.

Resting better than she had in days, Lucy still slept. Samuel was quite sure she would awaken sometime later today. He did need some rest before having to cope with the questions that would come. The foot stomping he pictured in his mind would not happen today. Lucy would not have the strength to stand. She wouldn't need to. She was adept at throwing daggers with her eyes.

"I need to stay down here," he mumbled. Ben's bed was too far from Lucy.

"You can sleep in the big bed. Your brothers filled the tick this morning, remember?"

He remembered his twin brothers' smirks and sly faces as they'd delivered the freshly filled tick to the door, and it still irked him. He enlisted Sarah's help readying the bed. She oversaw the tightening of the ropes with the paddle and then proceeded to point out every lump and made sure he whacked them down.

She reminded him several times that Lucy had promised she could sleep in the big bed but then decided she would sleep there just one night with Lucy. 'Cause Samuel was married now, and married people slept in big beds. Thoughts fueled by memories of last night's bathing filled his mind. He needed to stomp them down, and fast. After Lucy had her say, Sarah might end up spending months in the big bed while he lived in the barn.

"Come on, Samuel." Sarah pulled him toward the bed. Knowing his brothers were taking care of the livestock and figuring Sarah was more proficient at finding bread and jam than he was, he allowed himself to be led to the bed.

"Wake me up if anything happens," he mumbled.

Sarah nodded as she pushed him onto the bed.

"Take off your boots, Samuel," were the last words he heard as his head hit the pillow.

Lucy struggled to hold on to the fading dream as she always did when she dreamed of Samuel. This dream seemed almost real. His voice was deep and steady, and not once did he change into his younger self. Bits of other dreams fogged her mind—sick parents, Reverend Woods pronouncing her Samuel's wife, flying over snow-draped trees, Mr. Simms yelling at her. Sarah covered with jam.

Lucy blinked.

Sarah remained covered in jam, her face illuminated by the light that filtered through the window. Lucy tried to sit up or say something to stop Sarah.

How often had Mama told Sarah not to eat without asking? Yet, there was Sarah, covered with red strawberry preserves and sitting in Mama's rocking chair as if she were queen. And before breakfast! Or was it? The sun shone fully through the west window of her bedroom. It must be well past the noon hour. Why was she still in bed? Hadn't Sarah tried to wake her? And why was the chair in here?

Memories and voices swirled around in her mind, some with crushing clarity. It was just her and Sarah now. Considering how weak she felt, she was thankful Sarah had taken the initiative to feed herself. Once wouldn't hurt.

But who'd braided Sarah's hair? Buttoned her stays? Sarah could not do it herself. And the fire was burning brightly. Who else was here?

Trying to sit up again, she found she lacked the strength. She must have been extremely ill. The Wilsons must have come to check on them. Emma must be around somewhere. That would explain the strawberry preserves as Lucy remembered how they'd eaten the last of theirs.

"Emma?" The sound came out as a hoarse whisper.

"Lucy!" Sarah jumped off the chair. "You are awake! I knew you would wake up today. Samuel will be so happy."

"Samuel?" The confusion in Lucy's mind grew. She knew she'd dreamed about Samuel—a lot. One particular dream of him cradling her in his arms lingered, more vivid than the rest. But if she was awake, why was Samuel still a topic of conversation? Why would he care?

Lucy closed her eyes. Maybe she'd experienced some type of brain fever.

"Yes. Samuel. You married him," Sarah said matter-of-factly as she climbed back into the rocking chair.

Lucy's eyes flew open. She stared at her sister. The jam on Sarah's face made her smile appear ten times as big as it should've been.

"Married?"

Sarah grinned even wider.

Impossible. Lucy managed to roll over so she could see Sarah better. "To Samuel?"

Sarah nodded, bouncing in the rocking chair as she did so. The movement made Lucy dizzy. She closed her eyes, willing the room to stop spinning.

"Sarah, I'm not married." There were few things Lucy knew with complete certainty, things that only changed in dreams. If she was flying, it was a dream, and whenever she married in her dreams, she always woke up before the kiss. She knew she'd never kissed Samuel. She must still be dreaming.

"Yes, you are. Reverend Woods camed here and everything. And the Wilsons and a bunch of people who helped bury Mama and Papa and Ben. Samuel held you in his arms in the blue-and-green quilt out on the porch, and you said "Yes, Samuel," when the Reverend Woods talked. Then you was married! Samuel brought you back in and put you in your bed. And you have been sick ever so long. His ma has been bringing food, and they've been putting it in the basket on the porch, but we can't talk to them because of the quarter-tine. And he said when you're better, the quarter-tine will be all over, and then we are going to have to have a big long talk, and you're going to be angry." Sarah folded her arms to indicate she'd finished with her news.

Lucy's head spun but no longer from dizziness. Following Sarah's logic when she made sense could be difficult. Married? Impossible. Samuel had surely canceled the intentions when he'd called off the wedding. Or he should have.

"What is a quarter-tine?" Even as she asked the question, Lucy understood. *Quarantine.*

"Silly Lucy. That's when folks are sick and can't be visited by other folks. But Samuel came, and he stayed, and he didn't get sick. But he is really tired. He stayed up all night with you almost every night. He says that since you are married now, he is my brother. And he is the nicest brother in the whole world! He is even nicer than Ben, 'cause he doesn't tease me, but Ben is in heaven, so he isn't in the world at all. You should have married him before so he could have been Ben's brother too. Please don't be angry with Samuel."

Angry? The word didn't explain what Lucy felt. Confused, lost, and something else she couldn't name, but not angry. She hadn't been angry with him for weeks. Saddened? Yes. Hurt? Definitely. Her disappointment that he'd ignored her when he'd returned from Boston this fall and in his apparent choice of Elizabeth had made her heart ache more than the loss of Mama. She had been angry when she'd heard Elizabeth had kissed him. But Papa Marden had talked with her, and that anger had dissipated. Mostly. After all, with Elizabeth, there could be another explanation. A devious one.

Which brought her back to the impossibility of Sarah's story. How on earth could she be married to Samuel? Since he'd returned from Boston, he had not spoken a word to her. A man couldn't marry a woman he hadn't spoken to, even if intentions were published. Sarah must be mistaken. Or maybe Lucy still dreamed.

Before she could quiz Sarah further, Sarah bolted from her chair and ran from the room.

"Samuel! Samuel! Lucy is awake!"

Thump!

"What?"

She knew that voice. She'd heard it often enough in her dreams.

Lucy knew she wasn't dreaming. She was having a nightmare. She closed her eyes and tried to wish it away.

"Come on!" Sarah tugged on Samuel's arm, attempting to yank him up from the floor. "Lucy woke up! You need to tell her all about being married. I told her. She doesn't believe me."

Samuel scrubbed his hand over his face. Of course Lucy wouldn't believe Sarah about something so fantastical. Sarah explaining what had transpired was not the way he'd intended to tell Lucy of their nuptials. Using the bedpost as support, he pulled himself up, then rubbed his head, wishing the fall had rendered him unconscious. Gathering his courage, he walked out of the bedroom, steeling himself for the eruption he'd envisioned for days.

Lucy blinked several times. The image did not change. The man coming to her bedside with his shirt askew and a half a week's worth of whiskers *was* Samuel. She never dreamed of Samuel unshaven and with holes in his socks. Didn't Mrs. Wilson darn them?

Before she could open her mouth to speak, he asked, "Lucy, would you like some tea? Ma brought some of her herbs. I have some warm broth, too."

He wasn't giving her a chance to speak. It hurt so much to think.

Samuel picked up a cup, sat next to Lucy, and lifted her head to press the cup to her lips. Too weak to struggle, she allowed him to hold her.

The tepid mint tea never tasted so good. If she hadn't wanted it so badly, she might have been tempted to push it aside and demand answers. She'd resolved to never let her anger get the best of her again after the Christmas ball. She'd even promised Mama. She would not let her frustration turn to anger and into a tantrum like when she was younger.

Samuel needed to leave. He shouldn't be here. But she couldn't help basking in his presence. His help was both needed and comforting—and confusing, very confusing. Too soon he took the cup away.

"Not too much yet. You will make yourself sick. Would you like some broth?"

Lucy shook her head. "M-m-married?"

"Yes, Lucy, we are." He lifted a hand and brushed a few errant hairs from Lucy's brow, pausing to cup her cheek. "It was the right thing to do, Lucy. It was the only way I could stay and care for you."

She turned her head to break eye contact. "Samuel." Lucy drew out the word until it contained an entire lecture. He removed his hand and scooted back in the chair.

"He asked me for permission. I said you loved him," Sarah added, bouncing with glee at the foot of the bed.

Lucy cast a surprised look at Sarah, closed her eyes, and took a deep breath. This must be a nightmare. Everything was impossibly mixed up. For years she'd dreamed of marrying Samuel, but that was before he'd sent the letter saying he couldn't. Those dreams made more sense. Courting. Papa Marden giving his blessing. Reverend Woods's stoic expression as he'd presided at her wedding.

Opening her eyes again did not change anything. Sarah still stood near Samuel with her ridiculously large jam-enhanced smile. Samuel still sat there, all warmth and kindness, looking as if he cared deeply for Lucy. The stubble on his face and the circles under his eyes testified he'd cared for her as Sarah said.

Lucy's head pounded. The things she wanted to say battled for a chance to come out of her mouth. Everything seemed right and wrong at the same time. Lessons from Papa Marden on kindness kept her silent—not that she had strength enough to argue. Until she was strong enough to do something, it was better to do nothing. Besides, it took so much effort to change her thoughts to words. Her stomach turned. The tea was not enough.

"Broth?" The one-word question was almost too much effort. *The confusion must be because I am so tired and ill. Maybe I'm delirious. A good explanation since nothing makes sense. I am delirious. Just like when Samuel was a boy and was ill and thought George Washington was looking for him. Won't the family laugh about this one? "Remember when Lucy woke up and thought she was married?" This will be better than the General Washington stories.*

Exhausted from the effort of trying to sort out the world she'd woken up in, Lucy closed her eyes after consuming four meager spoonfuls of the broth. The fitful slumber that awaited her was filled with dreams only slightly less confusing than reality.

Twelve

EMMA GUIDED THE SLEIGH UP the Marden's drive. The sunshine sparkled off the diamond-coated trees around her, and the ground shimmered with sparkling crystals.

As she pulled up to the house, she saw that Sarah chased a barn cat across the yard. Samuel sat on the porch steps next to several empty crocks and lifted his head from his hands.

"Samuel? What is wrong?"

"The fever broke, and Lucy is awake." He moved to help his mother down from the wagon seat.

"That is wonderful news."

Samuel shrugged. "Sarah told her before I had a chance to explain."

"I see." Emma paused. "Did she kick you out?"

"Not yet." Samuel stood and rubbed the back of his head. "She is sleeping again."

"When did she wake up?"

"Last evening."

"Has she been up this morning?"

Samuel shook his head and started loading the empty crocks into the back of the sleigh.

"Then it is likely you will have the opportunity to explain again." Emma climbed down to join him. She touched Samuel on the sleeve, and he jumped back. "If she is well, you are out of quarantine. Give me a hug. I missed giving you one on your wedding day."

Samuel stepped into his mother's outstretched arms. Emma held on until Samuel relaxed. Stepping back, she rested her hands on Samuel's shoulders and searched his face, her concerned-mother look deepening. He was sure she could see more than a lack of sleep.

"You'll get your chance to explain. I've nursed my share of sick ones, and rarely did any clearly remember waking the first two or three times." Emma smiled. "One son in particular kept waking up after having the measles, insistent on talking to General Washington. He wouldn't believe General Washington wasn't at our home." Emma winked at him.

A grin teased the corners of his mouth. The story of his recovery from measles at the age of eight had grown into a family folktale. He had no idea why he thought George Washington had been there, but he'd been adamant and had insisted on talking to the general. The story had grown over the years to include him trying to leave the house in his nightshirt with a toy musket to turn Thomas Jr. over to the general as a spy.

"George Washington visiting during her illness might be easier for her to take," Samuel said with a wry smile before continuing to exchange the empty crocks for full ones. "Searching for General Washington seems normal compared to waking up married."

"I am mighty glad her fever has broken." Emma smiled. "It will be several days before she is up and about. I'll continue to bring you food for now."

Samuel placed a basket on the porch, the aroma of warm dried-apple buns floating up from beneath the cover.

"Ma? Is there a morning you can sit with Lucy?" Samuel sounded more pathetic than he intended to. "I need to get my things that got left at the house, and I don't want to leave her alone with Sarah for long."

Emma raised her brow. "Let me see what I can do later this week. Your pa doesn't think we are in for any more snow, so I should be able to get over here. Do you still need the twins' help?"

"No. They did a good job of setting things to rights in the barn. It looks like Mr. Marden finished preparing for winter before he took ill. I needed help to clean up the mess that was created by his illness." Samuel grinned. "The barn smells like a different place. They did a good job and didn't complain at all. They finished chopping more than enough wood on Saturday to see us to January. The barn and coop are so clean they may even surpass Pa's standards. What does he need them to do at home that they are so anxious to work over here?"

Emma laughed. "I believe it isn't so much what they want to avoid as the hunting trip your father has promised them."

Being able to go on the winter hunt would more than compensate for the work they'd completed. He would never tell them that Pa had asked him weeks ago to stay behind and take care of Ma and the little boys so the twins could go on the hunt this year. He wished now that he had not agreed. The cold hunting trip seemed warm compared to the reception he was likely to receive as Lucy gained strength. But running away, no matter how legitimate the excuse, would only make things worse. He'd learned that in the past three months.

Sarah danced across the yard, a gray kitten dangling from her arms. "Look, Mrs. Wilson, Sibby birthed kittens." She thrust a mewing ball of fur close to Emma's face for inspection. "She hid them in the loft. Did Samuel tell you? Lucy waked up. I don't think she is happily married like Reverend Woods said. She didn't look happy at all when she waked. She is sleeping now." Sarah paused for a breath. The kitten sunk his tiny claws into her arm. "Ouch, kitty! I need to take him back to his mama. He likes his mama better." In a flash, Sarah ran off to the barn again.

Emma laughed. "It is good to see her happy. I need to get going. I promised Carrie I would be by today. I am staying the night, so I packed you extra food."

Samuel assisted his mother back onto the sleigh seat. She paused to give him a kiss on the cheek.

"I'll keep you and Lucy in my prayers." She patted his shoulder, and, with a flip of the reins, left Samuel to sort out his problems.

Samuel thought she would jump at the chance to be with Lucy and smooth everything over. Now he wasn't sure. He believed Ma would put off coming again as long as she was able.

How would he do it without her? He needed her to help Lucy understand that he cared.

Thirteen

LUCY HEARD SAMUEL COME DOWN the stairs.

"Good afternoon, sleepy head. How do you feel?" He filled the doorframe. Had she never noticed how strong his forearms were?

"Like a tree fell on me. The huge one down by the mill pond." Lucy rubbed her head and sighed. Her head didn't hurt as much as before, but the dull ache lingered. Several times that day she had been aware of Samuel waking her and forcing more tea and broth into her mouth. She hadn't spoken because it took all her effort to swallow.

Samuel nodded as he sat down in the rocker. "Would you like some more broth?"

The last thing she needed at the moment was more to drink. There were other needs at the forefront of her mind, and she was determined that Samuel was not going to help her with them.

"Since you're still here, I take it you still think we are married." Lucy tried to move into a different position to relieve the pressure she was beginning to feel.

"We are married." Samuel used the same steady, low tone he used to cajole his horse.

No change of position helped. Her discomfort grew. Where was the chamber pot? Could she get Samuel to leave so she could find it?

"No. We are not. I think I would remember getting married." Lucy tried to sit up, but her arms shook with the effort.

"Careful there." Samuel put an arm around her to support her as she moved to sit at the edge of the bed. He didn't let go, even though she continued to try to move. "Whoa, there. Where are you trying to go?"

She squirmed. She was far too old to converse about her need to perform certain bodily functions. Without looking obvious, Lucy tried to see where the chamber pot was. She bent over to check under the bed, and the room started to spin. She leaned back before dizziness overtook her. The last thing she wanted was to be tucked back into bed.

"Where is Sarah?" she asked.

Samuel's gaze drifted up to the ceiling. "Upstairs sleeping. She played so hard this morning she fell asleep over her bread and cheese."

Lucy squirmed some more.

"Lucy? Is something wrong? Do you hurt?"

What is wrong is I need you to leave so I can take care of myself. And Sarah is sleeping and can't help me! Lucy wanted to scream, but to her horror she moaned. If she didn't find the chamber pot soon, her need would be revealed in a most embarrassing way.

"I need, uh..." She trailed off. "Don't you have some work in the barn?"

Samuel shook his head. Concern filled his face. He lifted his hand as if to help her but dropped it.

There was nothing for it, Lucy decided. She would either have to confess her needs or embarrass herself even more. She could feel the heat in her cheeks.

"Chamber pot," she stammered. "Where is it?"

Samuel's own blush crawled up his neck. He reached to the foot of the bed and pulled out the covered pail.

Lucy glanced at the container, then at Samuel. The heat crept higher on her face. She willed him to leave, but he just sat there, staring at her, his face as red as hers must be.

"Do you need any help?" Samuel did not quite meet her eyes.

Lucy found satisfaction with his need to blush. It served him right. Who did he think he was to offer to help her use the chamber pot?

She started to shake her head, and the room moved. "No," she rasped.

Ignoring her denial, Samuel grasped her arms and shifted Lucy toward the edge of the bed. His action stirred other feelings deep within her, feelings she wasn't comfortable with.

Samuel stood. "I think I will get a couple more logs for the fire."

Lucy watched him leave and let out a sigh. She knew he'd stay close enough to hear her if she needed help, but she was grateful for some privacy.

She pushed the quilts aside and proceeded to take care of necessities, grateful for Samuel's thoughtful placement of the pot—close enough to both her bed and the wall to allow her to support herself. By the time Lucy returned to her bed, her legs were shaking. She breathed a deep sigh of relief. She had not needed Samuel's assistance, nor had she fallen or overturned the chamber pot.

As she reached to pull the quilts across her lap, she noticed the embroidery on the cuff of her shift. None of her shifts had embroidered cuffs.

It was her mother's.

Samuel stomped back into the gathering room, his arms full of wood. Without a word, he retrieved the chamber pot and left through the lean-to door.

Lucy stared at the cuff. There must be an explanation. She recalled bathing Ben when he'd burned with fever. In an effort to cool him off, they'd bathed and changed him. Mama had also done the same for Papa. She tried to picture Sarah bathing her. Impossible. She was too small. Since they were quarantined, it was unlikely Mrs. Wilson had helped. Lucy leaned against the wall and came to one rather disturbing conclusion.

Samuel strode back into the room and replaced the chamber pot. "If you need some privacy again, just tell me."

Lucy did not look up.

He knelt down and put his hand on her shoulder. "You are shivering. Let's get you back under the covers." He lifted the quilt she'd dragged across her lap. Lucy allowed him to lift her legs and maneuver her into the bed. Then Samuel placed a folded quilt behind her to cushion her back where she leaned against the wall.

Was he this gentle while I was ill? Do his hands tingle from the touch as my legs do? An unbidden picture of Samuel washing and changing her came to mind. She needed to know.

"Samuel, did…did you…?" Lucy couldn't finish. Samuel sat in the rocker next to her, saying nothing.

"This is Mama's." She fingered the embroidery at her wrist. Her face warmed with embarrassment again.

Samuel slid forward in the rocker and wrapped Lucy's hands in his to stop her from tugging at the sleeve.

"Sweetheart?" Samuel lifted her chin with a crooked knuckle, still holding her hands in his other hand. Lucy still would not look up, so he moved his hand to her cheek and ducked his head until he caught her eye.

"You were very ill. It was necessary to bathe you to cool the fever. Rather than return you to your dirty shift, I put this one on. I didn't realize this was your mother's gown. If it upsets you, tell me where to find one of yours." Lucy pulled her hands out of his and turned her head away, but she missed his touch as soon as she broke contact—a loss she'd rather not explore. She tugged the quilt up to her chin and pulled her knees up and rested her head on them. Her head felt so heavy. She would not lie down for the remainder of the conversation. Lying there would be even more pitiful.

He bathed me! And he's not apologizing for it—just for getting the wrong shift. Does he really think I am upset about wearing Mother's clothes? Is he daft? She knew she should slap him. Any virtuous girl would, but she lacked the strength to lift her hand. Even if she tried, it would probably feel more like a pat on the cheek. Not the message she wanted to send. Completely improper. She should be outraged. She should be angry, but instead she felt embarrassed and ashamed. Slapping Samuel for it wouldn't solve her feelings. This wasn't like George trying to take liberties under the mistletoe.

Lucy knew what Samuel had seen and touched. She'd always known that someday a man would see her back. She'd hoped it would be Samuel, but she thought she would have time to prepare him, to say something to him before he saw the scars. Or ask Papa Marden to say something when he came to ask for her hand. She wasn't ready to explain. She wasn't that strong. She needed to know what he thought. *Could he ever come to care for me when he knows the truth? Would he think I deserved it or agree with Papa Marden?*

Papa had told her that the scars were Mr. Simms's sin, not hers, that the punishments had not been because she was evil but because Mr. Simms had been deeply troubled by what he'd experienced in the war. She accepted Papa Marden's explanation, and his love. But the scars were always there, casting doubt that a man even as kind as Samuel could live with a body as scarred as hers. Men were attracted to pretty women. Not only was her face plain, her back was ugly.

An unbidden tear slipped down her cheek. The humiliation over the need to relieve herself seemed minuscule compared to what she was experiencing now. Maybe if she could keep her eyes closed, he would leave. She buried her face in the quilt to hide her tears.

The bed ropes creaked as Samuel moved from the rocker to the edge of the bed.

She lifted her head to tell him to leave, but before she could, he cupped her cheeks in his hands and wiped away her tears with his thumbs.

"Lucy," he whispered.

"You saw." A sob racked her, and she buried her face in her hands.

What could he do? *God, help me!* He felt more helpless than he had since riding Old Brown into the yard on that too-still morning. He placed his hand on her shoulder and scooted closer until he could bow his head over hers. Then he wrapped his arms around her quaking body.

"Yes, sweetheart, I saw. You are a beautiful woman." He kept his voice low and even, just barely above a whisper.

Lucy shook her head and raised it enough for him to hear her. "The scars. You saw the scars."

The scars? Not the rest of her? Samuel gathered her tighter in his arms. He twisted until he could lift her into his lap and hold her even closer. He laid her head on his shoulder and was surprised when Lucy brought her hands up and clung to his shirt. He murmured reassurances as his shirt became damp with her tears. He called her every endearment he could think of, cradling her as gently as he could and hoping that she would understand in time that the scars did not matter. But her pain did.

Lucy's grip weakened, and her shoulders stopped shaking.

Samuel hoped she was ready to listen. "Yes, darling, I saw them. \I will not ask until you are ready to tell me." He placed a soft kiss on her temple and drew her closer, aware of the tears still falling onto his already soaked shirt.

Shadows moved over the walls as the sun started its western decent.

Lucy stilled and drew back, blinking at Samuel. She traced a tear with her finger. Samuel had not realized he was crying too.

The intimacy of the moment was broken when she squirmed and pushed feebly against him. Samuel turned and set her back on the bed, but he would not leave her alone.

"Would you like some soup now? Ma brought some fresh this morning."

"Yes, please." Lucy leaned back, thankful he'd chosen not to pursue the matter. Someday she knew she would need to explain, but she didn't have the strength right now. The tears had taken away everything. Inside, she'd discovered an emptiness the broth could not fill. Though something had started to fill at Samuel's touch. He had not been repulsed. And he'd cried, just like Papa Marden had.

While she ate, Lucy pondered. There were no recriminations. No demands for an explanation. No begging for the tears to stop. He'd simply let her be. But he had not let her be alone.

The bowl was almost empty when she realized Samuel hadn't commented on her scars directly at all. He'd said she was a beautiful woman. A funny sort of lump grew in her throat. Even with Papa Marden's reassurance that Mr. Simms was wrong to call her ugly and other names she could never repeat, she'd never dreamed that anyone, even Samuel, would call her beautiful. With her scarred back and boring brown hair and eyes, she was anything but that.

Samuel had seen her unclothed. He'd washed everything. Oh, my. Lucy's mind raced through all the ministrations he must have performed. Impropriety seemed too mild a word. It was beyond indecent. It was scandalous.

But he'd thought she was beautiful. His words filled her like butterflies in a meadow, fluttering and tickling her in places that left her in awe. Beautiful.

Lucy knew she was blushing. She dropped her eyes and studied the quilt. The spoon fell into the bowl, and she raised her eyes to his.

Samuel leaned forward, his gaze never leaving hers. "I meant what I said. You are a beautiful woman." It was as if he'd read her mind.

She felt the heat in her cheeks become more intense.

The sound of little feet on the stairway spared her further embarrassment.

Fourteen

LUCY SAT ON THE CORNER of her bed against the wall, hands wrapped around her knees. She was too awake to sleep and too weak to do more than think. She had much to ponder. Her thoughts dived and chased about her head like a flock of swallows on a summer evening. As soon as she could focus on one, another would take its place.

She pulled the quilt tighter around her. She wasn't cold. Samuel left a decent fire before retiring to Ben's room, but she found the action comforting. Everything had changed. Mama was gone, as were Papa Marden, the baby, and her brother. Tears filled her eyes.

Oh, Mama and Papa Marden, I miss you so much. I need you. What am I to do? She missed Benjamin, too, but she'd shed her tears for him earlier, with Papa. Without Mama and Papa, she felt like half of her was missing, creating a vast, empty place. A void Samuel was trying to fill. But she wasn't ready to let that happen. Not yet. She needed to feel the emptiness just awhile longer before she could consider filling the hollowness in her soul.

She had no one to ask for guidance and advice. Sarah was too young and seemed to be in favor of this bizarre marriage. Samuel was not a voice of reason or even reasonable when it came to the subject.

After tucking Sarah in for the night, Samuel came down to talk. He sat in the rocker across from her bed and recounted the details of their marriage. The conversation was somewhat awkward from the start, given the revelations of the afternoon they'd both tried to avoid.

Lucy's face registered shock when she realized she'd married wearing nothing more than her shift. How degrading! Even if no one other than Samuel and Sarah had seen it, her shift was not acceptable wedding attire. It was utterly shameful.

Samuel described brushing her hair two hundred strokes that day. He played with the ends of her braid while telling her. A braid he'd made. She could hardly fathom what the action meant. More than once she'd overheard Mrs. Wilson and Mama titter over Mr. Wilson's habit of brushing his wife's hair. Mrs. Wilson said it was how her husband said "I love you." *What did Samuel mean by it? Was he following his father's tradition? Two hundred strokes?* She often left off brushing her hair at fifty.

Samuel reaffirmed the account of the marriage as told by Sarah—a ceremony so strange Lucy could not believe stuffy Reverend Woods had officiated such a farce. Given his abhorrence to common-law marriage, he may have done it to try to prove a point to Samuel's parents. That the minister accepted a delirious woman's mumbling at the appropriate moment to mean she agreed before God and witnesses to be a wife was a stretch even for him. Both he and his witnesses were daft. The witnesses had all been Samuel's family. The other men who came had stayed up on the hill, unable to watch the proceedings. She did agree with Samuel on one point. Reverend Woods was wilier than he seemed. The village wives had been disappointed at their husbands' tales that night.

What of God? Would God honor such a marriage? God honored some odd marriages. Ruth, Esther, and Rahab were examples enough of that in the Bible.

She recalled her mother's wedding to Papa Marden in this very house. Lucy had sat in her new dress, doing her best not to fidget despite the stiff, itchy material. She'd listened as Reverend Woods had spoken almost as long as one of his sermons before telling Papa Marden to kiss Mama. The kiss Papa gave Mama had caused someone to clear their throat. Then Papa Marden had turned and swept her off the bench and into a tremendous hug.

Lucy wrapped her arms around herself, longing to remember every hug her beloved stepfather had given her.

Oh, what she wouldn't give for one of Papa Marden's hugs right now. No matter how tightly she pulled the quilt around her body, she could not duplicate the feeling. One of Samuel's hugs would do. Actually, it would more than do. She might never admit it out loud, but Samuel's hug this afternoon had been better than Papa Marden's. Being encircled in Samuel's arms left her feeling safe and warm, just like with Papa, but there was something more.

No. She could not think of Samuel's arms now. Those feelings would only confuse her. She couldn't think objectively about their marriage if she wanted to be held in his arms again. All she had to do was cry out and he would come bounding down the stairs to check on her. She could have the hug she longed for in just moments if she wanted.

Lucy's eyes drifted closed as she tried to imagine his reaction. She knew he would not be happy at being fooled into marriage. Mr. Simms said he'd been tricked, and he had not been happy. And Mr. and Mrs. Wilson had tricked Samuel into marrying her. It had been either risk his mother's health or be wed. That was not a choice at all. A good man like Samuel deserved a choice, not some bizarre version of a shotgun wedding. Even if she and Samuel had been engaged before. That was over.

She understood why he married her. She would have done anything to save her own mother, even married Mr. Sidewall and mothered his three obnoxious little boys if it would have spared her. Lucy hoped she was a better alternative than the unkempt widower and his little terrors.

Lucy, you are a beautiful woman.

Samuel thought she was beautiful. Her face did not compare with Elisabeth's or Marybeth's, but she did not think he was lying. His eye hadn't twitched, but maybe he'd grown out of that habit.

Lucy soaked in the words as she watched the flames dance in the fireplace through her open door. Papa Marden often told her she was pretty, but, as always, the memory of Mr. Simms describing how ugly she was and telling her that no man would ever want to marry her crept into her reverie. Could she believe Samuel?

A log dropped, breaking the spell and bringing her back to her dilemma.

Oddly, despite having been trapped into marriage, Samuel seemed determined to stay. Her feeble protests were met with a grin or a shake of his head. Little phrases like "our barn" rather than "your barn" peppered his conversation. At one point he'd even mentioned he needed to go to his folks' house to get the rest of his things. He'd laid claim to her house, farm, and sister, as well as her.

The farm had long been a coveted piece of land. If Samuel liked farming, she would have thought he'd married her for the land. But he'd wanted to be a doctor for so long. He hadn't explained why he'd given up that dream. Nor had they spoken of his relationship with Elizabeth. Lucy was too scared to ask. Owing that the tale involved Elizabeth, all might not be as the children reported the day of the kiss.

So why would he marry her now?

He'd always had a strong sense of duty. She'd once overheard Mrs. Wilson tell Mama that of all her children, Samuel was always the one she could depend on to finish what he started and to do it well. No denying Samuel was a good man. She knew he would stay with her until death parted them. The question in her mind was, would he be happy, or would he come to despise her like Mr. Simms had despised both Mama and her? She couldn't live with the anger again.

She harbored no illusions that he might have married her for love. Not once had he mentioned any feelings for her—just necessity, friendship, marriage being the honorable thing to do, and reputations.

Well, that, and he'd brushed her hair and called her beautiful. Maybe he was daft. What had happened to everyone while she was sick? They were all as crazy as Old Man Gibson who ran around in his nightshirt last winter every time it snowed, tossing snowballs at everything he could.

As for herself, she'd loved him for oh, so long. Crying in his arms this afternoon and being held so securely served to convince her there could be no other man for her. But she could not risk him regretting his choice, as Mr. Simms had. She would rather live alone than with such hatred again. She'd witnessed Samuel upset a few times but never in a rage. But he could change. She had been told that Mr. Simms had once been nice too.

How long had she been ill? A week? Longer? She wasn't sure. She couldn't recall the date. What day had she been married? How could a new bride not know her wedding date? Ridiculous! One more argument against this insane arrangement. Every bride knew her wedding date. But, then, every girl remembered her proposal, too.

Samuel apologized for not waiting until she awoke. "You weren't even aware, but I did kneel here by your bedside and asked you to please marry me. You were rude enough to not answer."

Even though he delivered it with a wink and one of his special smiles to lighten the mood, it didn't help.

He was still trapped.

The last night she remembered clearly was the Monday night she'd recorded the deaths in the family Bible. Something tugged at her memory. Something did not make sense to her when she read it. The dates and names were incorrect. Her name was not listed as Simms. Perhaps she'd read it wrong or the dates were inverted.

Lucy wondered at what she saw. Had she misread something? The night she'd written in the Bible her head had pounded, and her eyes were full of tears. She remembered praying the snow would not come and that someone would find Sarah. Her last thought had been that she would soon be in heaven with Mama.

She vowed to check the Bible. There could be a complication. If she was right, it might mean she wasn't married because her name wasn't Lucy Simms. Both Samuel and the Reverend would need to concede she'd married under a false name. She may have found a legal way out. For once she blessed the lawmakers. She could set Samuel free.

Her thoughts continued to wander. Like tadpoles in a pond, they swam about until it was impossible to focus on just one. They were so fascinating that she wanted to watch them as they wandered about, weaving and dancing.

Yesterday, when she'd first awoken, Lucy was sure she still dreamed. But her dreams of Samuel hadn't been of the haggard man who walked out of her parents' bedroom sporting several days' worth of facial growth. In her dreams, Samuel always appeared clean-shaven and go-to-meeting neat and never smelled of barnyard. He never smelled of anything in her dreams. When he touched her in her dreams, her heart didn't skip, and butterflies didn't race around her insides mixing up her feelings.

She wanted to be furious. A few years ago she would have tossed a temper tantrum. She wondered if he expected one. He'd witnessed plenty. But she had grown up and wasn't going to be like Mr. Simms and let anger rule her actions. Papa Marden had taught her better.

Sarah was happy. The grim bundles she'd hoisted to the roof were now snug in the ground up on the hill. No doubt the animals were cared for and the barn in perfect order. How could she be upset over care he'd given them?

But he insisted they were married. And he'd changed her shift! He'd seen the scars. Where not those reasons enough that she should be angry?

He'd also held her while she cried. That brought a very different emotion, which scared her more than her anger, for she did not understand what she felt. She wanted to run. But where? Into his arms or out of his life?

Samuel's arms around her when she cried today conveyed so much more than they had when she was little. No longer awkward, they were strong and sure. Safety, understanding, and —

Wait! He'd kissed her! She bolted upright. The quilt fell from her shoulders as her fingers flew to the spot on her brow where his lips had rested—more than rested. Caressed. Granted, he'd placed it on her forehead, but it was still a kiss. He never kissed her before when she cried. He never kissed her before at all.

The kiss was more confusing than the marriage. The kiss seemed like he meant it to be a promise. She couldn't even bring herself to be upset with the kiss. Her first. Or was it? Wouldn't Reverend Woods have told him to kiss her after the vows? Of course, being so ill, he probably hadn't kissed her on the lips, but maybe on the cheek.

Too tired to continue sitting, Lucy slumped to her side and watched the flames through half-closed eyes, remembering the warmth of Samuel's embrace and the tingle of the kiss.

She still had not come up with a suitable answer to the central question. Why had Samuel married her?

Duty? Maybe.

Love? Not likely.

The kiss? Her imagination. Undoubtedly.

She could not allow Samuel to be forced to stay in this marriage. He'd studied to be a doctor. Doctors didn't marry every patient they cared for. Surely no one in their little community would think ill of him for not marrying her. True, some of the old gossips would sully her name. But he would be free.

Then what would the future hold for Sarah and her? She could not run the farm alone. If she sold it and moved to Boston to find work, no one would ever hear any sordid version of this winter. Samuel would be free to marry Elizabeth or one of the other girls from town. She must consider Sarah. Securing a job would be difficult with a child in tow. Maybe the Wilson's would take her in.

In the waning firelight, Boston became the perfect solution. If she lived in Boston, she wouldn't see Samuel marry someone else, and no one would witness her heart breaking.

Lucy watched the flickering flames dance her into her dreams.

Samuel rolled over again on Ben's old bed. Even diagonally it was a bit short for him. He recognized the bed from the days when Mr. Simms had been alive and the house consisted of a one-room cabin and lean-to. The bed that had once belonged to Mr. Simms was too wide for the narrow room James Marden had built in the addition for Lucy, and so it was moved upstairs. Lucy's bed was longer. Maybe he could get Lucy to move into her parents' room. Then he could take hers and have room enough to stretch out. Of course, sleeping in Lucy's bed would thwart all attempts to sleep.

This bed smelled of little boy and the creepy crawly things all boys hid in their pockets. If it smelled like the lavender sachet Lucy kept tucked under her pillow, he might not be able to control his impulse to run downstairs and hold her close. Not a bad idea. She might even agree. His other thoughts presented a problem. His "lead me not into temptation" prayer may have worked while she lay fevered and needing his constant care, but the petition didn't help much now. His mind remembered the fine feminine details in a different light now, and he found himself wanting to revisit those details and to have permission to claim them as his.

Holding her this afternoon, while painful, felt wonderful. Holding his wife in that moment, he knew he could never let go.

And the kiss.

Had she even noticed? He'd wanted to lower his lips to hers and make it real, to try to make her understand their marriage was real. But he'd restrained himself, though not without difficulty. The timing was off, and she was too vulnerable. He'd wanted to kiss her again tonight when he'd recounted the wedding, to claim the kiss that should have ended the ceremony. He'd explained himself poorly. Her continued insistence that he be free was proof enough that she didn't understand.

Ugh! He flipped onto his back. The images of his beautiful Lucy would not leave him. There was no sin in a man wanting his wife. The big problem was his wife did not believe she was married. Admittedly, he would feel much better if they'd stood holding hands when they'd exchanged vows. The phrase "exchanging vows" wasn't accurate either.

When she fully recovered, perhaps he could talk Reverend Woods into repeating the vows so Lucy would have a chance to say yes and remember it. Or they could repeat them to one another as his parents had done.

If she said yes.

The look she'd given him while he'd explained the situation this evening did not instill much confidence that she would say yes. She hadn't lashed out at him as he'd expected, but the emotions of hurt, anger, and confusion had all played across her face, each fighting for prominence. There was also the bone-deep sorrow. Neither talked about her parents, but the pain of her loss never left her eyes.

He'd determined years ago to win her heart. At the time, he had not thought it would be difficult. The task may yet prove as impossible as becoming a doctor.

When she was about nine, she'd blushed in his presence for the first time. Unlike other girls, she never giggled around him, but after that one occasion, she would occasionally become tongue-tied. Their friendship had shifted ever so slightly. He'd avoided her for a while, and she'd stopped coming over as frequently. At first he hadn't missed her, and then Mr. Simms had died. After that, he saw Lucy frequently as he took his turn helping out with the livestock, but Lucy didn't hang around him much. Ma told him to give her time when he asked if something was wrong.

After James married Anna, Lucy started to smile again and even started to become a nuisance. Then one day something changed for him, and she was no longer an annoying tagalong. By the time he was fifteen, he set about to make her blush as much as possible. A year later, when he did try to make his feelings known, his plan went awry, with one gentle tug on a braid. But she forgave him that. Canceling an engagement, then getting married anyway? Not in his favor.

How can I convince her I want this marriage?

Sleep came, leaving his question unanswered.

Fifteen

LUCY LEANED ON HER DOORJAMB and rubbed her eyes. Samuel sat plaiting Sarah's hair. And Sarah was standing still. Sarah never stood still, not for anyone or any bribe. Why would she stand still for Samuel?

Unbidden memories came floating back. Had she been three? Her arm was injured. She'd lived with the Wilsons for several weeks.

"Stay still, Lucy. I can't do this with you wiggling all over."

"I can't, Sammy. It hurts."

"I'm not hurting you."

"No, you hurt hair."

"I'm sorry. I'll try to be careful."

"Mama do it better."

"Mama isn't here now."

"You are a boy. Boys don't help girls."

"Well, I do."

His first attempt at braiding had been far from tidy, but every day for most of a month the scene repeated itself—Samuel braiding her hair while his ma attended to baby Carrie. He became her champion, and she his shadow. He taught her how to read her letters during the month her broken arm healed. After several difficult nights, Emma permitted Lucy to sleep with him in his trundle, knowing her seven-year-old son could do more to chase Lucy's nightmares away than an hour of rocking could.

Sarah's giggle brought Lucy back from her reminiscing. "You did good, Samuel. Sometimes when Papa made braids it hurt. You never hurt my head."

"I've had lots of practice." Samuel wasn't looking at Sarah. He was looking at her—no, winking at her!

Lucy was mortified to be caught staring, and the heat rose to her cheeks.

"It appears we woke Lucy." He turned Sarah about so she could see her sister.

"Lucy! Are you better? Can you play?" Sarah bounded to the door, and for a moment Lucy was afraid her sister's exuberance would smother her. At the last minute, Sarah's leap was stilled by Samuel's hand.

"Gently, Sarah. Lucy is not quite well."

Sarah looked up at Samuel. "May I hug her?"

Lucy held out her arms. "Always, sweet girl."

Sarah snuggled into Lucy's arms, delivering a long, yet soft hug. When she let go, she turned to Samuel. "I was careful."

Lucy raised her brows. Sarah barely knew Samuel. He'd lived in Boston most of her young life. Why did the child seek his approval?

Samuel nodded and gave her shoulder a squeeze. "Will you set the table, please?" Sarah skipped across the room to the cupboard.

"Resilient, isn't she?" Samuel asked as he guided Lucy to the rocker near the fireplace. "I brought her out for the funeral at Ma's suggestion. She seems to have accepted the changes in life, for the most part. Although at night when I read the Bible verse, she curls up in my lap and talks of her parents and Ben and sheds a tear or two."

"You've been reading to her?"

Without asking, he spread a quilt over her lap and knelt to arrange it around her feet so they would not touch the floorboards. Samuel nodded. "I read to you, too."

Lucy gawked at him, her mouth forming a slight O. The look Samuel gave her was full of messages she couldn't decipher. She could not turn away. Her heart raced faster than a frightened deer in a hunter's sight. What she thought she glimpsed was impossible. It had to be the imaginations left over from her fever-fueled dreams. She saw the expression the Samuel of her dreams would wear. The real Samuel wouldn't gaze at her that way, the way Papa Marden had looked at Mama.

Samuel stayed on his knees.

Lucy felt love radiating from him. Scared, she wanted to run again, but there was no place to run. Her resolve to send him on his way once she was up and about was being challenged, and she had not even been awake five minutes. It was so tempting to accept this marriage as her new life. But she would not trap him. Lucy never knew Samuel to express anger like Mr. Simms, but trapped in a marriage to her when he wanted to be with someone else, Samuel might change.

Sarah dropped one of the pewter cups with a clatter, causing Lucy and Samuel to break eye contact.

"Sorry. It's not broke. See?" Sarah held out the cup for Samuel's inspection.

"No harm done, Sarah. You are doing a fine job," Samuel commented before bringing his attention back to Lucy.

Lucy pondered Samuel's reaction to Sarah. Definitely not like Mr. Simms. Breaking a pewter cup was near impossible. At Sarah's age, she would have been punished just for the noise.

"Would you like some porridge this morning? Made it myself." The corner of his mouth inched up into a lopsided grin. "Not bad with a bit of molasses."

Was Samuel flirting with her? The funny feeling in her stomach had nothing to do with hunger. Lucy didn't trust herself to speak, so she nodded.

He tugged the end of her long, messy braid. "Perhaps I should fix your hair today, too."

Lucy felt her cheeks grow warm. She ducked her head. This would not do at all. How could she ever tell him to leave when he acted as if he liked her? The Samuel who'd ignored her in September and

October would have been much easier to reason with. Not this one she wanted to...to...to what?

Just wanted.

Samuel lifted her chin with one finger until her eyes met his, then studied her face for a long moment. Lucy wondered if he were searching for something beyond her recovery.

"Your color is much better today. Let's get some food inside you and then decide about the rest of the day."

Lucy opened her mouth to protest. She needed to tell him before she got used to having Samuel around, but the words she needed to say would not come out.

Samuel placed his thumb to her lips and shook his head. "Lucy, this discussion can wait until tomorrow, but getting you well cannot." Samuel turned to the fireplace and retrieved the pot of porridge.

Could Samuel sense her resolve to send him away?

Sixteen

As Samuel eased the yarn out of Lucy's hands, her eyes fluttered open and she grabbed for the ball.

"What? Oh." Lucy looked sheepishly down at her wrapper. She'd intended to do something useful other than sleep. The knitting basket had been close at hand, so she'd started there, thinking to get up and dress after a bit.

"Do you need help to your room?"

Lucy reached for the yarn. "No, I am awake now. Where is Sarah?" She hoped the child hadn't gotten into mischief.

A teasing grin formed on Samuel's face, and he pointed his thumb over his shoulder to where Sarah lay curled up with her doll on the rug. "I put my special sleeping potion in the porridge this morning. It worked."

Lucy returned his grin.

"Shall I move her upstairs or let her sleep there?"

Lucy shrugged. "She is liable to wake as I did."

"If she does, I will get us all dinner. Ma sent chicken pies today."

Samuel returned a few moments later without Sarah. "Shall we eat?"

In answer, Lucy rose and shuffled toward the cupboard. Samuel caught her elbow. "Sit at the table. I can get this." He guided her shaking body to the bench and made sure she was seated before gathering the plates and unloaded the contents of the basket.

Lucy wondered what to say. Telling him to leave now would be useless. She knew he would never leave her without proper care.

Samuel started the conversation. "What happened?"

Confused Lucy looked up at him. *Quite a bit. If you must know, my parents are dead. According to you, I am married. And my sole accomplishment today is picking up a ball of yarn.* "What happened?" she repeated.

Samuel swallowed a bite he'd snitched. "The week of the blizzard—I know you came to the house and mentioned Sarah was ill, but what happened after that? I have only the dates in the Bible and what little Sarah has said. I am at a loss to figure it all out." He placed a full plate in front of her and set his on the side of the table opposite her.

"Oh." Lucy took a bite of the pie before answering. The crust melted in her mouth. She took another.

"After three days in bed, Sarah recovered much like her old self, but not so talkative."

Samuel chuckled.

"The next morning, Ben complained of a sore throat. He woke in the night with a high fever. For three days, I took care of him so Mama wouldn't keep going up and down the stairs. Papa Marden would take over at night. The last night, Ben kept moaning, then he fell silent. I thought he'd fallen asleep. The next morning Papa wrapped Ben's body in the green blanket."

Lucy blinked back tears and took a sip of warmed cider. She'd watched tears trail down Papa's face as he explained there was no time to try to dig a grave because of the falling snow. Lucy held the door for Papa to carry Ben's body outside, then helped him with the ropes. He'd drenched the blanket with a bucket of water before lashing the precious cocoon to the roof, where it would freeze and be safe from animals.

"The blizzard just started so..." Lucy gestured to the roof. "The following day, Papa didn't come back in from the barn after his morning chores. I went to the barn to find him. Mama fretted so."

Lucy sifted through the memories, trying to decide what to say next. "I found Papa Marden sitting on an upturned crate, his head in his hands, weeping." She'd sat down with him, and he'd held her while she cried with him.

"By late afternoon, I saw that Papa suffered from more than a sorrowful heart. Despite Mama's protests, Papa continued to try to take care of the farm. All the while, his cough deepened."

Lucy paused to take a few bites and compose herself. "On the second night after the blizzard started, I found Papa Marden lying on the barn floor, bleeding from a gash in his head. He'd tripped on the shovel. I washed off the blood, and he opened his eyes. He burned with fever. When he was able to stand, I helped him to the house."

She'd prayed for strength every step of the way as she'd half dragged him through the deep snow to the cabin. Had the wind not died down so she could see her way, she would not have made it to the house. She could not cling to both Papa and the guide rope. He was too heavy. Once inside, she helped Mama put Papa in their big bed and returned to the barn to finish what chores she could.

"Mama wouldn't let me help take care of Papa. I worried that she would..." Lucy waved her hand uselessly. "You know, because of the baby."

Samuel nodded and set his fork aside.

"Saturday morning I prepared to hurry over to your place for help. I heard Mama yell." Lucy played with her food a moment before continuing. "Papa Marden passed. She didn't want me to leave, but I should have gone anyway. It took both of us to hoist Papa's body up on the roof next to Ben's. The exertion was too much for Mama. I should have—" A sob cut off the rest of the sentence.

Samuel walked around the table, straddled the bench next to Lucy, and pulled her into his arms. "I am sorry. I should not have asked."

Lucy shook her head. "No, I want to tell you." She hiccupped. "It helps." She gave a wan smile and pulled back. Then she hiccupped again and took a long drink of the cider before continuing.

"Mama still didn't want me to leave. She said another storm was coming and didn't want me out on Hill Road. You know Mama and traveling in storms." Samuel nodded. Lucy's mother had always been skittish about storms. "I would have come anyway, but Mama took to her bed. I thought she was just tired, but I think she knew the baby was coming. I wish she had sent me for your mother."

Mama's predictions of another storm had proven right, but the storm had dropped only three inches of new snow rather than the foot her mother feared. That alone would not have prevented her from making a hurried trip over to the Wilson's house. However, the wind gusts were so strong Lucy doubted she could have made it there and back without becoming lost in the blowing snow. She'd prayed for help to come. It hadn't.

"Sunday morning, Mama couldn't rise from her bed. Her labor had begun. I dared not leave her alone to run for your mother or even one of the closer neighbors. I prayed someone would notice our absence from church and stop by to check on the family. When no one came, I wondered if there was an epidemic." *That would have explained why you didn't come. Why didn't you?* Lucy looked at Samuel but didn't ask the question.

By sunset, Lucy knew she would be forced to deliver the baby, who should not be coming for another two months. How she longed for the help of another woman. She'd attended Jane's birth two years previously and, five years before that, had helped with Sarah's while waiting for Mrs. Wilson to arrive. Those experiences did not give her the skills of a midwife.

"Mama did not have the strength to yell as she had when she birthed little Jane. She just whimpered. I didn't know what to do. I tried to remember everything your mother did. The baby came in the middle of the night. Mama was so weak she didn't even open her eyes to look at him before she died."

Lucy played with another bite of her food, taking her time to chew it so she wouldn't have to talk for a moment as she recalled details she'd rather not share. Little toes, little fingers. She'd held the tiny baby boy for but a few precious moments. He was as still as the night that surrounded them. Through her tears, she willed him to breathe. Rubbing him and even slapping his tiny backside failed to produce more than one little gasp, which was his first and last breath. Lucy stood alone in the darkness of the night to morn their loss.

She'd sunken onto Mama's couch with her brother held tightly in her arms and had cried until she was as empty as the cider barrel in spring. When there was nothing left to cry, she rose and prepared the bodies for burial. Her movements were slow and clumsy. She wanted to sleep, to be carried out of the nightmare into a dream world, but dawn would bring even more responsibilities.

"By the time Sarah woke, I had Mama and the baby wrapped in the quilt. I should have gone for your family's help then, but I was too stubborn, and I was angry that you hadn't come. I was also too tired to think through what I was doing. It took me most of the day to get them up on the roof." Only after she'd spoken did she realize she'd revealed more than she wanted to. But she was beyond caring. She wanted Samuel to feel some of the pain that ripped at her heart.

Samuel wrapped his arms around her and let her tears fall. "I should have come. I wish I had."

"I think I would like to lie down." Lucy pulled out of his arms and stood to leave the table, but her knees buckled. Samuel's reaction was quick. Before Lucy could protest, he scooped her into his arms and held her snugly against his chest.

A flash of movement caught her eye as they entered her room. Sarah had come down the stairs.

"Are you carrying Lucy to bed, too? I love it when I am carried to bed. Sometimes I wake up but pretend not to just so I don't have to walk. Are you pretending, Lucy?"

"Why, Miss Sarah, were you awake when I took you upstairs?" Samuel asked as he set Lucy on her bed.

Eyes wide, Sarah must have recognized her blunder. "Yes, Samuel. I am sorry."

"You little minx." His smile reassured both sisters that Sarah was forgiven. "Sit at the table. I will be out in a minute." He set Lucy on the bed. For a long moment, he stared at Lucy, and Lucy stared back.

"Do you need—"

Lucy shook her head and pulled up the quilt before he could finish his question, then turned to the wall, shutting out all discussion.

Samuel stood for a long moment before leaving the room.

Lucy traced a crack on the wall and wondered again why Samuel hadn't come when she had needed him.

Seventeen

SAMUEL BRUSHED OLD BROWN. THE horse turned his head as if to inspect the quality of his owner's work. "I know you are restless. The boys haven't let you out much. Do you like your new home? Or are you missing your old barn too much? This is a nice barn. Good feed, and John's mare seems friendly enough." Old Brown tossed his head. Samuel chuckled. "Don't you go showing her how spoiled you are."

With Lucy on the mend, he could take his time in the barn. He needed to inspect the livestock, feed, and implements. He hadn't planned on farming, but farming came with Lucy. And, gratefully, he found it wasn't as onerous as he'd considered it three years ago. Being in charge of a farm would be different in many ways than working on one. He needed to make plans. An inventory would help him know where to start.

The barn was one of the nicest in the district. Samuel's father once said Mr. Simms gave his barn more attention than he did his family. He remembered how magnificent the new barn appeared next to the squatty little cabin before John Marden added the two story addition. In comparison to his father's, the Marden barn was palatial. Several stalls sat unused even after James had purchased the sow and turned two stalls into her domain. The hayloft held more than enough feed and straw for even the longest of winters. Sibby and the other barn cats kept down the rodent population.

The barn even boasted a dedicated tack room. Most farmers in the area hung their bridles and ropes from wall pegs and used a corner of the barn for storage or, like his father, an empty stall. Most didn't own a barn this size, either. Samuel figured he could keep his carpentry tools in the tack room and rearrange the stalls so he could use the adjoining one as a workshop. Before he'd thought of becoming a doctor, he'd hoped to take up cabinetry like his pa. Winter months were plenty slow enough that a skilled farmer could make some extra money with woodworking.

Samuel looked around, satisfied. The building was solid. The wind couldn't find its way in between the boards. The doors swung on well-balanced hinges. The layout provided room for farm equipment, a wagon, and a buggy. He wondered what Mr. Simms had planned when he'd built such a monstrous barn in place of the old one. Perhaps raise horses? Whatever Mr. Simms had done in his life, at least he'd built an excellent barn.

Samuel never understood why Lucy hated this barn.

When they were small, she would play in his family barn with his brothers and sister, but she wouldn't get near her own. He figured Mr. Simms had told her to stay out. The man had been a fearsome yeller. Samuel recalled venturing past the door one day in search of Lucy. Mr. Simms, riding crop in hand, had stepped toward Samuel and yelled at him to get out. Samuel had been so frightened he'd run halfway home before realizing he'd neglected to deliver the gingerbread he had been taking to Lucy. He'd dropped the bundle when he ran but didn't dare go back.

Even after James became her new father, Lucy still avoided the barn. When sent on an errand to fetch Mr. Marden, she would stand at the door and call rather than set foot inside. Samuel had witnessed the behavior more than once, but that had been years ago.

Had she overcome her fear while I lived in Boston, or had desperation sent her to care for the animals when James Marden took ill?

Samuel put the brush back on its hook and took inventory of the tack room. The tack room door secured with a cross latch—not as long as a full crossbar but high enough that Sarah would not be able to reach it without standing on something. There was even a way to padlock the room, though Samuel did not see a lock around.

When Samuel was ten, he'd come into the barn, mostly to convince Lucy not to be so scared. But she'd cowered and cried outside, begging him to stay out. He remembered how a strong chain and lock secured the room then. He asked his pa about it. His father grunted and said Mr. Simms must have considered his saddles valuable. Deep gouges from the chain were still visible on the grayed walls.

The tack room proved to be neat and orderly, just as he expected James Marden to keep it. A shadow on the highest shelf caught his eye. Reaching up, Samuel found a riding crop.

Odd place to put it. Samuel ran his finger over the fine leather. He never used a crop.

James Marden hadn't used one either. But Mr. Simms had. He was using one to abuse the horse he rode the day he died. Samuel wondered if this were the same crop Mr. Simms had threatened him with as a boy. Lying on the shelf, it had become dusty, and the leather was cracked. The carved handle bore the initials "W. A. S." and was ringed with a serpent. He remembered seeing the mark often in his youth, on a sign hanging at the turn from the main road. This crop belonged to Mr. Welford Arthur Simms.

He slapped the crop in his palm. A disturbing image filled Samuel's mind. He dropped the crop as if it had burned his hand.

No. No man would do that to Lucy. Not even the cantankerous Mr. Simms. Surely Lucy would have told him. Kneeling on the floor, he bent to pick up the crop. From this angle, he noticed there were gouges in the wood around the door and a dark, hand-shaped stain on the wall. He covered it with his own. A child size print, ages old.

Samuel staggered out of the tack room, crop in hand. His stomach rolled. The stain was not paint. Only one thing made him this ill. Blood. Leaning against a rail, he wet his handkerchief in a trough and wiped his face. He still clutched the crop.

What to do with it? He wanted to burn it, bury it, or fling it into the river. If his guess proved correct, taking it into the house to the fireplace would unnerve Lucy. Ridding himself of the vile discovery would need to wait. He returned the crop to the shelf. Samuel sincerely hoped another version of events less cruel than he'd imagined existed.

He spent unnecessary time with each animal before he felt calm enough to return to the house. After Lucy's reaction to his seeing the scars, he was not ready to let her know he'd stumbled upon this. The nightmares, the scars, the barn—it all fit. He'd told Lucy when they were little that he would always be there for her. He had not been. If he had, his back might be covered with lash marks too.

After a second walk around the barn, he returned to the house. Sarah sat on the braided rug next to Lucy's bed, playing with two rag dolls.

Sarah raised her finger to her lips. She stood up and tiptoed over to him. "Lucy said it's time for the dolls to take a nap, but they are not tired."

The dolls were obviously not napping, but Lucy was.

Knowing Sarah could use some time out of the cabin, Samuel helped her with her cloak and mittens. As soon as she'd stepped out of the doorway, Sarah ran to seek out the barn kittens. She was not at all afraid to play in the barn.

Several choice words came to Samuel's mind. He was glad Mr. Simms was dead.

Eighteen

THE NEXT MORNING, AFTER BREAKFAST, while he worked in the barn, Samuel's mother pulled up in the wagon. Emma wasted no time in sending him to visit the house for the day with Sarah in tow.

What a curious feeling to return to his parents' home. He had been gone only two weeks, but it didn't feel like home anymore. He was a stranger, an interloper. Never in the three years he'd studied in Cambridge had he come home feeling like a guest. His home was with Lucy now. Samuel noted slight changes as he drove up. Most he attributed to the melting snow and further preparation for winter.

Thinking of his new home, even calling it Marden's or Lucy's seemed unfitting. Although "the Samuel Wilson's" sounded presumptuous, whatever it was, that house was now home. For the first time in his life, he felt like a visitor in his parents' home.

Emma poured steaming water into the bucket and added shavings of lye soap to it. The stench of lingering sickness and death and the dust motes floating about the home disappeared under Emma's care. Lucy rocked in the rocker, her pale face emotionless. She toyed with a ball of yellow yarn in her lap.

"I feel so useless, Mrs.—"

"It isn't Mrs." Emma wrung out the cloth. "I told you this past summer you were of an age where calling me by Christian name was permitted. Now that you are a married woman and my daughter-in-law, it is Emma, Ma, or even Mother Wilson if you must, but never Mrs. Do you understand?" Emma wagged her finger playfully.

"But you know I'm not really married?"

"What do you mean not really married? I witnessed it myself, right outside this door." Emma gestured to the door with the damp rag, sending a cascade of droplets over the floor she'd just swept. "Reverend Woods conducted it. No whispered vows in a snowbank for you."

"There were no vows, whispered or otherwise. I wasn't awake. It can't be." Lucy wrung her hands, causing the yarn ball to fly off her lap and roll across the floor, leaving a yellow tail behind. "How can God recognize a marriage when someone isn't awake to even turn down the proposal?"

Emma set the bucket down and wiped her hands on her apron before retrieving the ball of yarn. She sat in the chair next to Lucy's.

"I think God recognizes more than man gives Him credit for. What do you know of my marriage?"

"Mr. Wilson drove you home in the sleigh the night you announced your engagement. The sleigh got stuck, and the horse was lame. So you said your vows *verba de praesenti.*"

"Yes, under the lightly falling snow. There was a break in the clouds to the west, and we could see one star." Emma smiled, her gaze far away. "Reverend Woods claims our marriage is wrong. You've visited our house and seen us together. Do you think we don't have a real marriage?"

Lucy worried her lip and toyed with the yarn ball. She'd heard lectures from the pulpit about marriages needing to be performed in public. Her Puritan ancestors had created laws requiring marriage over 150 years ago. Not that the laws were always followed, as Emma had proved. The Reverend claimed unwitnessed marriages often led to heartbreak. More than one girl had exchanged secret vows to later find herself heavy with child and the man she'd claimed for a husband denying all. Lucy's marriage had been witnessed, but not by the bride!

"If I recall, you were at Sunday supper when Reverend Woods learned my Thomas and I hadn't said our vows before his predecessor. I don't think I ever saw a man of the cloth so red in the face." Emma giggled.

Lucy did too. "Then he spat his soup across the table. Poor Thomas Jr. and Samuel got it full in the face."

The image of both boys with soup dripping down their face sent both women into fits of laughter until Lucy started to cough. Emma hurried to bring her a cup of herb tea.

When Lucy could breathe normally again, Emma continued. "I think every sermon he gave for a month had to do with marriages being performed by clergy. My Thomas declared our marriage witnessed by God and took great delight in telling the good reverend on numerous occasions that we felt no need to repeat our vows before him, even after we'd paid the fine and the marriage was recorded. We refused to pay the fornication fine since all of our children have names and homes. Magistrate Garrett never pressed that matter." Emma deepened her voice and mimicked the reverend. "Thomas Wilson, you should be ashamed to have flaunted both the laws of Massachusetts and God, living in sin for two decades. What kind of example have you set?"

She lowered her voice a smidge deeper, matching her husband's. "Well, Reverend. I suppose we have set a good loving one. I've been faithful to her every day of our marriage. I don't come home drunk or beat my wife or children. Few men in your congregation can make those claims." Emma took a deep breath and continued in her own voice. "I then told him, 'Since we were lost in a snowstorm, we could have been in New York or New Hampshire. They were not so picky before the war. I've never been good with directions. Common-law marriages are legal there.' I don't think he believed me. Besides, I think you still needed a license and a witness in New Hampshire back then."

The sputtering reverend had opened and closed his jaw several times before he'd stormed out of the house and hadn't accepted another invitation to dinner until two years ago when Junior was married.

They giggled until tears formed at the corners of their eyes.

"You need to understand, we'd planned to make our vows in the spring. We'd even posted our intentions. Not saying our vows in front of witnesses had nothing to do with rebelling against God, as Reverend Woods is fond to lament. Our vows had everything to do with our situation. We both knew that by the time someone found us, I would be considered ruined, and Thomas would be forced to marry me as soon as the magistrate could be found. But the magistrate had been away for more than a fortnight."

A dreamy look filled Emma's face, and she released a sigh. "Getting married under the disapproving glares of our fathers didn't seem pleasant, so we simply said our vows under the open sky. We had quite a bit of talking to do when help did arrive the next afternoon, but my Thomas stood firm in declaring we were married, and we moved into the little cabin on his farm before nightfall. By spring, Thomas Jr. was on his way, and no one saw any point in bothering the itinerant preacher for vows. The magistrate, who was Mrs. Garrett's father, came back ill from Boston. So everything just was left unofficial. Agreeing to marriage vows in front of witnesses would not change the reality of our marriage."

Emma paused, a tender smile on her face, then placed her hand on Lucy's knee. "You may not feel married, but Samuel did pledge in front of witnesses, and Reverend Woods took your mumbling as consent. Ideally, you should have been completely coherent, but necessity dictated some variation. Like his father, Samuel is not going to abandon the vows he took."

"But we can't be. I thought I was dreaming."

"If you had known, would you have said yes?"

Lucy fiddled with the yarn and needles in her lap. A hundred times in her dreams she'd said her vows only to wake up unkissed and alone. If she had been able to stand next to him, or worse, been cradled in his arms because she was too weak to stand and he'd given her that crooked grin, she would have been helpless to refuse him anything. Just as Emma would have been considered ruined on that snowy night long ago, people would assume she was ruined if he had continued to stay without marriage. She knew she wasn't truly ruined. Samuel was not the kind to have taken advantage of her like that. However, he'd bathed her and changed her shift. There was no way she would be considered not ruined if she turned him away now. Every housewife in New England knew exactly what type of care he'd rendered. A single man caring for a woman that way would have sent her Puritan grandmothers into fits and fainting spells.

Of course she would have said yes, but only if she was sure Samuel wanted her to.

Her hands stilled. "I don't see what that has to do with it. I was unconscious. It doesn't change anything."

"Whether or not your vows are real has less to do with what was said in thirty seconds in front of a minister and more to do with how you live in the next thirty years as husband and wife."

Lucy wanted to argue, but she had no ammunition. Mama had been married twice in front of a minister, the words identical both times. But the marriages were as different as day and night. She opened, then closed her mouth.

Emma reached over and clasped her new daughter-in-law's hand. "As far as the Reverend Woods and the Commonwealth of Massachusetts are concerned, you are married. I do not deny that yours was an unconventional wedding. What type of marriage you have from here on out is up to you. There is no reason you can't say your vows between you and Samuel with God and the stars to witness it if you need to say them to feel married."

Lucy crushed her knitting together in her lap. "Emma! Why are you forcing your son to do this? I thought you would have not wanted him forced to marry, especially after you and Mr. Wilson didn't allow anyone to force you with yours."

Emma twisted the silver band on her finger, a gift on her first anniversary. "Samuel was not forced into this. He chose it."

"What type of choice was it? Leave me here with Sarah? Risk your becoming ill? At five years, Sarah could not care for me. Only a monstrous man would allow us to die. Samuel would never leave me to die. And you haven't been well. In no way would he put your life in jeopardy. Yours or mine. He had no choice!" Lucy ranted with renewed strength.

"I would have stayed, and told him so."

"But he had already been exposed. You know he wouldn't risk exposing you, too. Doctors and others care for ill people all the time, but they don't have to marry them. Sarah was here, and I was far too sick to be compromised. He doesn't need to be tied down by me. Now that I am better, he can leave."

"Can he?"

"Yes." Lucy folded her arms in front of her chest.

"You can take care of yourself?"

"Yes."

"Sarah?"

"Yes."

"The farm?"

"There isn't much to do at the moment." Lucy squirmed. She knew she couldn't care for the livestock yet.

"I don't think you are being completely honest." Emma gave her the look all mothers gave their children for lying. "You have had to rest at least twice since you started to knit that scarf." Emma gestured at the knitting lying in Lucy's lap. "I doubt you can even cross the room and stir the stew yourself. Let alone knead bread. You are recovering, but not quickly. You still need help. The question you need an answer to is, does he want to leave?"

Lucy sighed and glanced at the ceiling hung with dried herbs and vegetables. She couldn't answer as to what Samuel wanted. He'd said he wanted to stay. As for the rest, Emma was right, and she knew it. Alone she could survive, but not with Sarah and the farm. She wasn't even fully dressed. She'd donned her long wool stockings yesterday when Samuel went outside and then her heavy petticoats this morning. The effort tired her so that she had not put on her stays; rather, she'd completed dressing in an old, shapeless overdress.

"Lucy, there is no shame in accepting help."

Tears filled Lucy's eyes. "I don't mind the help. But he is stuck with me for the rest of his life. One week should not ruin the rest of his life."

Emma rose and started to scrub the table. Several minutes passed before she asked the next question. "Do you not like him? I thought you were quite fond of my son. You were engaged and had your intentions posted. I know something went awry with those plans. But did your feelings die?"

"I did…I do like him. But you know what happened with mother. Mr. Simms didn't go one day without reminding her how she ruined his life by trapping him."

Emma stopped scrubbing and turned to face Lucy. "That isn't what happened."

Lucy studied Emma, her eyebrows pinched in confusion.

"I know you heard Mr. Simms accusations and worse for years, but did it ever occur to you that his story wasn't the only version?"

Lucy stared at Emma.

"There is much more to the story." Emma paused for several moments, then shook her head. "I promise I will tell you all as soon as you are well enough to walk to the road. But for now, will you trust me when I tell you that Mr. Simms was not trapped into any marriage, as he so often said?"

Lucy nodded, wide-eyed. What story could Emma possibly have to tell? She opened her mouth to ask a question, but Emma shook her head.

"Not today, but as soon as you can walk far enough to prove you are well, I will tell you everything I know."

Lucy nodded and sunk back into the chair.

"Take a nap, dear, while I finish setting the house to rights. When you wake up, we can give you a bath and wash your hair. A good bath will make you feel so much better." Emma gathered the knitting and set it in the basket, then assisted Lucy to her room. Emma closed the door slowly and almost missed Lucy's murmured, "No need. Samuel did."

Samuel found himself with his father in the workshop. Thomas was chiseling a dovetail joint into the new chest he'd been fashioning. He blew the sawdust out of the joint and experimentally pieced the sides together.

"Make yourself useful, son. Those boards need to be planed for the lid." Thomas gestured to a stack of wood balanced on sawhorses.

Samuel placed a board in the clamps. He checked the angle and sharpness of the blade and glided the plane over the surface. Curls of wood spiraled to the floor. He ran his hand over the smooth board. Few things felt as good as a board cleaned of bumps and slivers and the release of the new-wood smell. He'd missed this in Boston, creating an entirely new object from what had once been a tree. He removed the board from the clamp and eyed it to see if his work was straight. After his third board, his father started talking.

"See how well these sides fit?" Thomas held two sides of the chest together over his workbench, slipping them together like a puzzle. "Just like a good marriage. It takes more work to make dovetail joints, but they're stronger than tongue and groove or any other way of joining this corner."

"Both boards carry equal responsibilities; they don't need extra help from nails or glue to stay tight. Some carpenters don't care how long the drawers or chest will last. They just want it to look nice now, not giving a thought to ten, twenty, or even fifty years from now. Remember the stool Junior made?"

Samuel winced and suppressed the urge to rub his backside even as he laughed. He had been the one to sit on the wiggly stool when it went crashing to the floor.

"It seemed sturdy enough, but it lacked the strength it would've had, had he taken the time to listen and do things right." Thomas took a mallet and tapped the joint into place.

Samuel recalled the lessons learned from the crushed chair. Thomas Jr. hadn't followed Pa's instructions, insisting he could build a chair his own way. He had even taken the time to carve an apple in the seat back. Samuel teased that the unskilled carving looked like a wormy apple. He should have known not to sit on it.

"Son, I hope you and Lucy can have a dovetail marriage. It is going to take a lot of work. Lucy isn't any piece of wood. No, she is like this maple burl." Thomas moved from his workbench to pick up a chunk of misshapen wood.

To the untrained eye, the knotted mass appeared destined for firewood, but Samuel knew the wood was as strong as it was beautiful and rare. Mallets and beadles created of the wood made some of the finest tools. Bowls carved from it rarely cracked.

"Your girl reminds me a lot of this wood. Workable in some places and hard and challenging in others, like your ma, I suppose." Thomas studied the wood a moment, running his hand over the rough surface. "What would happen if you planed this wood using the same pressure you are using on the oak?" Thomas waved to Samuel's work.

"I'd end up gouging and chipping it."

Thomas nodded as he put the burl wood down and returned to his bench. "You'd ruin it. Some men might blame the wood. God made the tree. Wouldn't be its fault some fool of a man didn't know how to work it right. It takes more patience than your average wood. This chunk will make a beautiful little piece someday, something for a lady—a box for her trinkets or sewing, or a mortar and pestle."

Thomas returned to piecing together the chest he was making.

Samuel laid the planed boards side by side, moving them around to create a design with the exposed grains. He planed a couple more spots before he deemed them ready for his father's inspection and for gluing and clamping them together.

"Fine work, son. Always were good with your hands. Best woodworker of all my boys so far." Thomas nodded his approval and returned to his work.

Samuel was somewhat surprised when his father started in on the lecture again.

"Did you want to marry her?"

"Sure, Pa, I wouldn't—"

Thomas cut Samuel off. "Thought so. Marriage is a lot of work, you know. Some young bucks think it is all in the courting and figure once they get hitched they're all set, that they never have to work at winning her again. Those boys are fools." Thomas shook the chisel in his hand for emphasis. "I'm sure your fancy medical school taught you everything about making babies, but I doubt they taught you about making a wife."

Samuel's face warmed. One couldn't grow up on a farm and not understand the rudiments of procreation. Medical school delved into more of the internal workings of the process. Samuel was sure he was more versed on the subject than his father.

This was not a talk he wanted to have with his father. He couldn't ever look at Ma's mended rocker without rehearsing Pa's lecture on sharing. He'd avoided the inlaid lamp table for months after the "Being a man doesn't mean you chase skirts" lecture. He hoped this chest was to be sold to someone he didn't know. But with his luck, it would be a wedding gift, and the trunk would sit at the foot of his bed.

"Not going to embarrass us both by discussing that part of marriage. I suspect you know the fancy names and all. I am sure they don't tell you most of making a baby doesn't happen in the bedroom."

Samuel's color deepened and he ducked his head as he worked on the wood.

"Starts with the ears."

Samuel looked up, surprised.

"Didn't teach you that, did they? You need to listen to your wife; not only to what she says but what she doesn't say. Yup, women are just like burl wood. You can think everything is going along smoothly, then bump, there is a knot that needs to be worked out. Could be a simple thing, like letting her get a nap because it is tough work carrying a babe around in her belly. Or it could be a hard one where you got to use your ears a whole bunch and keep your mouth shut.

"A wife is meant to be at your side, like Adam and Eve. Some men only want a woman who'll cook and wash their clothes or warm their bed and they miss out on the joy of having a woman as a companion and friend." Thomas returned his attention to the board he was working on. "Burl wood—work it slow and easy or it will chip. Yup, your Lucy will make a fine wife if you treat her right."

Double lecture day in the shop. Lecture on marriage from a chest and treat Lucy right from the maple burl. Samuel took a minute to process that Pa was giving the "treat my daughter right" talk he would have gotten had he been able to ask for Lucy's hand. James Marden would be pleased.

Thomas held up the four-sided body of the chest, each side locked into the next, all perfectly square and solid, no glue added into the joints. "A dovetail marriage, son, is what you want to build."

Clang! Clang! Emma made a racket in the other room, intentionally, no doubt. Lucy yawned and stretched as she stepped out of her bed and into the gathering room.

Emma slid the last of three rounded loaves off the board and into the baking oven. Replacing the soaked wooden oven door, she sighed. "Best fireplace north of Boston. That is what your mother always claimed, and she was right." Made of river rock rather than brick, it cooked everything just a bit better. The bread would be done as soon as the door stopped steaming itself dry. No wonder Anna had insisted on keeping the old cabin as the kitchen and gathering room when James had offered to build her a new house.

"Mmm, smells good." Lucy closed her eyes and inhaled. While she enjoyed the food Emma had sent, nothing compared to fresh-baked bread.

"About time you woke up, sleepyhead. Let's get you cleaned up and your hair washed." Emma poured the steaming water into the copper tub near the fireplace.

Lucy looked nervously around the room. "When will Samuel be back?"

"Not for at least an hour." Emma tested the water. "Don't worry. If he and Sarah return early, I will send them out to the barn."

Lucy crossed the room on shaky legs. As much as she hated to admit it, she was still too weak to take care of the farm and her sister.

"Can you get in on your own? I want to brush your hair out before we wash it." Emma disappeared into the large bedroom to retrieve the brush from Anna's table.

Emma was correct. The bath felt heavenly. Lucy hadn't realized that even her toes had carried the strain of her illness. Emma gently brushed and then washed Lucy's hair. Then she scrubbed her back, reminding Lucy of when Emma had rubbed salve on her back years ago.

Lucy lifted a strand of her damp hair to her nose. "Emma, it smells like summer flowers."

Emma patted her shoulder. "It is one of Carrie's soaps. She is getting much better at her creations. Do you remember some of her first ones?" Both women smiled. One of her soap experiments had smelled like a wet dog and was declared unusable even for bathing animals.

"She sent this bar up with her husband on your wedding day."

Lucy raised a brow, but she was too tired to argue the point with Emma. She would not find an ally in her mother-in-law. Moments later she wished she'd fought the subject of her marriage as Emma determined to make it a topic of conversation.

"Did Anna tell you much about the ways of a husband and wife?"

Lucy's flaming cheeks had nothing to do with the steaming bath water. *Not this. Definitely not while I am bathing!* Lucy peeked from under her tresses, gratified to see that Emma also suffered from unusually rosy cheeks.

"Of course, she told me some. We live on a farm." Lucy didn't know if she knew all Mama would have told her, but she hoped Emma was not going to tell her more now.

Emma's shoulders relaxed. She helped Lucy out of the tub and wrapped her in a warm towel. "Then, sweet girl, it is time you read the Song of Solomon. What happens between a husband and wife is beautiful enough for even a king to feel the need to sing about it." Emma turned Lucy to look directly into her eyes.

Lucy's color deepened. She'd spent too much time wondering what a real kiss would be like.

"I brought you a new shift, suitable for a bride. We won't don it now, but when you are feeling better, I hope you will wear it."

Lucy was glad when Emma turned around as she slipped her old shift over her head. An image of Samuel doing the same in reverse came to mind. Lucy looked down at her feet. Was it possible to blush all the way to her toes? It certainly felt like it was.

Lucy closed her eyes and sighed. Thinking of herself as a bride was something she was trying to avoid. Though Emma's conversation was short, it had been more embarrassing than the one she recalled with her mother on the subject of womanhood. And not because of her state of undress. This time her husband had a name.

Samuel loaded the last of his belongings into the wagon. He had forgotten he'd made several pieces of furniture intended for his future home before he'd left for Boston. Though some of the larger pieces were not needed at the Marden's, he took them anyway. They could be stored in the barn until he decided what to keep and what to sell off. As he placed the last chair in the wagon, Thomas approached carrying a chunk of wood. Samuel recognized it as the piece of burl wood they discussed earlier.

"I think you will know what to make out of this better than I do. My daughter-in-law deserves something from a piece of wood as rare as she is." He laid the wood inside of the wagon.

"Where are your tools?"

Samuel pointed to the workshop.

"Better take them to your place. Won't do you much good here."

Samuel hurried to the shop. The sun would soon set, and he wanted to get back in time for his mother to make the trip back in the daylight.

Samuel lifted a sleeping Sarah out of the wagon. She'd played hard with Mark and Daniel all day.

Emma met Samuel at the door and ushered him in with his bundle, indicating for him to take Sarah upstairs. Samuel noted Lucy's bed sat empty and that the straw mattress had been removed.

"Lucy?"

Emma tilted her head in the direction of the closed door of Anna and James's bedroom. When Samuel came back downstairs, Emma handed him an empty crock and followed him out the door.

"How was it with Lucy?" He surveyed the contents of the wagon, searching for the items he needed in the house.

"Well, I got the house cleaned, and she had a warm bath. The stew is done, and there is fresh bread."

Samuel lifted a crate out of the back of the wagon. "And about our marriage?"

"We did talk, but I cannot convince her that your marriage is real. That is for you to do. Marriage has to be more than words. It has to feel real. And I am not talking about what the two of you will do in there." Emma once again inclined her head toward the closed door. "If that room is the only place she feels married, then she is right. She isn't. Her entire life changed this last month. She lost family and gained you. Give her room to think and grieve, but not so much room she can push you away."

"She doesn't want me here." Samuel leaned against the wagon. The rest of its contents would be better off stored in the barn for now.

"She needs you here." Emma handed Samuel the basket of soiled linens from Lucy's bed. "You washed and changed her while she was ill." Not a question.

Samuel nodded, hoping his mother wasn't going to attempt a marital talk with him as well.

"Was she awake?"

"No, Ma." Samuel raised his brows. Was his mother guessing? Or had she spoken about it with Lucy? He sighed with relief when his mother discontinued her line of questioning.

"She trusts you. I hope she trusts you enough to tell you the stories you need to hear. Listen without judging her." Emma handed her basket to him. "Whatever she says, she has never done anything wrong or deserved what happened. Now empty the rest of this while I make sure I have everything."

Samuel pulled the wagon up to the porch. Emma grabbed her cloak, shut the door behind her, kissed her son on the cheek, then climbed into the wagon. She took the reins in hand but did not move the wagon.

"Samuel, one more word for you. Wait until she is well to make her yours. But don't wait a single day before letting her know you want her to be yours." Without giving her son a second to respond, she flipped the reins and ordered the horses to move off.

Samuel stared after her, red-faced. Getting marital advice from his father was not half as shocking as hearing it from his mother. Did she think him callous enough to rush things? He'd learned about the female body at school. Even a dropout knew it unwise to get an ill female in the family way. He had the uncomfortable feeling his mother spoke about more than healing from the illness Lucy had been battling.

Samuel carried his crate into the house and wondered where he should put his clothes. He knew eventually they should go in the bedroom where Lucy napped, but he did not feel putting them in there now would do anything to endear Lucy to him.

So up the stairs he went.

Nineteen

A THUMP OVERHEAD WOKE LUCY.

Strange.

Who would be on the roof?

It took her a moment to realize she lay in her mother's room. Her room now. Emma had left her little choice. Four windows gave the corner room more light than any other room in the house. Her mother preferred to sew sitting on the sofa tucked in the corner. The sofa had belonged to Papa Marden's mother. Most of the furniture in the room had also come from Papa Marden and was much finer than the furniture built by her grandfather. The bed originally had a feather-filled mattress. But it made Papa Marden sneeze and his eyes water, so they'd sold it.

Lucy would need to go through the chests and wardrobe soon and determine what to keep and what to give away. She wondered if Samuel could fit in Papa Marden's clothes. Samuel was about an inch taller, his shoulders broader. She shook her head to dislodge the image her mind conjured up. Samuel would not be staying. His footfalls echoed overhead. Emma must have left.

Not wanting to give Samuel a reason to come into the room, Lucy wrapped herself in her mother's dressing gown and slipped out the door. Her gaze drifted to the open door of her little room. Emma removed the bedding and mattress from her bed and pulled down the curtain as well. Lucy wondered if Emma would return the empty tick along with the quilts next week or wait as long as possible.

Samuel froze halfway down the stairs. Lucy stood near the table with her back to him. Her thick braid hung clean and smooth down her back. His immediate response was to go to her and loosen it, but he refrained. Lucy turned and caught him staring. Color flooded her cheeks. For a moment, neither moved. Samuel descended the last five steps as Lucy retreated a few inches until the table blocked her way. With trembling hands, Lucy pulled the wrapper tighter, unaware her attempt at becoming more modest had the opposite effect. The tightened garment outlined her silhouette all the more.

Samuel swallowed and tried to push his thoughts down. He doubted his kisses would be welcomed. "You look much refreshed."

Lucy pulled her braid around and toyed with the end before nodding stiffly. "We washed my hair." She looked at every part of the room except where he stood. "Your mother made dinner. Have you eaten yet?"

"No, I just arrived. Sarah fell asleep on the way home. I figured I'd eat after I finish in the barn. What about you? Would you like me to dish you something?" He stepped toward the fireplace and Lucy.

"Not yet, thank you." Lucy's voice was no louder than a whisper. Her legs trembled, and she started to sway.

Samuel reached out to steady her. "Why don't you sit near the fire?" He led her to the rocking chair. He didn't want to mention how faint and tired she appeared. Her entire countenance had drained of color in the few moments he had been in the room. He hoped he was not the cause.

Samuel lifted his hand to her brow, pretending to check for signs of fever. There were none, but a stray strand of hair needed to be smoothed. His hand lingered before sliding down her face. He placed a kiss where the errant hair had been. Neither of them breathed. Eyes wide, Lucy watched Samuel step back. He held her gaze a moment before retreating to the barn.

Samuel dared to look back at the house only when he reached the barn door. Had he looked back sooner, he might have returned to place another kiss on Lucy's head—and her lips as well. Her skin was so soft under his fingers, and the lavender scent of her hair was so sweet. He could no longer detect the stench of illness, and he wanted to celebrate. God had given him a wife!

Whistling a happy tune, he strode into the barn. Unaccustomed to that sound, Old Brown flicked his ears and snorted.

Lucy stared at the closed door, her fingers inspecting the spot Samuel had kissed. Surprisingly, it was not warmer than the surrounding skin to the touch, but in her mind it tingled with warmth.

She wanted him to stay, but she couldn't let him.

Above her she heard her sister moving about. Sarah gained speed as she hurried down the stairs, then ran across the room and into Lucy's lap, smothering her sister with a hug.

Lucy wrapped her arms around Sarah and held her tight as she listened to every detail of the day recited at high speed. Dogs, cookies, and searching for a mitten were highlights. Lucy let the words flow over her, smiling and nodding when appropriate, but her thoughts were more upon the man in the barn than on his brothers.

When Sarah mentioned a wagon full of furniture, Lucy interrupted Sarah's tales. "Furniture? Where?"

"In the wagon." Sarah rolled her eyes.

"What kind of furniture?"

Sarah shrugged. "Chairs?"

Lucy looked around the room. There were no new additions. Sarah must be mistaken. "What else did you do?"

"That is all. Samuel and I camed home. What did you do? You smell pretty and not all sick and yucky. Did you take a bath?"

Before Lucy could answer, she became aware of Samuel standing in the open doorway. She was not going to discuss her bath in front of him. Her mind filled with thoughts of another bath, the details of which she'd imagined more than once. She looked away before her blush could come to full bloom.

Samuel shut the door. "Ready for supper?"

"I'll set the table!" Sarah climbed out of Lucy's lap.

Dashing around the table, Sarah stopped by the open door to Lucy's room. "Lucy?" Sarah pointed.

"I moved into Mama and Papa's old room."

"Can I sleep in the big bed with you tonight?" Sarah had remembered her promise. As much as she needed more sleep, Lucy knew she needed peace. Her sister would badger her every hour until the promise was kept. She nodded her head in acquiescence, and Sarah clapped her hands.

"Hurry and finish the table, little one." Samuel laid out the food before Lucy could find the strength to get out of the chair. By the time she walked the four feet to the table, everything was ready. She scolded herself for her slowness. She would never convince Samuel to leave if she couldn't even walk across the room. After the kiss this afternoon, it was imperative she get him out soon. If she'd lifted her chin, she could have turned the kiss into a real one. She couldn't let that happen. How long would her resolve hold against such temptation?

Sarah kept up the dinner conversation on her own, oblivious to the silent adults who were thankful for her chatter. As long as they needed to interact with Sarah, they were safe from one another.

Too soon the meal ended. Lucy started to gather the empty bowls. Before she could stand, however, Samuel was by her side, removing them from her hands. She tried to hold on to them, but she doubted he even noticed, her attempt was so feeble.

"Let me wash them tonight, please. Another day or two of rest and I am sure you can snatch them from my hands." He winked before turning to the dry sink.

Another wink! He is flirting with me. This can't be happening. Lucy realized her mouth hung open as she watched Samuel rinse the plates.

What could she do? There was no place for her to escape except to the bedroom. Going in there would be admitting she did not feel well, but her entire body yearned to fall into the big bed and sleep. With luck, Sarah would fall asleep without needing to talk. Chattering and wiggling children were a form of torture. But there was no way to put her sister off another night. And having Sarah with her was preferable to being alone with Samuel.

Sarah had not yet mastered the art of eating over her plate and bowl. Lucy swept the crumbs she could reach into a pile, anything to ignore the man washing dishes. He wasn't even grousing about it. Mr. Simms had never lifted a finger. The door closed, she looked up, and found herself alone. She hadn't even heard Sarah ask for Samuel to accompany her to the privy. She let out a sigh. She knew she should move from the table, but she lacked the strength. She wondered if it would be more embarrassing to have Samuel find her fallen on the floor or still at the table. Stifling a yawn, she laid her head on her arms. She would hear the door open when they came in, but for a moment she could sneak a rest.

A sudden noise brought Lucy awake and she looked up to see that Samuel had placed the Bible on the table near her. She was embarrassed at being caught asleep.

Sarah came around the table and touched her cheek. "You have sleep wrinkles."

Lucy turned away, trying to smooth her cheek, as Sarah giggled. For a moment she thought she heard Samuel start to laugh too. A peek at his face revealed he could not possibly be laughing.

"Tonight we are reading from Ecclesiastes, chapter 11. Sarah and I finished Proverbs and decided to continue reading the Old Testament."

Lucy listened. She'd never read the entire Old Testament in order. Papa Marden had always skipped around, reading only the stories and joyful verses. Mr. Simms had always read the verses about obeying parents and eternal punishment. Lucy suspected he made some of them up. She struggled to understand what Samuel read. The verses seemed to be a mix of both joy and rebuke. Her mind wandered as she listened. She tried to remember what came after Ecclesiastes. She started reciting the books of the Old Testament beginning with Genesis, Exodus...Psalms, Proverbs, Ecclesiastes, Song of—. Lucy gasped just as Samuel finished the verse.

He looked at her quizzically.

She returned the look. Surely he would not read the entire Old Testament in order. Papa Marden had once told her the Song of Solomon was to be read by married people. And just this afternoon, Emma had told her now was time to read the pages. Lucy had peeked years ago and knew it started off with kissing. Samuel could not read it aloud in front of Sarah. He couldn't read it out loud in front of her. Kissing!

Samuel studied Lucy and looked back at the last verse he read. He continued reading.

Lucy tried to follow the words. If Samuel inquired about what had disturbed her, she needed a different answer.

He closed the Bible, but before he could stand to put it away, Sarah kissed him on the cheek and spun to tug on Lucy's arm. "Hurry, Lucy! Tonight we get to sleep in the big bed!"

Lucy leaned on the table to support her wobbly legs as she stood from the bench. Samuel was soon at her side, cupping her elbow for support. "Are you ready for this?" he asked in a low voice.

Lucy nodded. "I dare not put her off another night. She is so excited." Lucy shuffled to the bedroom, leaning on Samuel more than she liked. There was a pleasant wood spice about him tonight, mixed with the usual smell of him. Lucy chided herself for noticing.

Sarah bounced onto the big bed.

"Oh, Lucy! Isn't it wonderful? But tonight is the onlyest night I can sleep here. 'Cause then it is Samuel's bed too."

Samuel and Lucy both stopped midstep as Sarah continued. "Samuel's brothers told me all about it. They said I was silly to want to sleep in the big bed with Lucy 'cause married people sleep in big beds so they can have big families."

Lucy stiffened and heard Samuel's sharp intake of breath.

"Sarah, darling, what exactly did Samuel's brothers say?" Lucy managed to ask as she sank onto the corner of the bed, her arm wrapped around a bedpost for support.

"I told them you promised we could sleep in the big bed. Joe asked me when you promised. And I told him before you got sick. Then he said you wouldn't want to sleep in a bed with me now 'cause you were married, and married people enjoy sleeping together. But I told him you promised, and you always keep your promises. He laughed at me. So I stomped my foot and told him it was true. Then John said he was sure it was and he was sure you would keep your promise. Then he said Samuel made his bed and would have to lie in it. And I told him Samuel always makes his bed, and he laughed again." Sarah crossed her arms and lifted her chin.

Lucy let out a sigh of relief that the twins had not said anything more by way of explanation to her little sister. She wondered if she could knock their heads together.

"So is it true Samuel, do you want to sleep in this bed with Lucy?" Sarah asked innocently.

Lucy wondered if she would faint.

Samuel cleared his throat. "Sarah, until your sister is completely better, I will sleep upstairs." Lucy did not miss the emphasis on completely.

"Why?"

"I get up early to do the chores in the barn. I don't want to wake her up."

"Oh, Lucy, should I wait too?"

"No!" Lucy and Samuel shouted in unison, and Sarah slipped into the bed. "Tuck me in, Samuel, please?" she pleaded. When he came around the bed, Sarah threw her arms around his neck. "I love you, Samuel. You're the bestest brother."

"Are you forgetting something?"

"Prayers!" Sarah leaped from the bed and knelt to pray. Lucy took advantage of both sets of closed eyes to slip out of her robe and ease under the covers. When Sarah finished, she climbed back into the bed.

"Lucy, aren't you going to kneel for your prayers too?"

She hadn't thought about praying, just not being seen in her shift in front of Samuel. No way was she going to get out of the bed and kneel with him watching. He'd seen that and more, but now she had a choice.

Samuel came to her aid. "Sometimes we don't kneel when we pray. Like at dinner. Lucy might get too cold if she kneels. So tonight she is going to say her prayers in bed."

His eyes met Lucy's over Sarah's head. Lucy mouthed "Thank you." To which Samuel replied with a wink.

Sarah nodded and scooted down in the bed. Samuel kissed her on the forehead and started to leave the room.

"Wait!" cried Sarah.

Samuel halted in the doorway.

"You need to tuck Lucy in, too."

Samuel advanced toward Lucy's side of the bed, his eyes never leaving her face. Lucy pulled the covers up to her chin as she sank deeper into the bed. By the time Samuel reached her, there was nothing left to tuck in. As Samuel lowered his face to hers, Lucy's eyes grew wide. At the last moment, he changed course and landed a kiss on her cheek.

"Sweet dreams," he whispered in her ear, sealing the thought with a second kiss before leaving the room.

Lucy couldn't be sure in the dim light, but she thought he'd winked at her again.

Sarah snuggled into Lucy's side and gave a contented sigh.

Lucy was not content. As she drifted off to sleep, she heard the footfalls from the ceiling overhead and wondered what it would be like to...

Twenty

SAMUEL SHOVED OPEN THE BARN door. The cock had yet to crow, but he found the sleep that had been slow in coming had fled before the first fingers of dawn had crept through his window. He thought it best to occupy his mind with things other than Lucy.

That proved impossible as he milked Lucy's goat, cleaned the stalls in her barn, and wondered when her new calf would be born. Contemplating the birth of the calf reminded him that Lucy's birthday was about a week away. He wasn't sure if it was Tuesday or Wednesday, but his ma or the family Bible could provide the information.

What does one get a reluctant bride for her first birthday as a wife? Old Brown's ideas were unhelpful and self-serving. Apples and carrots. The pigs were worse. Samuel contemplated the beautiful wood Pa had given him. The swirled burl would make a fine trinket box. Between the tools he'd brought with him and the collection James Marden left behind, he had everything he needed, other than time. To carve a box the way he envisioned, it would take more than a week.

His eyes fell on the tack room. Inspiration hit. The box could wait for Christmas. He bent to examine the door. He could fix the room in a day or two, and if he could find some whitewash stored either here or at his pa's, he knew the perfect gift for the woman who seemed to have an aversion to the room. An added bonus—between the two projects, he could stay out of the house most of the day and for several days to come. Being in the same room with Lucy was not easy. He spent half the time fighting the desire to pull her into his arms and the other half wondering if she wanted him to.

Being near Lucy was like walking along the top of a ridgepole with a basket of eggs in one hand, an anvil in the other, and a fine china plate on his head. So much to balance. He wanted the type of marriage his parents had. They were so…he didn't have a word for it. *Together* wasn't big enough, but the word was the best he could find. They worked and laughed together. They were two halves of the same whole. So far his marriage could be summed up in one word—lonely. He couldn't blame Lucy. She was as weak as the newborn kittens hidden in the hayloft. It wasn't as if she had been throwing herself at him the past two months, nor had he made any effort to see her. He hoped time would fix these problems. Well, time and a lot of prayers.

The sun streaming through the window woke Lucy. The spot where Sarah slept had cooled. Lucy stretched. Sarah was not a comfortable bed partner. Lucy might even sport a bruise or two to prove it. She'd forgotten how much Sarah tossed and kicked in her sleep. Other than the weeks after Mr. Simms had died when she'd slept with her mama, Sarah was the only other person with whom she'd ever shared a bed, that she could remember. What would it be like to share a bed with Samuel? She didn't remember sharing it with him sixteen years ago, and even if she did, it would be different now. Would he toss and kick like Sarah, or would he keep her warm like Mama? Shocked at her thoughts, she leaped out of the bed she'd shared in her mind.

Too sudden. The room tilted, and she had to brace herself on the bedpost.

She chided herself. The sooner she got that man out of her life, the better.

It took her longer to get dressed than normal. Mama's couch came in handy to rest on between layers. Her stays did not fit correctly, and she found she needed to tighten them considerably, as she had her skirt and petticoats. The illness had drained her of what little excess weight she carried. Her fingers could feel the definition of each rib through her shift. She shuddered. What would Samuel think of such a skinny wife? He'd called her beautiful, but he might not have noticed how her bones stuck out.

"You must stop thinking of him that way," she muttered aloud.

The gathering room was empty. The clock on the mantel read ten minutes before eleven. Sarah must be with Samuel out in the barn. Three fires currently burned in the massive fireplace. The smallest consisted of a dozen glowing coals. As she suspected, the pot nearest it contained some still-warm pease porridge. Lucy stared at the fires. Emma had taught her son well. Most men unfamiliar with cooking would set only a single fire. A peek at the pot hanging on the crane confirmed her suspicions. The beans had started to cook. Had Samuel done all of this? Perhaps Emma had stopped by to help.

She remembered his mother teaching them both how to make her baked beans. Samuel had groused about having to learn to cook anything, but his father had set him straight, pointing out how Emma's lying-in with the twins had been longer than most and if he hadn't known how to cook a few things, they would have been hungry, even with the food Lucy's mother and others provided.

Alongside Carrie and Lucy, Thomas Jr. and Samuel had learned the mysteries of baking beans, johnnycake, pease porridge, and fried ham. She smiled at the memory. The boys had turned it into a competition. Sadly, they learned the hard way that beans could not be hurried with a bigger fire.

Her stomach rumbled. Though there would be a meal in about an hour, she dished herself some of the warm porridge and indulged in a cup of goat's milk.

Sarah giggled as she rode on Samuel's back across the yard. She had a secret, and as a reward for keeping it, Samuel had promised her a full week of piggyback rides to and from the barn. Since she didn't enjoy getting her shoes muddy, she declared her silence a perfect trade. The melting snow left the yard riddled with puddles. They froze over at night, but by noon the muddy spots were difficult for one with such short legs to avoid.

The pair stomped into the house but stopped when they noticed Lucy snoring softly in the rocking chair. A half-finished sock hung precariously from her knitting needles. Sarah covered her mouth to keep another giggle inside. Lucy's mop cap had slipped, covering one eye.

"Look, Samuel. Lucy is a pirate, like your story." Sarah pointed over his shoulder and giggled.

Samuel set Sara down and closed one eye, making the pirate face he'd used earlier.

Sarah couldn't contain her laughter any longer.

Lucy woke with a start, and the stocking and needles clattered to the floor.

Samuel turned to hang up his coat—and to hide his smile.

Sarah hung up her cloak and wasted no time in regaling Lucy with stories of pirates and how Lucy had looked identical to one when they'd come in.

Lucy laughed with her. Pulling her cap at a more rakish angle, she grimaced and growled, "Nay, matey, a privateer I be!"

Sarah laughed so hard she could not even speak and fell to the floor holding her sides.

"Sam-ah-u-el is a pi-i-rat to-too," she squeaked out, pointing at her brother-in-law before collapsing in another fit of giggles.

Samuel squinted one eye closed and limped across the room on his imaginary peg leg. Lucy laughed so hard tears began to form. He stepped around Sarah, pretending to balance on his peg leg.

"I be Pirate Sam. And ye be my bonny wench." He pulled Lucy out of the rocker and planted a loud kiss on her cheek before he buried his face in her neck and tickled her with his whiskers.

Lucy shrieked and clung to him. Samuel pulled his head back and looked at her out of his one eye for a long moment. Turning to address Sarah, he growled, "What say ye, matey? Shall I make this wench me wife?"

Sarah laughed even louder and nodded her head vigorously.

Samuel snaked his other arm around Lucy's waist and drew her closer, then placed his lips on hers.

Lucy stopped breathing, her eyes wide, then she slowly closed them and leaned into the kiss. When Samuel started to pull back, she followed up on her toes until the connection was broken.

"And a fine bride she be," he said in a hoarse whisper.

Sarah's clapping and shouts of "Hurrah for the pirate's wife!" filled the room.

Lucy blinked and leaned back.

Samuel did not relinquish his hold on her. All thoughts of pirating fled. Had he stolen a kiss or had it been freely given? She looked as astonished as he felt.

Sarah's chants grew louder, reminding him they had an audience. Samuel dropped his arms. "We should get dinner on."

Lucy's hand flew to her mouth as she turned to the cupboard to hide her reddening face from her sister.

Samuel vanished into the lean-to.

Unspoken strains of "What have I done?" echoed through the house.

Dinner would have been a quiet affair full of self-recrimination and covert glances had Sarah not been present. The little chatterbox kept a constant conversation going requiring minimal answers from the adults, who barely paid attention. If they could have, they would have steered the conversation into safer waters.

Lucy had just started to sip her cider when Sarah declared, "Lucy, you should have seen your face when he kissed you. Samuel, I told you she loved you!"

Lucy had the uncomfortable feeling the cider was going to spray out of her nose. She couldn't swallow. With much effort, she managed to spit the cider back into her cup. A quick glance at Samuel told her he was having the same difficulty with the bit of bread he was chewing on.

Before either of them could respond and change the subject, Sarah continued, "So now you are really married, right Lucy? You kissed him, just like Reverend Woods told Carrie to do. And you should only kiss people you marry."

Lucy opened her mouth to answer, but no response would come out. She wasn't married. But after such a display, how could she deny she wanted to be? Samuel wasn't all at fault. She kissed him back and clung to him not wanting the kiss to end. Just as a pirate's wench would have. Her face heated again, she took an intense interest in the ham on her plate.

Sarah didn't stop for an answer. "Timmy tried to kiss me behind the church last summer, but I told him I was never going to marry him, and he should go way. He doesn't smell nice like Samuel does. Timmy always smells like the barn cats. I'm never going to kiss Timmy."

Samuel managed to finish his supper, although it took a monumental effort. More than once he had been afraid he might choke to death. A couple of times he'd sneaked a peek at Lucy to make sure she wasn't choking as well. He worried at one point she might spew the contents of her mug all over the table. A niggling in the back of his mind told him in a few years the story of their first kiss would be one they would laugh at. At the moment, the kiss was not open for discussion or repetition. Even if Lucy had kissed him back.

He hid a smile behind his cup and wondered how long before there would be a successful repeat performance. Next time he would kiss Lucy without Sarah as a witness.

Sarah's conversation ended as she finished the last of her milk.

"Nap time." Lucy looked as if she couldn't live through another moment of her sister's prattle.

"Can't I help Samuel in the barn?"

Samuel shook his head. He also needed to be away from Sarah's nonstop chatter. Hearing about the kiss again would not help him sort things through. He hadn't planned on kissing Lucy so soon. Not that he regretted it, but he needed to revise his plan.

Sarah dropped her shoulders and, to both adults' relief, climbed the stairs to her room.

Samuel started to pick up the supper dishes, but Lucy waved him off. After a mumbled excuse, he escaped to the barn.

As soon as he left, Lucy fell into the rocker and covered her mouth with her hand and began to giggle. Her first real kiss still played on her lips. He may have been playing the pirate, but he had not stolen the kiss. She'd given it.

Twenty-one

SAMUEL WASN'T SURPRISED TO FIND Lucy asleep in the rocker or the dinner dishes still on the table when he returned to the house a half hour later. He debated with himself a half moment before scooping her into his arms and carrying her into the bedroom. She would be much more comfortable on the bed, he reasoned, ignoring the truth that he just wanted an excuse to hold her again. He took a moment to study her after covering her with a quilt. Lucy sighed in her sleep and sort of half smiled. Samuel hoped she was dreaming of him.

He cleared the table and added some molasses to the beans and leftover pork from their dinner meal. Tomorrow was the Sabbath, and the beans could serve as their after-meeting meal as well as tonight's supper.

Samuel rubbed the back of his head. Saturday night baths. That could be a bit complicated. Lucy had taken one yesterday, and considering how much she still slept each day, she wasn't well enough to attend Sabbath services. Lucy could help give Sarah hers after supper, and he would sneak down and take his bath after everyone went to bed. He would be sure Lucy slept peacefully first.

Samuel remembered the other thing he wanted to do when Lucy was out of the room. He pulled down the family Bible and opened it to the back, where Grandfather Stickney had kept the family records. He found Lucy's mother and Mr. Simms's marriage. Lucy's name was not written where he expected it to be. When he found it, he recognized the same hand from his own family's Bible—his mother's elegant script. Surely his mother had made an error. Lucy was listed as a Stickney, not a Simms. But her birthday of December 12 fell three months after Anna's wedding date to Mr. Simms.

Samuel stared at the page. He'd heard unkind things about Anna and Lucy from an old gossip or two. When Mr. Simms died, there had been comments made by even the more pious members of the congregation, but he'd thought little of it. So general was the dislike of Mr. Simms he thought it natural.

Anna Stickney Simms Marden was his mother's closest friend and not the type of woman who would bear a child out of wedlock. She'd married before Lucy's birth. Traditionally Lucy should bear Mr. Simms's name. And publicly she had. He'd never heard her called by any other. A few people did call her Miss Marden, but they'd moved here more recently and would assume she had her stepfather's name. His mother must know something about it as she'd written it in the Bible. He wondered if Lucy knew. She'd never corrected anyone when they called her Simms.

He turned the page to where he'd written in their marriage information and read it several times before it dawned on him. He'd married Lucy Simms, not Stickney. The reverend had used the name Simms. Was their marriage invalid? Lucy must not know her name was listed as Stickney or she would have used that argument. He didn't know who to ask about the legality. An incorrect question to Reverend Woods could start a series of embarrassing sermons to both of them. Magistrate Garrett could not be approached for fear of Elizabeth learning of the conversation. Perhaps he would corner his mother tomorrow.

More pressing, the twelfth was next Tuesday, which left him precious little time to complete his birthday surprise. Samuel went out to the barn to work on it.

Supper was more relaxed than dinner, mostly due to the subject revolving around tomorrow's church meeting and all the friends Sarah hadn't seen in weeks. Both Lucy and Samuel reassured her she wouldn't need to tell anyone of her parents' deaths as Reverend Woods would have taken care of the announcement.

After hauling out the tub and preparing Sarah's bath, Samuel headed to the barn and made himself scarce. By the time he returned for Bible reading, Lucy sat brushing through the last of Sarah's snarls as the little one's hair dried near the fire. Lucy sent him a quizzical look when he emptied the tub, but she made no comment. She wasn't about to bring up the subject of Samuel's needing to bathe.

Sarah had no such qualms. "Samuel, aren't you going to take a bath too?"

"Later," he mumbled.

"Is Lucy going to help you wash your hair and back?"

Mortified, Lucy shook her head. "No!" she blurted the same time as Samuel.

"Samuel is a big person. He can do his own hair and back," Lucy explained not daring to look at his sandy hair or broad shoulders.

"But Mama used to help Papa. I would hear them laughing up in my room."

Lucy closed her eyes and breathed deeply, hoping an answer would come before her face turned as red as a cherry. Mama and Papa Marden's habit was to take their baths locked in their room late Saturday nights, and more than once Papa's rich laughter had floated down from the room.

Again, Samuel came to the rescue. "Lucy has already helped with your bath tonight. I think she will be too tired to help with mine."

Sarah accepted the answer and dropped the subject.

"Shall we read?" Samuel asked, getting the Bible down and opening to the last chapter of Ecclesiastes.

"Can I help you read? You point at the words, and I will tell you the ones I know." Sarah bounced as she asked the question. At Samuel's nod, she climbed into his lap.

Together they read the chapter. After two or three verses, they fell into a rhythm, with Sarah reading all the small words and Samuel filling in all the words in between.

"Remember..."

"...now thy"?

Samuel nodded at her pronunciation before continuing. "Creator"

"...in the..."

". . .days of thy youth, while ..."

"...the..."

"...evil days come not, nor ..."

"...the ..." Sarah beamed.

"...years draw nigh, when thou shalt ..." Samuel smiled at Sarah as she scrutinized the next word.

"...say"

"I have..."

"...no ..." Sarah almost shouted the familiar word.

"...pleasure in them."

When they got to the end of the chapter, Sarah pointed to the large words at the top of the next page. "The S-song of—What's that word?"

"Solomon." Lucy noted the color rising in Samuel's face as he answered.

"So tomorrow we are going to start the Song of Solomon? I didn't know they wrote songs in the Bible."

"No, I think we will skip to"—Samuel turned the pages—"the book of the prophet Isaiah." Samuel pointed to the title.

"But you said we would read everything as long as there were not any *begats* 'cause they are long and boring."

"Well, the Song of Solomon is all about the *begats*, so that is why we are skipping it."

"Oh, all right, then." Sarah patted Samuel's arm. "Tuck me in?" she asked, jumping off his lap. Samuel followed her up the stairs.

Lucy scooted over into the seat Samuel had occupied earlier and turned back several pages. Curious, she began to read the Song of Solomon. She paused at the second verse. She'd tasted wine several times. The first time was at Mama and Papa Marden's wedding. It had tasted like vinegar and grapes, and she'd spit it out. Samuel's kiss tasted much better than the wine. Why would the Bible say love was better than wine? Maybe they didn't press fresh apple cider in the fall to compare it too. Samuel's kiss tasted much more like fresh-pressed cider than wine. But how did love compare?

Lost in her musings, she did not hear Samuel come down the stairs or walk up behind her. Her index finger rested at the side of the second verse. Straddling the bench next to her, he covered the hand on the Bible with his own. Startled, Lucy lifted her head, her mouth hanging open slightly, unsure what to do. She looked down at the Bible and tried to extract her hand while shutting the book, but Samuel's hand prevented her from doing both.

"What are you reading, Lucy?"

"Nothing," she lied.

Samuel used his free hand to lift Lucy's chin and turned her face to his. His eyebrow quirked, questioning her integrity.

"I mean, I was just reading the Bible." She trailed off, seeing the twinkle in his eye. No use lying. He knew.

"You know the Song of Solomon is pretty heavy reading for a woman who claims to be unwed."

"I was just…" Lucy fidgeted, no excuse coming to mind. She met his eyes for a moment longer before dropping her gaze to his lips. The verse filled her mind.

"I believe you were reading 'Let him kiss me with the kisses of his mouth: for thy love is better than wine.'"

Lucy's eyes bounced back up to his as he closed the distance between them. Lucy knew she should jump up and leave, and he was giving her enough time to do just that, but her body wouldn't listen. Instead, she heeded the Bible verse and let him kiss her, leaning into him to make it easier. Her eyes fluttered closed. *Definitely better than new cider.*

When the kiss ended, she found her hand resting on his shoulder, her heart betraying her mind's command. Samuel rested his forehead on hers.

"Until you are resolved that we are married, I suggest you don't read any further." The huskiness of his voice resonated all the way to her toes. Lucy pulled back and shut the Bible.

"I think you are right. It should not be read by someone who is unwed."

"But are you?"

"Am I what?"

"Unwed?"

"I think so," she answered shakily, for at that moment she wanted to be wed.

"You are no longer sure?"

"Samuel." She drew his name out the same way her mama did when she was exasperated. "I can't trap you. I won't have your life ruined because I took sick and you chose to save my life."

"Do I seem trapped to you?" Samuel held out both arms, a grin brightening his face.

Lucy studied him. He still sat close, though no longer touching her. She would need to move two or three inches to rekindle the connection and place her lips back on his. Samuel looked much more relaxed than she felt.

"No, you don't seem trapped now, but what about next year? What happens when you realize you made a big mistake?"

Samuel raised his hand and cupped her cheek. "Lucy, you are many things, but never a mistake." He placed a kiss on her brow and stood to leave.

Lucy grabbed his hand. "You are sure?"

"Yes, sweetheart, I am sure." Samuel walked out the lean-to door without his coat.

Lucy stared at the vacant doorway, feeling more confused than ever. He seemed determined to maintain their sham marriage. Maybe he would change his mind after going to church tomorrow. Elizabeth was sure to be there. She would make him see the mistake he was making. The thought of church reminded Lucy that Samuel had yet to bathe, so she hurried to the bedroom and shut the door. Noticing the slide bolt, she decided to use it. Not so much to keep Samuel out as to keep her in. After that last kiss, she wanted more, but she suspected that, just like drinking too much cider at pressing time, too many of his kisses would cause a stomach ache. Or worse.

Samuel needed to cool off. Sitting inside, he'd had to fight the urge to pull her into his lap for a better kiss. Lucy needed to come to her own conclusions about their marriage. Too many kisses would press an unfair advantage. Or one exceptionally good one. He'd pressed her as far as he dare tonight. If she were smart, Lucy would go to bed while he was outside and would lock the bedroom door.

Twenty-two

ELIZABETH GARRETT FLOUNCED INTO THE little white church. She timed her entrance perfectly, as usual, making sure she had the maximum audience to admire her new dress. She opened the frog on her cloak, resting the fabric as far back on her shoulders as possible. The deep-red block print drew every eye. She knew the ladies were eyeing the delicate rose print. The single men, and perhaps a few of the married, were wondering if their good fortune would include witnessing Elizabeth removing her fichu from the daringly low neckline. Her gaze slid to the Wilson pew. Samuel was not there—again. She knew he would be back to church, and for her, soon. Her brother had told her and her mother all about his ridiculous marriage.

Elizabeth rolled her eyes. No one would take it seriously. Her father said that he heard Lucy hadn't even been completely awake, but since the intentions had been properly posted, he could not find legal fault with the nuptials. More than once, Mother had insinuated that Lucy had been born on the wrong side of the blanket. "Like mother, like daughter. Trapping some innocent man." Her mother's exact words echoed through her mind. Of course, Lucy would need to live to catch Samuel permanently. Her father doubted she would. The wedding was of little concern. There had been eleven deaths so far this winter attributed to illness. Perhaps Lucy had passed. The reverend would announce her passing along with the others.

What an evil thought to think while walking down the aisle in church! She didn't wish Lucy dead—well, not genuinely dead, as that would be unchristian of her—just not married to Samuel dead. Movement caught her eye as she passed by the Marden pew. The little Marden girl bobbed with excitement as her father whispered to her to calm down.

Wait! Mr. Marden was dead.

She swiveled her head in a most unladylike manner. Samuel?

Apparently, he was taking his role as head of the household seriously. Lucy was not there. Perhaps Samuel was a widower. It would be her Christian duty to console him. The little Marden girl wasn't a bad sort. She could even be nice to her. She was old enough to help with chores. Or Samuel's mother might take in the child. Elizabeth's smile widened a fraction.

Elizabeth gave the slightest shake of her head, letting the lone ringlet bounce, and slowed a bit to make sure Samuel had time to admire her new outfit before slipping into the Garrett pew across the aisle.

Sarah quieted down, and Samuel turned to the front of the chapel just as Elizabeth settled into her pew. She flashed a smile in his direction—the same smile she'd used at the cider pressing. Her boldness struck Samuel. She must have timed her entrance solely to show off her new dress—a rather vulgar affair that promised to show more of her assets than acceptable at church or most places respectable people frequented. Had she always been so vain? Why hadn't he run like Joseph from Potiphar's wife when she'd approached him?

Next to him, Sarah stuck out her tongue and crossed her eyes. Samuel gave her a frown and shook his head. He doubted Elizabeth had seen the face she'd made, but he didn't want to encourage Sarah, even if he agreed. At the same time he wanted to laugh. He could picture Lucy making that very face in Elizabeth's direction more than once when they were school age. He was sure Lucy would applaud Sarah's actions.

He turned his attention to the announcements, knowing Lucy would want to know who had been born and who had passed. He was surprised to hear his name called and his recent marriage recognized along with the fact that the Marden pew was now the Samuel Wilson pew on the tithe rolls. A hushed murmur went up at this; whether in response to his new marital status or the inheritance of one of the prized front pews, he could not be sure. He concentrated on looking straight forward, pretending not to notice. Sarah tugged on his sleeve.

"Samuel, they're talking about you." Her whisper echoed, and some heads turned in his direction.

Samuel nodded and patted her arm, glad she was not tall enough to see over the pew without standing. The reverend moved on to list those who'd died this week. Samuel sorrowed for the three families who'd lost members. Thankfulness filled his heart that Lucy was not among those mentioned.

The start of the hymn signaled the end of the hushed gossip. Samuel sighed, the worst part of the meeting concluded. No one would think of him from here on.

The sermon was benign enough, one of dozens given at the beginning of Advent, making it both easy to focus on and let his mind wander at the same time. Samuel couldn't see his family sitting three pews back, but he wondered what type of mischief his brothers were concocting. Rare was the Sunday that at least one of them didn't earn a reprimand from Pa on the way home.

Sarah leaned her head into Samuel's arm and kicked her feet in an unidentifiable rhythm. Samuel wondered how it would be to have Lucy on his other arm. Perhaps next week.

The closing hymn was sung. Families gathered children, Bibles, and hymnals so they could dash out of the cooling church and into the warmth of their own homes.

After the prayer, Samuel scooped a sleeping Sarah into his arms. Elizabeth Garrett and her mother halted his exit from the pew. Elizabeth leaned close, presumably to give Samuel ample opportunity to admire the dress framed by her unfastened cloak.

"Oh, isn't she the sweetest?" Elizabeth gushed. "It is so good of you to help the Marden's in their time of need."

Samuel ignored the blatant flirtation and kept his eyes above her head, searching for his parents. He shifted Sarah in his arms, hoping to avoid further conversation.

"Is Lucy...She hasn't passed, has she?" Elizabeth made a show of looking around and rested her hand on her bodice.

Samuel kept his eyes above the height of her hair, discovering that the best part about a short woman was not having to look at her at all.

"My wife," he emphasized the word, "is recovering nicely. We felt the strain of riding into the church may be too much for her still."

Behind Elizabeth, Mrs. Garrett raised her brows. "My son told me of your marriage." She twisted the word into something ugly while continuing to smile. "He said the ceremony was rather unusual." Samuel knew her Nathan had been up on the hill filling in the grave along with the other spies. He would have not been able to see or hear anything from that vantage point.

Samuel did not volunteer any more information. He nodded and attempted to pass them to meet his waiting parents. "If you will please excuse me, ladies, my mother is waiting."

Mrs. Garrett let out a huff and stepped back. Not so easily deterred, Elizabeth laid a hand on his arm and batted her eyes at him.

"If you ever need anything, Samuel, you know you need just ask."

"Miss Garrett, as your mother has acknowledged, I am a newly married man. I ask you to please address me as Mr. Wilson and kindly remove your hand." The last part of his statement was delivered in a low growl.

Elizabeth dropped her hand, stepped back, and pulled her cloak closed. In a voice disguised as a whisper but meant to carry, she addressed her mother. "Well, I never thought I would see the day *Mr.* Samuel Wilson would be rude to a lady."

He bit his tongue so hard he was afraid he would draw blood, lest he respond there was not a lady present beyond the one sleeping in his arms. As he passed his parents' pew, his father stepped out beside him, his mother close behind. He did his best to ignore the Garretts and the gossiping friends who followed them out of the church. Still, snatches of the conversation reached his ears. Samuel was thankful Sarah slept and could not hear the cutting remarks made about her sister. He kept his jaw locked tight enough a headache started to form. He wondered if the good reverend had heard the slanderous comments and if they would soon listen to a sermon on gossiping.

"Will you come for dinner?" Emma asked as they left the building.

"Not today. I need to get back to Lucy."

"Do stop at the house on the way. I made an extra pie to send home with you."

"Sure, Ma." Samuel hurried to his buggy. He wanted to get a blanket on Sarah and avoid any further conversations.

By the time Samuel pulled into his parents' yard, Sarah was awake and talking and talking and talking. The temperature dropped, and snowflakes started to fall. There would be no time to ask his mother any questions. Telling Sarah to stay in the buggy, he hurried into the house after his mother.

"Here is the pie and a couple of biscuits to get you home."

"Ma, I know we don't have time to talk…" Samuel cast a nervous glance out the window. "But I need to ask you about what you wrote in the Marden Bible."

Emma's face registered shock. "How do you know I wrote it?"

"I know your hand, Ma, and you just confirmed it."

"You need to leave before the snow starts falling harder. If the weather is good on Tuesday, bring Sarah over for the day, and we will make a cake for Lucy."

"And we will talk?"

Emma shooed him out of the door. "Hurry home, and I'll see you on Tuesday."

Samuel was in the buggy before he realized his mother had not answered him. He hoped for good weather on Tuesday so he would have time to corner his mother again.

Emma spent the rest of the day worrying about what Samuel knew, or thought he knew. Had he heard the gossips mention Lucy's birth as anything but normal? Or had he just read the entry in the Bible?

"Woman, you are going to tear the hair clean out of your head if you keep doing that." Thomas eased the brush out of his wife's hand. Emma had made such a tangle of it he'd needed an extra fifteen strokes to get it smooth and tangle free. He continued to brush her hair.

"So out with it. You have been tied up in knots since we returned from church. It wasn't those old gossips, was it?"

Emma sectioned her hair and started to braid it. "No, it's Samuel."

"Again? I thought the marriage had settled everything."

Emma turned to face her husband. "He read the Bible." Seeing the confusion on her husband's face, she amended, "Father Stickney's Bible, where I wrote of Lucy's birth."

Thomas sat down on the bed.

"He wants an explanation."

Thomas nodded.

"I don't think Anna ever told Lucy."

"That is quite a problem."

"I was going to tell Lucy this past week, but she was so weak I didn't dare. But I said enough that if she knew anything, I would have known." Emma made a mess of her braid and moved to start over. Thomas stilled her hands and braided her hair.

"Lucy needs to know before Samuel finds out. Perhaps I can request his help later this week in the shop. Then you can ride over and have a long chat with her," Thomas suggested. "I might even be able to lay some of the groundwork. Our boy isn't old enough to remember how things were during the war."

"Would you do that? Would Thursday work? Lucy's birthday is on Tuesday, and I'd rather not deliver the news then."

Thomas dropped a kiss on his wife's cheek. "Thursday it is." He turned down the lantern and tugged her into bed. Emma burrowed into his side and tried to shut out the images of the night two Marys died.

Twenty-three

MONDAY MORNING DAWNED BRIGHT AND clear. A dusting of the snow that had fallen last night had washed the world in white. Lucy studied her face in her mother's mirror as she tied the end of her braid. She'd slept much of yesterday away, an excellent way to avoid being alone with Samuel, which also resulted in the hollows under her eyes fading. There was still the issue of their marriage. She was afraid he might convince her they were married if he kissed her again. She couldn't remember Mr. Simms ever kissing Mama, but, then, she was so little she might have missed witnessing any intimacies they shared. They must have at some point.

Lucy stepped into the main room. A glance at the clock told her Samuel should be in the barn. Sarah had yet to arise. Finally, she had a chance to prove she was recovered and he could leave. She set about making a simple breakfast. She sliced some of the old bread to fry for breakfast. With the leftover boiled eggs, it would serve as a simple but hearty meal.

She considered baking bread for the dinner meal but settled on doughboys. The fried dough was one of Sarah's favorite treats and didn't require her to heat up the baking oven. Nor did they require as much kneading. They would be an excellent dinner addition.

Samuel had left beans soaking overnight in one of the pots. Some days Lucy detested beans, but food was food, and beans were what they had. Beans and doughboys for dinner it would be. Not fancy but filling. Maybe tomorrow she would feel equal to the task of making bread. She would set out the leavening tonight. Planning for tomorrow invigorated her. How long since she had planned for the next day? From the time Benjamin had taken ill, she had been just trying to get through each day before worrying about the next.

What day was tomorrow? Tomorrow was her nineteenth birthday! How had she forgotten her own birthday? Tears filled her eyes. It was ridiculous to cry because Mama would not be here to bake a cake or Papa Marden would not surprise her with a new set of slippers or a dress length of cloth. She put down her knife and leaned on the table as her sobs came in waves. The round loaf of bread blurred before her vision. She turned away from the table, blindly searching for the chair. Suddenly, strong arms wrapped around her, and she found herself nestled against Samuel's chest. Where had he come from?

Samuel looked over Lucy's head for a clue to her distress. Had she cut herself? He hadn't seen any blood. More importantly, he didn't smell any. Fainting with Lucy in his arms would be disastrous. Her arms crept around his waist, and Samuel stepped back into the rocking chair, bringing Lucy with him. He lifted her into his lap, and she curled up, clinging to his now-damp shirtfront. Having no better idea, he held her close and rocked her back and forth.

Finally, Lucy stilled. Her head came up, eyes red and face wet with tears. She moved to get out of Samuel's lap. He tightened his grip, holding her in place.

He slowly shook his head. "No running off until you tell me what happened."

Lucy used the hem of her apron to dry her face.

"It…uh…was nothing…really." She fanned her hand as if waving the incident away and tried to get up again.

"Lucy…" Samuel raised his brows. He didn't believe her for a moment.

Lucy looked up with red-rimmed eyes. "I miss Mama."

"Of course you do, sweetheart." Samuel pulled her head back into his shoulder and rocked her again. Lucy sank into him. Samuel would have rocked Lucy much longer, but Sarah came rushing down the stairs.

"Lucy, is you sick? Samuel, don't you know Lucy is a big girl? Big girls don't need to be rocked."

Lucy worked her way off Samuel's lap with a bit of his cooperation and by way of a little shove to her backside.

"You've been crying." Sarah gave Samuel an accusing glare. "Did he hurt you?"

Lucy bent to eye level in front of her sister and put her hand on her shoulder. "No one hurt me. I was missing Mama and Papa and Benjamin. Samuel was letting me cry."

"Samuel let me cry, too. He is a very good crier."

Lucy smiled. "I think someone needs to get dressed. I was going to fry some of the bread for breakfast." Lucy hurried to finish her preparations as Sarah ran back up the stairs.

"Lucy?" Samuel waited for her to look at him before continuing. "We need to talk."

He wasn't sure if Lucy nodded or just bowed her head over the cutting board.

"Would this afternoon while Sarah is napping do?" Samuel waited for a response. The fire popped, the clock ticked, he could even hear the knife as it sliced through the bread. Lucy did not look up while he waited.

When she finished slicing the last piece of bread, she said, "We can't put it off any longer, can we." It wasn't a question.

Samuel stepped up behind her. "No, we shouldn't. It's been a week since you first woke up. You avoided me all yesterday. We can't continue like this."

Lucy bit her lip and nodded.

Samuel turned her into his arms.

Lucy stopped him. "Samuel, no more kisses. I feel too mixed up when you kiss me."

Samuel mentally shouted for joy. Lucy was just as affected by his kisses as he was hers. But he agreed. "I won't initiate any kisses." *But I am not going to stop you.*

Lucy let out a sigh of relief. They could take care of everything this afternoon and he could be moved home by tomorrow. She didn't want him leaving on her birthday, but freedom was a gift she could give him.

The morning flew by. Every time Lucy glanced at the clock, it seemed to have moved by an hour. Perhaps the clock hands were broken, but the doughboys rose just as fast as the clock hands revolved. She practiced her speech over and over again. Samuel was not going to distract her from her plan. She would need to make sure she stayed far enough away that he couldn't touch her.

It had been stupid to tell him he couldn't kiss her. He would know how much his kisses affected her. Did all kisses do that? No wonder they wrote about them in the Bible. The verse should have warned how dangerous kissing could be. More dangerous than a viper's den.

Samuel sucked on his thumb. It was the third time his hammer had slipped this morning. Since Sarah was nearby, he stifled the few choice words running through his head. The problem was, there was too much going through his head. He wasn't sure he could convince Lucy to remain his bride. The troubling bit about her name might pose a legal problem, but the fact that Ma knew about it alleviated his fears. His biggest problem was that he couldn't remember what he'd told Lucy when she was sleeping and when she was awake, or if he'd ever told her at all because he'd rehearsed all he'd wanted to say in his mind so many times it all blended together.

Lucy's stipulation of no kissing made him wonder if he could have gotten by without talking at all. Lucy had been willing enough Saturday night but still far too weak for more than what they'd shared. If he did a thorough job of seducing her, there would be no question as to the status of their marriage. He smiled at the thought, even though he wouldn't pursue it, yet.

"Samuel? Why are you smiling when you hit your thumb? Doesn't it hurt? Papa's thumb always hurt when he hit it. He would shake it and say funny things."

Samuel studied his reddened thumb. Thinking of Lucy even dulled pain.

After three doughboys, baked beans, and ham, and talking for fifteen minutes straight. Sarah was ushered up the stairs for her nap.

Lucy toyed with her half eaten doughboy, using it to push the last of her beans around on her plate.

Samuel pushed his empty plate aside. "Would you like to walk up the hill to see the graves? It's a bit warmer today."

Lucy had not expected to start this conversation with the topic of death. She longed to see the graves. Just seeing that the blanket cocoons were no longer on the roof would be helpful. And she had not taken a single step outside since recovering. Lucy stood and started to clear the dishes but Samuel touched the back of her hand.

"Leave them. We can clean them up when we return." Samuel pulled on his coat and held out Lucy's cloak for her.

"Is this your muff?" he asked, holding up a soft fox-fur muff.

Lucy shook her head. "Mama's."

"Would you like to wear it?"

Lucy reached for the muff. If both of her hands were inside of it, she could not reach out and touch Samuel. The muff may be more useful than she realized.

Samuel held open the door.

Much of last night's snow had already melted, and icicles now hung from the eaves.

Samuel cupped Lucy's elbow as they stepped down from the porch.

A tremor moved up her arm. She should tell him no touching at all. But without his assistance, it could be difficult to ascend the hill behind the house. "What was it like the day you buried them?" *The day you married me?*

"Much like today. The snow was melting, and the sun shone brightly in an ice-blue sky. For the funeral service, Ma had me bring Sarah out, saying it would be better for Sarah to witness the funeral than always wonder, especially with your health so precarious."

Lucy didn't respond as she stepped up the icy slope. One of the drawbacks of the muff was that she couldn't use her hands to balance herself when she slipped. Samuel's hand moved to her back. He walked close enough that Lucy could feel his heat. He would not let her fall. He never had, not even when climbing trees or crossing streams as children. The one fact she had always been sure of was that Samuel would never let her fall.

Why did she doubt him now? He'd proven daily that he was nothing like Mr. Simms.

The path up the hill was slick with snow and mud. Perhaps this wasn't a good idea after all. She could stumble and twist an ankle. That would complicate things. He would have another excuse to stay.

Lucy's boot caught on a snow-covered rock. Before she could even register she was falling, she found herself pulled tightly against Samuel, his arm encircling her waist. Lucy pushed down on his arm with her muff. He relaxed his arm, and she continued her climb.

Half covered with snow, the mounded dirt that marked the grave lay cold and uninviting.

"They are all in one grave?" Lucy did not lift her eyes from the snowy mound.

"Yes, even though the ground was not frozen through, the digging was difficult. They decided to dig one grave large enough for the four of them. The reverend was careful not to mention the baby during the service. Ma warned him that Sarah didn't know."

Lucy nodded, unable to speak for the lump in her throat. She blinked back tears. It would not do to repeat this morning's performance. She concentrated on the breeze that rustled the branches and tried to imagine Reverend Woods standing there in his black coat, his Bible open in his hands. If Samuel had not been by her side, she would have been tempted to say something out loud to her parents. But there was nothing left to say that she hadn't said when she'd put their bodies on the roof. Their remains were safe from the animals and elements now. She hoped that they were happy together in heaven.

A bird called from the branches high above them. Papa Marden could always identify winter birds from their call. Lucy needed to see them. As she tilted her face to the sky and searched the branches above, her hood fell back, exposing her face to the sun.

Samuel joined her in the search and spotted the mourning dove first. He pointed over her shoulder so she could locate it too.

Papa Marden has sent a mourning dove. A silly thought, she knew, but watching the plump, light-brownish-gray bird, it seemed to be a sign from above for her, just as the dove with the branch had been a sign for Noah. Papa Marden and Mama were still watching out for her. For a moment, she could almost feel the warmth of their embrace. After another mournful coo, the dove flew away. Lucy shielded her eyes and followed its flight toward the sun and out of her sight.

When she dropped her face and hand, she found she was looking into Samuel's eyes. Her heart skipped a beat.

"Ready to go back?" He held out a hand. Lucy knew the trip down the trail would be harder than the journey up. She extracted a hand from the muff and placed it in his ungloved one. He tucked it close, forcing her to step nearer to him.

No words passed between them as they picked their way down the hill. At the base, Lucy slipped her hand out of his grasp and back into her muff. Samuel gestured for her to lead the way. She veered for the back of the house, stopped, and looked at Samuel.

"May I take a few moments?" She glanced at the privy.

Samuel nodded and continued to the house as Lucy stepped around the garden.

She needed to collect her thoughts before speaking with Samuel. Not an ideal location for thinking, but it guaranteed privacy. She closed the door and took a dozen deep, calming breaths, glad it was not summer. In the cold, the privy smelled much more pleasant.

Samuel had been considerate to show her the graves rather than starting in on a conversation about their marriage. She hadn't realized how much she'd needed to see them buried. She wiped her face with the back of her hand. There had been enough tears today.

Not daring to stay longer lest Samuel come to check on her, she returned to the house through the lean-to. She found Samuel with his back to her, washing the dishes at the dry sink. She watched him for a moment. He sure seemed determined to stay. Removing her cloak, she sat down in the rocker knowing the closest he could get to her would be to pull up Papa Marden's chair. She considered the bench at the table, but the risk that he would sit next to her rather than put the table between them was high.

The rocking chair creaked slightly as Lucy sat down.

He dried his hands and carried the high-backed chair as close as he could to the rocker. The rocking of the chair sped up. "Do you have any other questions for me?"

"What?"

"About the funeral?"

"Oh no." Now that she sat next to him, he had no idea where to begin. "There is one question I thought you would have asked me by now. I am surprised you haven't."

Lucy quirked her brow.

"You haven't asked me why I came back from Boston, and why I am not a doctor."

"Why did you come back?" Her tone was flat.

Samuel looked at her solemnly. "I faint at the sight of blood."

Lucy sat up straight, causing the rocker to stop midcreak. "What? Since when?"

Samuel gave her a half smile. "I explained the whole thing to you the night I proposed. I guess you don't remember. I attended lectures as often as I could, and after a year and a half, I got an apprenticeship to follow Doctor Warren. At first, blood just made me feel uncomfortable, but my aversion to it grew. Eventually I became ill. There was a child—he didn't live. It got worse. In September the doctor asked me to help with a surgery—I don't even remember seeing the patient. The next week he asked me to help suture an arm. I fainted again. We had a long talk, and I came home."

"Oh, Samuel, all your hard work and all the money you earned to study at Harvard. Didn't you know before you left?"

Samuel rubbed the back of his neck and shrugged. "It didn't bother me when you had scrapes. Animals don't seem to bother me either. Just people."

Lucy covered her mouth to stifle a giggle.

"What is so funny?"

"I'm sorry, but it is funny. A doctor who faints at the sight of blood. Who would've thought?" Lucy continued to giggle. Samuel smiled. It was a ridiculous notion. He hadn't seen much humor in it earlier this fall, but when Lucy put it that way, it did seem funny. He enjoyed the sound of her laughter as it dispelled the tension in the room.

Lucy reached her hand out and touched his. "Samuel, how horrid of me to laugh. I truly am sorry. I know how much you enjoy helping people. You wanted this so badly." Lucy sat back in the rocker, all evidence of humor gone from her eyes.

"It was difficult at first. When I came home, I was ashamed to tell anyone. With you gone, I think that is why I talked with Elizabeth Garrett. She is so vain she never once asked me why I came home. I knew you would, and I didn't want to disappoint you."

Lucy's jaw dropped. "Disappoint me?" she echoed.

"Probably the dumbest excuse in history for ending the engagement. But it is the only one I had. I should have ridden to Gloucester as soon as I realized you were there. The longer I waited, the harder it got. I didn't want you to see what a failure I was."

"For not being a doctor? Do you think I would be so shallow?" Lucy asked, her eyes wide, her voice bordering on shrill.

He should have never underestimated her. "No." Samuel rubbed his neck again. "I felt like such a failure. I didn't want you to see me as one too."

"From where I sit, you must be a pretty good doctor." Lucy held her arms wide. "After all, I am not in the hill with Mama."

Samuel smiled. "I am not bad as long as no one is bleeding. Best you ask Ma to deliver our children."

"Our children?" Lucy's eyes widened.

Samuel kicked himself. That was not what he'd meant to say, but he couldn't snatch the words back.

"But we are not married. We are not going to have any children. You are going to leave and go back to Elizabeth. I am not going to ruin your life. You deserve to be happy. You may not be a doctor, but there are other options. You make beautiful furniture. There is always farming. I'm to sell this place when I go to Boston. It is a good farm." Lucy clapped both hands over her mouth.

Samuel raised his brows. "Well, that is a lot to discuss, isn't it?"

Lucy did not move her hands from her mouth and nodded.

"I think you missed the part where I called Elizabeth vain and told you I should have never even talked to her. I didn't initiate that kiss in the orchard. But I did end it very fast. If the children had stayed longer, they would have heard an earful."

Lucy dropped her hands. "But she is so beautiful and fits like a little bird under your arm. Everyone says you would be good together."

Samuel leaned forward his elbows on his knees, lowering himself to Lucy's eye level. "Elizabeth Garrett is not the woman for me. She is not kind. She is vain and has a terrible habit of spreading malicious gossip. She does not have soft-brown, honest eyes, nor maple-syrup hair and a kind heart like the woman I love. I am afraid I ended up hurting that woman very much." He wanted to reach out and pull Lucy into a kiss. Putting everything he was feeling into words was so difficult. He looked up to see Lucy staring at him.

"Who is it? Martha has brown eyes." Lucy dropped her gaze to her hands.

"Lucy. It's you. It always has been."

"No." Lucy's eyes widened. "You can't. You can't!" Faster than he thought possible, she leaped out of the chair and scooted around him and into the bedroom.

Lucy slid down the closed door, wrapped her arms around her knees, and cried.

"Lucy?" Samuel's voice came through the closed door.

Lucy raised her face to the ceiling and wiped away her tears but didn't respond. *Please God, let him leave. Help him to see he can't love me. I'm not good enough.* She stopped her prayer, realizing she was about to list the reasons Mr. Simms named, and most of them were too profane for God's ears.

Samuel tapped on the door. "Lucy, please?"

Lucy closed her eyes and muttered her prayer again and again. *He can't love me. He can't love me. He can't love me.*

She could feel Samuel standing at the door as the clock ticked away the minutes. After ten, she heard him walk away.

Lucy let out a sigh as the front door closed. Maybe God had answered her prayers. Exhausted, she crawled over to the bed and climbed in. Sleep came quickly, but her dreams were troublesome.

Twenty-four

"So, Old Brown, where did I go wrong? Was I too direct when I said I loved her? Does she not love me back? I was sure I saw it in her eyes." *I felt it in her kiss.* Not that he would say that out loud, even to his horse. Samuel hung his head. Old Brown nudged him, seeking a carrot or leftover apple. Samuel rubbed Old Brown's nose and reached for one of the apples that sat in a nearby barrel. "I know what you are after. You just pretend to be wise. There you go, you big beggar."

Old Brown took the apple and stepped back.

Samuel walked over to Lucy's birthday gift. It could use one more coat of whitewash.

An hour later, he was stretching to reach the top of the last wall when Sarah burst into the barn. He flipped the brush in his hand, raining white droplets all over his face.

"Samuel! Come quick!"

He dropped the brush in the can and wiped his hands and face with a rag.

Sarah grabbed his hand and tried to drag him out of the barn.

"What is it, Sarah?"

"Lucy is having a bad dream. I tried singing, and she won't wake up."

The shove Sarah gave him was unnecessary. Samuel sprinted across the barnyard with Sarah running behind him.

He threw open the door and entered the large bedroom. Lucy was pounding on the headboard and screaming, "No! No! I am the bad one."

Samuel scooped her into his arms. Lucy struggled and landed a solid punch to his chest, causing him to spin around and fall onto the bed, which allowed him to free one arm. He grabbed both of Lucy's fists in one hand and brought them to his chest, then began to rock her.

"Lucy, sweetheart," he cooed.

"No tack room. No tack room," Lucy screamed, working one hand free. A wide swing caught him on the jaw.

Gasping for air, Sarah leaned on the doorjamb. "Sing!"

Samuel recaptured Lucy's fist more securely this time and started singing, "Lavender's blue, diddle diddle, Lavender's green, When I am king, diddle diddle, You shall be queen . . ." He skipped over the verses Sarah had omitted before. On the third time through the song, Lucy relaxed and stilled. Waiting a moment to see if she would wake up, Samuel continued to hold her close. When she didn't wake, he placed her back in bed. After the abrupt end to their conversation this afternoon, Lucy would not react well to waking in his arms.

He left the room but did not close the door all the way.

"That is the worstest she has ever been," said Sarah authoritatively.

"Do you think she will have another one?" Samuel felt foolhardy soliciting the five-year-old's advice.

Sarah thought for a moment, her finger on her chin. "No, she never has before."

"Sit and play here at the table. I need to finish in the barn. I'll be in as soon as I can. If you need me, come to the porch and yell. I will hear you. And if Lucy wakes up, don't tell her I sang to her."

Sarah nodded solemnly. "May I get my dolly?"

"Of course. I must go out to the barn now. I left the lantern burning, and one should never leave a lantern in the barn."

Sarah nodded and scooted up the stairs.

Lucy woke with her throat raw and her hand bruised. The nightmare. She groaned. It had been years since she'd had a nightmare bad enough to leave her throat burning from her screams. She wondered if she had awakened Sarah or if Samuel knew. Of course not. She'd heard him leave. She hugged herself to dispell the remnants of the dream. Mr. Simms shouting at her that no one could ever love Anna's ill-begotten daughter. *Lucy, you are a brat not worthy of any man's love.* Names far worse than "ill-begotten" mingled with her memories. He'd called her mama an evil shrew and Lucy the devil's child before dragging her to the barn more than once.

Lucy took several deep breaths. She remembered Papa Marden rocking her and singing until the dreams left and she felt safe. Where was Papa now? She needed to hear how he loved her and how Mr. Simms had lied. Lucy stood and walked to the open door, intent on finding him. Then it hit her. Papa was dead. Who had sung to her this time? Maybe Papa had come as an angel.

Sarah looked up from the table where she sat playing with her doll.

"Sarah, did I wake you with my nightmare?"

"No..." Sarah drew out her answer. "I was already awake."

"Did you sing to me?"

"Yes, but it didn't work."

"It didn't work?"

Sarah tilted her head, then shook it slightly. "No, it didn't work when I sang."

"I dreamed Papa Marden sang to me." Lucy hugged herself, wishing for his secure arms around her. "I could feel him. It must have been an angel."

"It wasn't an angel, it was—" Sarah clapped both hands over her mouth, eyes wide.

Lucy relaxed her arms and looked quizzically at Sarah. If not Papa in a dream and if Sarah knew, it must be Samuel! Lucy's hands flew to her hips. "Sarah Beth Marden, was Samuel in the bedroom? Did he sing to me?"

Sarah kept her hands over her mouth and mumbled something, her eyes downcast.

"I asked you a question. I expect you to answer." Lucy took a step nearer the table.

Sarah pulled her hands a fraction of an inch from her mouth, blurting "I can't say" before clapping them over her mouth.

Lucy closed her eyes and counted to ten. Samuel. It had to be Samuel. She'd confused the lingering odor of hay and wood with Papa Marden's scent. Samuel hadn't left. Her heart did a funny sort of dance. Samuel had stayed. Her heart was happy, but her mind was upset. Lucy slumped into the rocking chair, confusion clouding her thoughts.

"He stayed. I can't believe he stayed," she murmured aloud.

"Who stayed? Samuel? Of course he stayed. He is in the barn," Sarah said.

Lucy had not meant the question for Sarah. Glancing at the clock, she jumped out of the chair. "I best get supper on." She would pretend nothing happened unless he brought it up.

Without saying another word, Lucy checked the beans and whipped up a batch of johnnycake. She wasn't sure how long it would be before Samuel came in, and she wanted the food hot. She needed to apologize for running out and make him understand. He needed to go. He had to be mistaken. He couldn't love her.

She could hear Papa Marden telling her someday a man would love her just as much as he loved Mama. "I'm afraid I'll cry the day you leave me, but they will be happy tears because, sweet one, you deserve love." He was forever telling her she was loved by him, by Mama, and by God, almost as if he knew she didn't quite believe it.

His reassurances were hard to believe, especially when the nightmares came. Mr. Simms would yell at her that no one could ever love something as disgusting as she was before leaving her alone to repent of her sinful nature in the tack room.

Which voice was right? Mr. Simms was so bitter about being trapped in his marriage to Mama. He yelled almost daily at Mama.

Lucy had no idea how Mama had trapped Mr. Simms. She never replied to his outbursts. She never explained them.

Lucy remembered what she had seen in the Bible. Checking the johnnycake, she decided she had enough time to reread the entry. She laid the thick book on the table and flipped to the back pages. She was running her finger over her name when the door opened and Samuel stepped in.

"Reading before supper? Or am I late?" Lucy shut the Bible before he could see where she'd been reading, stood and placed the Bible back on its shelf.

Before Lucy could ask her question, Sarah launched herself off the bench and wrapped her arms around his knee. "No, you are not late."

Samuel raised an eyebrow in question. Sarah glanced at Lucy, her eyes wide. She tugged on his arm and cupped her hand to whisper in his ear. "I didn't tell. Honest, I didn't. But she figured it out, and now she is all funny. I'm sorry."

Samuel gave her a quick squeeze. "Can you set the table, little one? I smell johnnycake. Do you think your sister will let us eat a bit of honey with it?" He gave Lucy a lopsided grin.

Caught off guard, she whirled to grab the honey crock from the cupboard and set it on the table. She thought he would say something about the dream or her running from the room. But he didn't even seem upset, even with Sarah for telling. She couldn't help but stare at him just to be sure there was no trace of anger on his handsome face.

Samuel winked in response.

Lucy's face flamed, she turned to the fire to hide her blushing while removing the beans and johnnycake. Could it be true? Did he love her like Papa Marden said would happen, even after seeing the scars? Papa had shared his love with all of them daily. And not a day had gone by that she didn't catch Papa kissing Mama at least once. He told her that the right husband would want to do the same with her.

Samuel and Sarah kept the dinner conversation going.

"Your hair is wet."

"Yup, I needed to wash it."

"Why?"

"It got all messy."

Sarah opened her mouth to say something else, but Samuel changed the subject. "Oh, I forgot. Ma invited Sarah to come for the morning. She said something about needing help with baking a cake."

"Bake a cake? With currents and nuts?" Sarah asked, her mouth full of beans.

Samuel nodded, and Sarah clapped her hands.

They remembered my birthday. With Samuel and Sarah gone for the morning, maybe she would have enough time to solve the mysterious entry in the Bible.

"Can I Lucy? Can I?"

Lucy realized both Samuel and Sarah were waiting for her to respond.

"I don't see why not. You will listen to Mrs. Wilson and stay back from the fire?"

Sarah nodded exuberantly, her curls bobbing about her head.

"Well, it is time for girls who are going on visits to get ready for bed," Samuel announced with a grin.

Sarah hopped up and ran up the stairs.

Before Lucy could get up from the table, Samuel reached across and clasped her hand. "I didn't mean to upset you earlier." He rubbed his thumb back and forth on the back of her hand.

Tingles ran up Lucy's arm. She stared at their joined hands for a long moment before raising her eyes to meet his. What she saw stopped her breath—there was no anger; not even the disappointment she expected, just blue eyes full of concern. Funny, blue had always reminded her of cold. But this blue was warm, like the blue flames that occasionally danced in the fireplace.

Samuel opened his mouth to speak just as Sarah came skipping down the stairs. "Later." He promised, giving her hand a squeeze.

Lucy scooped the dishes into the dry sink while Samuel opened the Bible. Lucy had no idea what Samuel read. She barely registered Sarah begging him to tuck her in. Nor did she remember starting to clean the dishes. It was not surprising when she didn't hear Samuel come down the stairs and stand behind her.

"Lu—"

Lucy dropped the plate and dishrag into the pail, splashing them both as she stepped back into Samuel's chest. He wrapped his arms around her waist as they balanced themselves. Lucy moved to step out of the embrace, but his gentle hold was firm.

"Lucy, we need to finish our conversation. We can't do it if you run away." His words tickled her ear. She could feel each breath he expelled. She wondered if she could even remember how to breathe. Samuel loosened his hold and stepped back, then turned her by the shoulder to face him. "I can't force you to stay and talk, but, please, will you?"

Closing her eyes, she took a deep breath. When she opened them, she saw the same blue flames she'd seen earlier.

How could she deny him? How could she not talk with him? Maybe Papa Marden was right and the truth would set her free or, rather, it would set Samuel free, and he would leave.

Lucy's shoulders slumped, and she nodded.

Samuel picked up a cloth and started to dry the dishes. "I'll help you finish first."

They finished in silence.

Samuel pulled a chair over near the rocker and sat down. Lucy dried her hands as she circled the table and settled on the bench on the far side.

Samuel cocked his brow.

Lucy pretended to ignore the unasked question. She was not going to tell him she was not taking any chances that he might touch her. Butterflies were still dancing where Samuel's arms had been wrapped around her. She traced her finger around the knots on the table top. She'd never noticed how the knot she was currently tracing resembled a heart before. She stopped tracing it and placed her hands in her lap.

"Samuel," she began in a steady voice. "I think it is best if you stop insisting we are married. You have options in what you could do. You don't need to be tied down to this farm and me." Her hands came from under the table, and she emphasized her words. "I can sell it and move to Boston. No one need know my reputation is in question. We both know nothing ever happened that would have left me ruined." She drew in a breath, continuing before Samuel could respond. "You have been better than any friend or doctor to do what you have done. I thank you. I owe you my life and probably more than I can ever make up to you. What I can do is release you from this sham marriage you agreed to. I want you to be happy." At this, she met his eyes, hoping he would see she was in earnest.

Samuel studied her for a moment. "What will you do in Boston?"

Lucy shrugged one shoulder. "Get work cleaning and cooking. I sew well enough. I might find a job at one of those big dress shops."

"What of Sarah?"

"She can stay with me."

He raised his brow.

"Or maybe she could live with your parents?"

"I am sure Ma would take her in a trice. But you are all that is left of her family. Do you want to abandon her?"

Lucy shook her head. She could feel tears forming. She could not let Samuel see them. Sarah was the biggest hindrance to her plan. If Lucy got a job in one of Boston's grand homes or even in one of the pubs, it would come with a room, and the employer would not likely want a small child underfoot. The dress shops might provide board, but she would be forced to leave Sarah alone all day. Even leaving Sarah with the Wilson's would still be abandoning her and would leave a hole in both of their hearts. "No, I don't want to leave Sarah, but I must think of what is best."

"Would living in Boston be best for you?"

"My reputation—"

"Not your reputation. There is naught wrong with it now and won't be as long as you don't send me packing. What is best for you?"

Lucy stared at the knot in the table and traced the heart again. What would be best for her was the worst for him. Unable to answer honestly, she shrugged.

"If I understand, you believe it is best for me not to be married to you. What if I disagree? What if I think marriage to you is the best choice I ever made? What if I don't want to choose something else? What if I want to stay?" Samuel's voice rose the slightest bit.

Lucy fidgeted. "You can't want that. You don't know how bad it will be."

He leaned forward, his voice returning to normal volume. "What do you mean?"

Lucy placed both hands on the table. Unbidden, her fingers traced the heart again and then drew a large *X* through it. "Every day Mr. Simms would yell at Mama, claiming it was all her fault he was trapped in the marriage and he couldn't be successful. I think he hated her. He was always so angry. He claimed to want children yet hated seeing me. He would call us both terrible names. The older I got, the angrier he got. I don't want you to have regrets. You had little choice but to marry me—that, or let me or your ma die. I don't think I could survive if you became angry like Mr. Simms. It was a terrible choice they forced on you. I won't be the cause of your ruined life. Already you raise your voice at me. How long will it be until you hate me too?" She kept drawing an *X* through the heart.

Samuel closed his eyes as if in prayer. When he opened them, his voice was calm. "When you have dreams like you had today, are they of Mr. Simms's yelling?"

"Yes." *And other things.*

"Did James ever yell at you or your mother?"

Lucy's chin shot up. "Of course not. He loved Mama and wanted to marry her. Mama and Papa disagreed sometimes, but he never yelled."

"But wasn't James Marden trapped too? If not for James, your mother would have to sell the farm. She couldn't take care of it all herself. She needed a husband fast."

"How do you know that?"

Samuel looked embarrassed. "I heard her tell Ma soon after the funeral."

Lucy thought for a moment. "But it was still different. Papa Marden wanted to be married to Mama."

"What if I want to be married to you? I did propose all those months ago in my letter. Yes, I had my plans change because I could no longer set up housekeeping with you, but I never stopped wanting to be your husband."

Lucy had no answer.

Samuel continued. "I knew when you were thirteen that I wanted you to grow up so I could marry you. Lucy, you were always my plan."

"Impossible."

"Possible. You are the only part of the plan that has worked out—sort of." Samuel rubbed the back of his head. Lucy sat speechless. She'd run out of arguments, save one. Samuel claimed he wanted to be married to her. It wasn't the best decision he had made. It was the worst. Not only would he not be a doctor, he would be on a farm. He didn't enjoy farming. It would only take a few harvests to drive him away.

She would have to pull out the last piece of information she had. Her reputation would be in tatters, and he would leave.

"Who did you marry?" she asked.

"You."

"No, what name did Reverend Woods use?"

"Lucy Simms."

"Then it is a sham marriage because I am not Lucy Simms. There is no Lucy Simms. Just Lucy Stickney."

"I know."

Lucy stared at him in stunned silence. What did he know? More than she did, apparently.

Twenty-five

A HORSE AND RIDER ENTERED the yard minutes after Samuel finished milking the goat. In the early morning light, he was not sure which of the twins dismounted and started to the house.

Samuel whistled to get his brother's attention, and the twin loped across the yard. Samuel still had no idea who came toward him. The blue muffler could easily be exchanged for the red one and was no guarantee of identity.

"Morning, Sam." The twin unwound his muffler but left his hat on, effectively concealing the scar that would identify him.

"Whatcha doing here?" Samuel did not call him by name. Getting the incorrect one would set them off in a series of pranks.

"Ma asked for a volunteer to come get Sarah-girl."

"And you won the wrestle."

A grin brightened Joe's face—he was pretty sure it was Joe. "I'll take the little chatterbox over cleaning stalls any morning."

"Speaking of the little chatterbox, you need to be careful what exactly you mention about married life to her." Samuel took a step forward, his face hard.

Joe threw up his hands. "All we told her was that you might want to share a bed with your wife. No way would we say anything Ma would tan our hides for."

Samuel backed off. There was no point in putting the twins in a spot where they decided they needed to get revenge. "Sarah is probably still in bed. I planned to bring her over in a couple of hours. Why did Ma send you so early?"

"Maybe she wanted to get an early start on the cake. Or"—he grinned mischievously—"she thinks you and your bride need some alone time."

Samuel's fist didn't connect with his brother's shoulder as he expected. The force of the unlanded blow caused him to stumble forward a step, and his right foot landed in a mud puddle, sending splatters up his boots and pant legs. Joe stepped out of range.

Samuel rubbed the back of his neck. He was not doing a good job of keeping his emotions in check. He had gotten little sleep last night after the abrupt end to his conversation with Lucy. When she realized he knew her name was not Simms, the color had drained from her face. She'd looked as if she might faint. He'd offered to help her to her room, afraid she might fall, but she'd refused and stumbled to the bedroom, not looking back. He'd debated about going to her, but the stricken look she wore stopped him. And so he'd lain awake, listening for the nightmares that never came.

"Ma says you and Lucy should come for a late dinner around one o'clock or so." Joe walked backward toward the house. "How soon can Sarah be ready?"

"As soon as you finish the chores." Samuel strode past him. "I'll get her up. Stalls still need mucking." He may not have landed the punch, but there were other ways to get back at the twin that must be Joe. At least he was pretty sure it wasn't John.

Lucy jumped when the door banged open, and her hand flew to her heart.

"Sarah up?" Samuel didn't look at her as he asked the question.

"Not yet," Lucy answered quietly, eyes wide. Samuel didn't smile. Had their discussion last night taken hold so soon? *Did I succeed in getting him to leave me because of my illegitimacy? Please, not because of that.*

"One of the twins is here to take her to Ma's. You'd better wake her." Samuel closed the door as he returned outside. He popped the door open again. "Don't bother with dinner. Ma has invited us over."

So Samuel wouldn't be gone with Sarah this morning. Perhaps he would keep his distance and stay in the barn as he had the past few days. Lucy did not want to be alone with him. Now that the marriage was over, she wanted him gone. His being in the house made things harder. She wanted a good cry, but he could never know her heart was breaking.

All too soon Sarah was settled with Joe on the horse, waving her good-byes. Lucy had nothing to do. Having forgotten to set out the leaven last night, she could not make bread today. With the invitation to dinner, she didn't need to cook either. She wandered about, searching for some chore to occupy her. As she hadn't been to the second level since her recovery and there would be some cleaning to do, she started up the stairs. Sarah's room was neater than usual. Lucy tightened the bed ropes more out of boredom than necessity. She paused at Samuel's room. Did she dare enter?

Pushing the door all the way open, she was surprised to see the bed neatly made. His shirts hung on wall pegs. In the corner, several crates stood in a neat stack. Stepping back, Lucy breathed deeply, relieved she did not need to go in. She knew if she did, she would break down for sure at the essence that lingered there.

She walked downstairs, still searching for something to do. Knitting more socks seemed to be the best option left. There was going through Mama's and Papa Marden's things, but she wasn't ready to sort through the memories. That could wait until the farm sold. She could get her tick and linens back from Emma and move back to her room tonight. Then she would shut the door to her parents' room. Too often as she lay there, her mind wandered to what it would be like to share the room with Samuel. Even after his revelation last night, she'd still dreamed of him.

She'd just reached the bottom step when Samuel walked in, a grin on his face.

"Ready for your birthday surprise?"

Lucy stood still on the step. "What?"

"Your birthday surprise." Two strides brought him to the stairs. He placed his hand on the banister above her hand. Still on the bottom step, Lucy found herself at eye level with him. Lip level with him. She dispelled the thought before it could take hold. His blue eyes twinkled. The half grin he gave her reminded her of the look he'd given her when he had played the pirate just before...

His grouchiness of an hour ago had vanished. What had changed? Wasn't he leaving? Confused, Lucy waved her hands, unable to come up with the right word. "I don't think it is appropriate"—her hands twisted her apron—"considering..." She let the sentence hang in the air, unable to voice the last part, *you are leaving.*

"Considering what? That I am your husband? Can't a man give his wife a birthday gift?"

"Yes. I mean no. We are not. You shouldn't." None of the answers that came out of Lucy's mouth made sense even to her.

One corner of his mouth edged up into the lopsided grin that made her heart skip a beat. "Well, I made it, and I can't exactly change that. So I guess I should give it to you regardless of your answer."

"Oh, well, then." Lucy held out her hand, palm up. Instead of placing a gift in it as she expected him to, Samuel took her hand in his and rubbed his thumb across her palm, sending chills up her arm.

He was not leaving. Lucy's heart sang. No matter what gift he gave her today, he wasn't going to leave, and that was the best gift. She only needed to choose what to do with it.

"It's too big to wrap." He coaxed her off the stairs.

She looked up at him, unable to form a coherent thought. "Oh?"

Samuel held up her cloak. "Put this on, and we shall go see it."

Curious, Lucy complied. When she had her cloak on, she turned to Samuel, who held a scarf in his hand.

"Surely we are not going so far that I need a scarf."

"No, but seeing I can't hide the present, I thought I would hide your eyes."

Lucy stepped back. Curiosity turned to fear.

"Please, no." She struggled to breathe out. "I don't like having my eyes covered."

"Then promise to close your eyes tightly when I ask?"

Lucy nodded as she took a deep breath.

Samuel held out his hand to her. Tentatively, she placed hers in his, and he closed his hand. Its warmth engulfed her as he guided her out the door.

Lucy's heart raced again, but it was different than when it had raced at the thought of the scarf being tied over her eyes.

Samuel tucked Lucy's hand in the crook of his arm to draw her closer. She wondered if he was as affected by their touch as she was. She wanted to be held much closer. Had he nearly kissed her at the bottom of the stairs?

Reaching the barn, he stopped. "Close your eyes."

Lucy crossed her arms and quirked a brow.

"You promised." Samuel pulled open the door.

"But I might fall."

Samuel clasped both of her hands in his. "Never." The husky words had a quality that both warmed and frightened Lucy. She dare not look up lest she see the blue fire in his eyes again. She'd already fallen. He just didn't know. If he did catch her, she hoped he would never let go.

She obediently closed her eyes. The clean scent of hay tickled Lucy's nose. How different this smell was than the sour odor that had permeated the building last time she'd stood in it. Someone had fulfilled the promise to the animals she hadn't been able to keep.

Samuel stopped and lowered their hands. "Keep them closed for a moment. I am going to turn up the lantern."

One of the horses snorted. Lucy turned at the sound. "Bart, is that you?"

"No, it is Old Brown. Be kind, old man, this is my Lucy, and I won't take any of your sass about her."

Lucy tilted her head. *My Lucy?* She wished she could see the expression on Samuel's face. His voice sounded as if he were laying claim to her and warning his horse off. She started to peek only to find Samuel waving his hand before her face. She closed her eyes tighter.

Samuel chuckled. "No peeking. Just one more moment." He guided her a few more steps, then placed his hands on her shoulders, turning her around.

Lucy could feel the warmth of Samuel behind her. Just a half step back would place her in his arms. She stood rigidly to avoid such temptation, but Samuel leaned forward, closing the space between them, his hands still on her shoulders. "You may look now."

Lucy's eyes popped open. It was the tack room, but not the one that haunted her dreams. The whitewashed walls both inside and out glowed in the light of the lantern. From a new window cut into the outside wall, a patch of sunlight fell onto a freshly sanded floor. Lucy took a tentative step forward. The rings for the chain and padlock were gone. The door had been split in two, making an upper and a lower door.

Samuel stepped around Lucy through the doorway and into the little room. He shuttered the window, then opened it again. "Lets in light and air but can be closed against the elements and at night. Don't need that old coon finding his way in here." He pulled the lower door partway shut. "See this latch? It locks on the inside of the room and can be closed by leaning over the door from the outside." He stepped around the door to demonstrate closing, then opening it, and closing it again. "The upper door closes like so, into this latch on the outside." He closed the top door and slid the wooden bolt over.

Lucy stared, wide-eyed, and her knees began to shake. Samuel came up behind her, wrapped his arms around her, then rested his chin on her shoulder. "It is impossible for anyone to get stuck in the room even accidently."

He pointed to the lower door. "From the outside, a child a few inches taller than Sarah can't open or lock the door. Yet from the inside, a child, even smaller than Sarah, can open the door and get out."

Lucy's shaking slowed as Samuel rubbed her arms, keeping her tight against his chest. "How? I don't understand."

"I'll show you, but I'll need your help to lock me in." He dropped his arms to her waist and gave her a squeeze.

"I could never..."

"Trust me. You can't lock me in. Sarah and I tested it. She gets out every time."

"Sarah?" Lucy asked eyes wide. "You locked Sarah in there?"

Samuel loosened his grip around her waist and stepped in front of her. "Yes, Sarah was in there. It is not possible to lock her in. Please help me, and I will show you."

Samuel leaned over and opened the top part of the door. Reaching through, he opened the bottom. He stepped into the tack room and closed the lower door. Lucy jumped a bit at the sound of the bolt closing. Samuel shut the top door. "Lucy, I need you to throw the latch."

"I can't."

Samuel opened the top door. "Sure you can, sweetheart. I'll be safe." He stuck his arm out of the window and waved it. "I have light and air. If something goes amiss, I could climb out. Now bolt the top door, honey, and I will show you how Sarah gets out."

Lucy took a reluctant step forward as Samuel closed the door again. Her hand shook as she reached for the bolt. She couldn't bring herself to touch it.

"Trust me. I can't be locked in. Just do it." Samuel's voice came through the door.

Lucy threw the bolt, locking the door faster than she would toss a snake out of the woodpile. She stepped back, her hand over her mouth, heart pounding. *What have I done?*

Lucy watched in awe as the lower door opened and Samuel crawled out on all fours, then stood and dusted himself off, a grin on his face. Lucy could see the patch of light through the open door.

"See?" He gestured to the door. "Impossible to get locked in."

Lucy's hand dropped from her mouth. She stepped forward and tentatively touched the still-closed upper latch. "What if someone places a barrel in front of the door?"

Samuel unlocked the top portion and opened it. "The lower door opens in. A barrel wouldn't block it."

"Is it really impossible to get locked in?"

Samuel's smile grew. "And a young child can't get in accidently either."

Lucy examined the door. She closed the bottom door, then opened it.

"Why did you do this?

Samuel took Lucy by the shoulders. "Mr. Simms used to punish you by locking you in here, didn't he?"

"How do you know?"

Samuel shrugged. "Good guessing mostly. I wanted to make this room into something different so you wouldn't dream about it."

"Oh." Lucy studied Samuel's face for a moment before rising on her toes and placing a kiss on his cheek. "Thank you."

Before she could escape, Samuel placed his hands on her hips and closed the gap between them. He paused a moment, giving her a chance to back away. Then he gave her the kiss his eyes had promised her on the stairs. The kiss that said, "I am not leaving you." Lucy rose up on her toes to deepen the kiss. Samuel's hands slid to her back and pulled her closer.

When the kiss ended, Lucy rested her head on his chest. *How can I tell him to leave now? I never want him to. I have not the strength. Please, God, I must know. Should I let him stay? Can this marriage become real?*

Samuel stepped back and waited for Lucy to look him in the eye.

"I found something while I was doing this." He kept one hand on her back as he turned them to face the tack room again. "I was going to destroy it, but I believe the honor belongs to you. I thought of burning it, chopping it up, and even taking it to the river and tossing it in."

Lucy tilted her head, confused.

Samuel stepped into the tack room and took something down from the highest shelf. When he turned to Lucy, he held the riding crop in the palms of his hands. Lucy gasped and stepped back.

"Lucy, if you wish, I can take this and destroy it, or you can. Either way, it will never be used again."

Lucy reached out, then snapped her hand back. "I can't touch it."

Samuel nodded in understanding. "Shall we burn it, chop it, or drown it?"

"Someone might find it if we threw it in the river. Can we burn it?"

Samuel nodded.

"But not in the fireplace."

"We can burn it in the fire pit."

Lucy followed Samuel out of the barn.

In no time a small fire burned brightly in the pit. Lucy thought it a shame to waste the firewood on the riding crop, but she did not have time to do the laundry today. It gave Lucy a moment of perverse glee to know that such a waste of firewood would have made Mr. Simms angry.

Samuel held out the crop in his open palm. "Would you like the honor?"

Lucy hesitated a second before she grabbed the crop out of his hand and cast it into the hungry flames. Together they watched as fiery red tongues licked at the wood and leather. Samuel wrapped his arm around Lucy and pulled her into his side.

She did not protest. She fit so perfectly there. He brushed a kiss across her brow and pulled her into a full embrace.

"He used to whip me with it. He told me I was a bad seed and it was his duty to drive the evil out of me."

Samuel tightened his grip, drawing her as close as greatcoat and cloak would allow. "Sweetheart, I've known you your entire life. You don't have a drop of wickedness in you. You never did."

Lucy lifted her face, searching his eyes for any evidence of untruth or flattery. She found none. "Even when I threw rocks in your fishing hole?"

Samuel gave her that crooked grin of his, then reached up and tucked a stray hair behind her ear. "That was far from evil, and I deserved it for trying to ignore you."

She leaned her head against his chest. "He called us terrible names. I didn't understand them until much later. Now that I have seen the Bible, I understand why he did."

Samuel waited a moment before he tilted her face so he could see her eyes. "Lucy, we *don't* understand why he said those things. All we know is that in the family Bible, you were not given his surname. Your mother was the best woman I know, excluding my own ma. I refuse to think ill of you or her because of an entry in a Bible or the names a mean man called either of you. That doesn't change the woman you are. The woman I love. The woman I married."

"But—"

Samuel placed a finger on her lips. "Nothing changes who you are. I love you. I always have. Your name doesn't change that." He replaced the finger with his lips.

Lucy's arms settled about his waist. When the kiss ended, she snuggled into his chest and watched the fire burn. Inside, her heart soared. *He said he loves me. He changed the tack room. He burned the crop. He is holding me, and he knows everything.*

"He was wrong, Mr. Simms was absolutely wrong. Papa Marden said someone would love me one day like he loved Mama." She searched his eyes all blue with fire, "I should have never doubted." Words failed her so she rose on her tiptoes and pressed her lips to Samuel's. He wrapped his arms around her and held her in place. Lucy ended the kiss and returned to watching the fire.

She sighed. Samuel's hand came up and smoothed her hair. The crop was disappearing in the flames. A loud pop accompanied the final destruction of the handle.

"Never again," she whispered.

Samuel's hand dropped to her back where the worst of the scars were. "Never, ever again," he repeated his vow before kissing Lucy's brow.

Lucy lifted her face. Samuel added kisses to her eyelids, the tip of her nose and then her lips. Lucy melted into him. One hand settled on his chest as if she was unsure to push him away or pull him closer. As Samuel deepened the kiss, her hand slid up behind his head and pulled him closer.

So this is what the Song of Solomon is about, this is love. No wonder they wanted to sing about it. I want to sing about it. I still think apple cider is better than wine.

Lucy found her answer.

Samuel broke the kiss. Lucy slid both hands to rest on his chest. Bringing his forehead to meet hers, he sighed.

"Lucy, please let me stay. Please be my wife."

Lucy stood still for a long time. "We are not really married."

"We could say our vows here, as my parents did in the snow bank."

Lucy stepped back. Not far enough to break contact but, far enough. "No, I heard the rumors and the names all my life. I must find out what happened. Then we can repeat the vows in front of the Reverend using my real name. I can have no shadow over our marriage. Or us."

"I think Ma knows. She would not tell me when I asked about her handwriting in the Bible. She said the story was for you to hear."

"Oh, she did say she had something to say of Mr. Simms to me. Perhaps I can get her to tell me today." Lucy brightened. The sooner she knew, the sooner they could get married for real.

"What if she doesn't know? Will you still become my wife?"

Lucy stepped back into his embrace and placed a kiss on his lips. She pulled back far enough to whisper 'yes,' before kissing him again. When she broke the kiss, she buried her head in his shoulder amazed at her own forwardness.

Samuel leaned down. "So we are married and engaged to be married?" Samuel gave her a crooked smile potent enough that Lucy wanted to say they were married and risk being late to his parent's place. But her resolve was not completely shaken.

"Just engaged. We won't—" Lucy fluttered her hand, her color deepened.

"Consummate?"

"Not until we are really married."

"Where shall I live in the mean time?"

Lucy shrugged. "Everyone thinks we are married now. I guess we can stay as we are with you upstairs."

Samuel pulled her back into another kiss. When it ended, he added, "I think it would be best if you lock your door at night."

Lucy blushed crimson and turned to the fire.

All that remained of the crop was three metal pins glowing red against the coals.

Lucy looked around the table. She lost a family and gained another family in just a month. The empty place inside was filling up like a water barrel in the rain.

Not all New Englanders celebrated birthdays. Papa Marden learned of making treats for birthdays from some of the Hessians he fought with during the war, a tradition he brought into his home. Each member had a favorite cake or treat made on their birthday that they were to cut and share with the family. Papa Marden often gave a practical gift such as a dress length of fabric or a book. The Wilson's adopted the tradition years ago.

Emma had outdone herself. Daniel and Mark took turns turning the spit with its savory roast for much of the morning. Pea soup and fresh bread had been prepared in addition to the currant cake and little jumbles. No wonder she'd sent for Sarah so early.

The dinner lasted longer than normal as no one seemed in a rush to return to the work of the day.

The twins spoke of the hunting trip they were to take in three days and could not contain their excitement. The hunt would last a week—the first winter hunt for the twins. Each bragged about what his take would be and what they would bring home for Christmas dinner. Thomas Jr. would be joining them, as well as Carrie's husband, Paul.

Lucy caught Samuel's eye. "Going?" she mouthed. Samuel shook his head. Lucy frowned. She did not like the idea of him missing out because of her. They'd discuss it later.

Dinner wound down, and Emma brought the currant cake to Lucy, who sliced and served each piece, teasing her new brothers by offering them much smaller pieces than they requested.

"Mmmm." Daniel licked his lips. "I'm glad you are my new sister. Now we get cake twice more each year!"

"Twice?" asked one of the twins his mouth full.

Daniel nodded and swallowed a rather large bite. "We get Lucy and Sarah!" Samuel reached over and playfully knocked his brother's head.

"Just think, when Samuel and Lucy have babies, we get even more!" exclaimed Mark.

Lucy and Samuel both reddened at the loud guffaws of the twins. One of them hummed the chorus to "Poor, poor, Samuel." Thomas cleared his throat. Emma followed suit by changing the subject.

"Lucy, dear, we know James got you some gift each year. I hope you don't mind, but as your mother and father-in-law, we would like to give you something in James's honor."

Lucy found it difficult to swallow. Emma got up and brought a brown paper package over. Lucy untied the string to reveal two lengths of blue cloth, one floral print and the other solid. There was also a matching length of ribbon, and lace Lucy recognized as Emma's handiwork. Tears filled Lucy's eyes.

"Thank you, Emma and Thomas, and everyone." She hugged the package to her. Samuel reached over, giving her knee a squeeze. She smiled at him.

"Would you look at that," announced Thomas, gesturing to the window. "It is starting to snow. Son, better pack up your wife and Miss Sarah and head on home."

"But the dishes—" Lucy started to protest.

Emma waved her concern away. "I have plenty of helpers."

Joe spoke up. "They could stay."

"No, they should go. It won't hurt you a bit to do some dishes."

Lucy glanced at Samuel. They would not get answers if they couldn't get Emma alone.

Emma nudged her husband and gave him a pointed look.

Thomas said, "Samuel, can you come on Thursday? I have half a dozen orders needing to be finished before we leave on Friday."

"Sure, Pa."

"Lucy, why don't you and Sarah come and we can have a baking day? Or I could come over there."

Thomas chuckled. "Lucy, she'll be inviting herself regularly now, just like she did with your ma. Claims your oven is the best around. She is always finding excuses to bake bread in it."

Lucy smiled. A baking day would be a welcome change, and she would get to ask Emma about the writing in the Bible. "Come use it, then."

"Thursday it is."

Twenty-six

THE NEW STATUS OF "MARRIED engagement," as Samuel dubbed it, came with a new set of challenges. Not the least of which was keeping their not-really-married courting chaste. Sarah would pop up unexpectedly, putting an end to any little intimacies they indulged in. The fear of their little chaperone did a good job of keeping his kisses shorter than he would have liked, which was for the best.

Lucy urged him to go hunting with his father and brothers. Samuel explained he would have been staying home anyway to watch over the farm. He'd agreed to take care of his parents' farm duties as well as theirs. Lucy still did not like him being left out but was relieved that at least she was not the cause. Waiting for answers would be easier if he was not always so near.

Each night she locked her door against the temptation to accept their marriage vows as they were. The fact that Samuel slept in Ben's bedroom helped. Sarah would surely hear them if Lucy did make it up the stairs without them creaking. If Samuel heard her on the stairs, he would send her back down. Of that she was reasonably certain.

She doubted the wisdom of Emma's advice to read the Song of Solomon. She'd followed that advice Wednesday afternoon while Sarah had slept and Samuel worked out in the barn. There was much of the song she didn't understand, but she wasn't about to ask. What was spikenard, and why did it smell? Did she need some? Should she ask Emma? Other sections made her blush when she read them with Samuel in mind. She pictured Samuel's teeth as sheep and laughed. Whoever had written the passage must have never stood downwind of sheep. Lucy decided Emma was trying to get her to see how beautiful married love could be. Or else how lovers acted like fools and spoke nonsense. She couldn't wait to say her vows regardless of what her last name might be.

Best of all, she had not had a single nightmare. She'd even walked into the barn without shaking when Sarah insisted on proving again that the tack room had the "bestest door in the world."

Thursday morning Emma arrived soon after Samuel left for the day. The two women began a double batch of bread, then Lucy started some laundry in the outdoor kettle. After a light dinner, Sarah went upstairs for a nap. Her protests lasted as long as it took for her to be tucked in with dolly.

"Why don't we knit on your mother's couch?" Emma picked up her knitting and headed for the bedroom. "We have much to discuss."

They took their seats on either side of the couch and pretended to be interested in the socks they were knitting.

Then Emma took charge of the silence. "What did your mother tell you about your birth?

"Nothing, but I heard the rumors about my being natural born." Lucy's face heated. "Then there is the Bible. When I wrote their deaths in it, I noticed something else that doesn't make sense."

Lucy set her knitting aside and retrieved the Bible. Returning, she opened it to the pages recording the last four generations of Sticzneys. She found her name and pointed to it.

"Samuel says this is your handwriting."

"So you two discussed this?" Emma raised a brow.

Lucy nodded. "It says my last name is Stickney, not Simms. Were you there? Is that why you wrote it? Can you tell me who my father is?"

"It is time for you to hear what you should have been told long ago."

Lucy fidgeted. Emma was taking too much time getting started.

"I wish your mother had done it before, but—" Emma dropped a stitch and worked to retrieve it before speaking again. "Do you have any doubt your mother loved you?"

"No. She loved me very much."

"Good. Now, where to begin..." Emma set her knitting aside and pulled the Bible into her lap.

"Perhaps this date will help." Emma turned back a page to show the first marriage of Anna Stickney to Welford Arthur Simms and the second to James Marden.

Lucy read the dates. "Mother married Mr. Simms three months before I was born."

"Now your grandfather's death date. Notice he died the week your mother married." Emma pointed to a different entry on the opposite page, to a name Lucy had rarely heard mentioned. "Mary was your aunt. You will notice she died as winter ended the year you were born. March 22, 1778. I remember the date well. It was six weeks after my own dear little Mary was born. She also died that day. It has always been a comfort to me to think of my two Marys together in heaven.

"The early months of '78 were difficult in many ways. My Thomas was away fighting the redcoats. There had been a couple of skirmishes with them farther south. He had been gone for three months by then. He never did meet our little Mary.

"Many of the men left to fight, including James Marden. He left Anna with a promise to return and marry her. Your grandfather believed that at sixteen she was too young to be wed."

Lucy looked at Emma in shock. Her mother had known James before?

"Your aunt Mary was three years older. Your age now. You resemble her, especially your eyes. She too had a soldier who had been fighting for more than a year. Welford Simms."

Lucy sucked in a breath. Her aunt had been in love with Mr. Simms? She could not reconcile anyone being in love with him. Mama had said he was different before the war, but for someone to be in love with him was beyond possible.

"Your grandfather refused Mary permission to marry Mr. Simms and did his best to discourage the romance. Grandfather Stickney never told anyone his reasons, but he was not fond of Mr. Simms. I think forbidden love was why Mary pursued him. She had a bit of stubbornness to her.

"On that day, your mother and Mary came to our place to help, as they had each day for several weeks. I had not had an easy lying-in, and Mary was a sickly baby. Samuel had just celebrated his third birthday at the time, and Thomas Jr. was five. Both boys were driving me to distraction. I was so afraid one of them would topple into the fire. Your mother and aunt were a great help to me.

"That night they left later than I would have liked. The sun was setting, a light snow falling. I asked them to stay, but they thought they must return home to help your grandfather, who had been having problems with his heart.

"As they walked up the road, they met some men—deserters from the skirmishes to the south, most likely. Cowards from both sides hiked the road during those years. Your mother was never specific about how many there were. They chased the girls into the woods and attacked them. In fighting them off, your aunt hit her head on a rock buried in the snow. After the men finished with her, she lay in the snow, unmoving. Your mother fought back. For her efforts, she was beaten as well as violated. She crawled over to your aunt and curled up. I think your mother expected to die. One of the men must have felt some remorse because he returned and covered her with an old worn blanket. The blanket and the warmth of Mary's dying body kept Anna alive."

Lucy fiddled with her yarn. Poor Mama. No wonder she'd never liked Lucy out after dark.

"Your grandfather came searching for them just past dawn the next morning. I was still up having lost my Mary mere hours before. He could barely stand, so I left him by the fire with my boys and went to search. Oh, how I wished Anna and Mary would have stayed with me. I found them both in the snow." Emma paused, and tears filled her eyes. Emma pulled a handkerchief out of her pocket and dabbed at her eyes before continuing.

"The effects of that night stayed with your mother her whole life. Your grandfather suffered as well, his health declining even more. By summer, your mother realized she was with child. When your grandfather found out, he took to his bed, never to leave." Emma put away the handkerchief.

"Several of our men came back to us in the late summer, including my Thomas and Welford Simms. They had both been wounded. As you know, Mr. Simms walked with a limp the rest of his life. By then James Marden had gone farther south and joined General Washington, where he became a valuable spy. I often wondered if things would have been different, if James had returned home with the others."

"When Welford Simms learned of Mary's death, he was furious. He blamed me since the girls had been at our place helping. He and Thomas came to blows over it before Thomas sent Mr. Simms away." Emma paused and stared out of the window.

Lucy gave up any pretense of working.

"Your mother ran this farm with the help of a twelve-year-old boy until Mr. Simms came. Your grandfather was dying and worried about how Anna would survive, so he signed the farm over to Mr. Simms after extracting a promise from Mr. Simms that he would care for your mother and give the unborn child his name and protection. Of course, every gossip in town knew what had happened. You were not the only child with an unknown father from those years of war. In those days, every woman knew it could be any of them, so we all politely pretended nothing was amiss.

"He wasn't forced or trapped into the marriage. He wanted the farm and a family. He got both. Mr. Simms married your mother under the big tree near the barn. The next Sunday they attended church and stood when the minister announced their nuptials. Mr. Simms turned and placed his hand on your mother's stomach. You should have heard the gasps."

Emma paused to chuckle at the memory. "I thought old Mistress Murdock was never going to be able to breathe again. He declared this was his son and any who disputed it would face his fist. And more than one person was acquainted with those fists.

"Your grandfather died in his sleep a few days later. Mr. Simms seemed to live up to his agreement for the next two months. The farm thrived. Every place he visited he spoke of the coming birth of his son.

"One stormy night, he sent for me. Anna was having a bad time." Lucy nodded.

"Mr. Simms paced back and forth all night. His uneven gait echoed through the cabin. It did little to settle Anna as all that separated them was the curtain drawn across the room. He finally left and went to the tavern.

"Your mother was nervous. She was worried what would happen if you were a not a boy. When she realized you were a girl, her joy was replaced by fear. She begged me to take you and keep you to replace my Mary. My heart still was too broken, and I had no milk. If I had known your future, I would have taken you and raised you. But then Samuel would have been your brother." Emma waved a hand.

Lucy didn't want him as a brother.

"Your mother fell asleep cradling you and crying. I thought it was the effects of the lying-in. I could not comprehend her fears. I stayed with your mother until the next day when Mr. Simms came through the door, demanding to see his son. Anna was feeding you.

"'I'm sorry Welford,' your mother apologized. 'She is a girl.' He let out a roar and stepped toward your mother, intent on grabbing you. Your mother shielded you with her body.

"She cried, 'Welford! Welford! Please, there will be more. Don't hurt her. She looks so like Mary. May we call her Mary?'"

"I think the thought of you resembling Mary stopped him. 'You may call that child anything you want,' he barked. 'But two names you may never call her—Mary and mine.'" He then turned to me and said, 'This whore has born a daughter. Write whatever name she bids in the Bible but make sure the last name is Stickney so all will know she is a daughter of a whore.'

"He slammed the door and left. I stayed with Anna for a week. He did not return for two."

Emma pointed to Lucy's name. "I wrote this. Your mother debated what to do. She believed Mr. Simms would not harm you. And for years, he did not—until the day you called him Papa and he broke your arm."

"I never knew he broke it because I called him Papa." Lucy puzzled over the revelation.

"I don't know if he meant to hurt you. Setting your shoulder back into place was so painful you fainted. You walked to our place with your mother often, so you knew the way. I am still not sure how you did it on your own. Imagine my surprise that morning when Samuel brought you in from the barn instead of the eggs. You were covered with scratches and dirt."

"So I am not Mr. Simms's daughter. That is why he refused to let me call him Papa." Lucy looked down at the Bible. Things were clearer now. "Why did mother not tell me?"

"I begged her to. I don't think she thought you were ready to hear or understand. I don't think she wanted to remember it. You were not conceived in love, but she loved you, and she needed a husband. Unfortunately, Mr. Simms was available at the time. As hard as life was with him, it would have been worse without him. She couldn't run this place on her own. At least Mr. Simms wanted the land enough to make sure she never starved."

"He kept promising to change. When he took you home after breaking your arm, it was a while before he hit you again. Anna was right. Even then you resembled Mary. I think as you got older it annoyed him more and more. By then it was too late. We couldn't take you away from him. Publicly he let you use the name Simms. I think that is even what is recorded in the parish record. As the war ended and we tried to move on, no one wanted to remember the deserters or what had happened to innocents like your mother and Mary.

"Anna and I encouraged you and Samuel to spend as much time as possible together. It was a safe place for both of you. He became your protector, which kept him out of trouble, and you were away from the farm. As you got older, we saw the potential for a lifelong romance, and we both hoped you would marry someday."

Lucy raised her brows. "What does Samuel know about this?"

"I told him nothing beyond what he's read in the Bible." Emma clasped Lucy's hand. "This is your story to tell."

"I mean about your plans for us to wed."

"He knows I've never been opposed to it. I give you my word I didn't force him to marry. As to your story, he may remember bits and pieces. He was three when your aunt died and I brought your mother to my place while she recovered. I've never asked him about those days, so I don't know if he remembers anything or not. He was young enough that he might not. I do encourage you to tell him soon—tonight, if you can."

Lucy kept silent for a while and then slowly nodded her head. "I will. It is hard knowing Mama was violated. But it is better than thinking she was one of the awful names Mr. Simms called her. I am glad to know I am not Mr. Simms' daughter."

"I think your mother tried to console herself that the deserter who showed some remorse and left his blanket was your father. I think he came back once during the summer and tried to apologize. There was a young stranger outside the church one day. He came up and tipped his hat to her. "Miss, I am truly sorry for all your losses and pain." Then he gave her a small leather pouch and left. Anna didn't say a word; wouldn't talk about who he was. Never said what he gave her either."

"Ach! I smell the bread burning!" Emma hurried from the room. Lucy didn't smell anything burning. She simply sat and stared out the window. A cardinal flew down to snatch something from the snow. How red he was against all the white.

Twenty-seven

LUCY SAT SHOULDER TO SHOULDER with Samuel, the Bible open before them. The clock ticked away the silence. The story became more real to her having retold it. Mama had been only three years younger than she currently was the awful night Aunt Mary had died and Lucy was conceived. Mama had survived one nightmare only to begin another. Mr. Simms had, in a way, kept his word. Though the Bible held her real name, she had been enrolled in school as Lucy Simms, and she and Mama had always had food and shelter. Knowing her mother was not any of the names Mr. Simms called her helped her love her mother all the more.

Never had she considered her mother a weak woman, even though she wished she would not have put up with Mr. Simms's bullying. Lucy could not comprehend the strength her mother must have had just to live with her circumstances.

Samuel ran his thumb back and forth over Lucy's palm. He gave her hand a gentle squeeze. "So when shall we arrange to say our vows?"

Lucy shrugged her shoulders. She had not been thinking about the future as much as the past all day. How like Papa Marden Samuel was, making him the best man she had ever known. Knowing the truth had changed nothing for him. If anything, he seemed more accepting of her. Papa Marden must have known the truth about Mama, Mr. Simms, and her. Lucy came to the conclusion he must have loved Mama more for it, not less. The same feeling emanated from Samuel. In the silence, she became more his partner than she had been an hour ago. The shared secret bound them closer. Perhaps that was what marriage was about—sharing burdens.

It was all Lucy could do to wait until she could retake her vows. With a twist of her head, she could start a kiss that would go on and on, ending beyond the closed bedroom door. Why had she wanted to wait? Oh yes. She needed to remember her wedding and do it with her real name.

Samuel brushed his fingers on her cheek. "Sweetheart, did you hear me? When shall we say our vows?"

Right here, right now. "Tomorrow?"

"Pa and the boys are leaving in a few hours, at dawn. If we want them there, we will need to wait."

"I would like to have your parents there."

"Then a week from Sunday after church? If Ma invites the reverend to dinner, he can't be too upset by having to repeat himself."

Lucy counted on her fingers. "It is Christmas Eve."

"Then it will be the best Christmas gift ever." Samuel sealed his sentence with a chaste kiss.

Samuel stepped into the kitchen, a sack over his shoulder.

Emma looked up in surprise. "I didn't expect you until later." She eyed the bag suspiciously.

"Lucy and I talked last night and decided it would be best if I moved home—"

Emma's gasp interrupted him. "No, Samuel, you must not."

"Move home for the week, Ma. We decided to get married again, or, in Lucy's mind for the first time, on Christmas Eve, when Pa is back."

Emma sat down. "Ach, son, you almost made my heart stop. So you are getting married again?"

"Providing the reverend agrees. If not, we will take our vows *verba de praesenti* that afternoon in front of you and Pa. Lucy says she wants to feel she is married before…um, well, before…" Samuel knew he turned as red as a ripe apple, and he couldn't complete the sentence.

Emma stifled a grin and nodded.

"I'll ride over each day to care for the animals. Just do the reverse of what I planned with yours. Besides, I can work in Pa's shop. I've got something special to finish up." Samuel flashed a grin before heading up the stairs two at a time, whistling the entire way.

Twenty-eight

"Absolutely not!" Reverend Woods roared. Lucy tried to shrink back into the high-backed chair in the reverend's office, and Samuel leaned forward as if trying to insert himself between Lucy and the irate minister.

Reverend Woods stood, his face a sickening shade of red. "I will not perform your marriage again. There is no need. I did it correctly the first time. I don't care what your name is in the family Bible. It is recorded in the parish record as Simms, signed with your father's own hand as I have shown you." Lucy was somewhat mollified to see that Mr. Simms had publicly kept his word about claiming her as his own.

She interrupted, realizing too late that it would only fuel the preacher's tirade. "But I did not agree to my vows the first time."

"Are you calling me a liar? All present heard you distinctly agree at the appropriate time. I signed my name to the record. Your marriage stands." He turned to Samuel. "I hold your parents responsible for this outrage. Flaunting their unsanctioned marriage has given your wife unacceptable ideas. Instead of bowing to her demands, I suggest you take her home and take her in hand." The reverend pointed to the door.

Realizing that engaging the reverend further might result in excommunication or worse, Lucy gathered her wrap and the Bible and hurried out of the room. She wondered if the reverend would use her selected scripture as the text tomorrow, keeping with the tradition for the bride to choose the text the first Sabbath after she'd wed. Samuel had been curious as to her choice, but she'd refused to tell him. Most brides found a way to poke a bit of fun at their grooms with the verse they chose. Lucy had written hers on a scrap of paper she'd handed the reverend when they'd first entered.

Reverend Woods gave an amused smile when he read the paper. Their meeting had started as well as it could. The discussion as to the validity of the marriage had gone well up to a point. The reverend had seemed more concerned about records than he was their feelings on the matter.

Lucy huffed. "That did not go at all well."

"I think we are lucky he didn't threaten to remove us from the pew and the church rolls." Samuel wrapped Lucy's cloak about her as a protection from the lightly falling snow. "I'd best get you home before this gets worse. I'll talk to Ma about saying our vows in the parlor next week after church."

Lucy tilted her head toward the privy behind the church. "Give me a moment?"

Elizabeth rubbed her bedroom windowpane to clear the frost that had accumulated on the cold glass. She couldn't believe her eyes. Samuel was coming out of the parsonage gate alone with a bundle in his hand. She could not be certain what he held through the wavy glass. Had he managed to annul his ridiculous marriage to that boorish Lucy Simms? Or had Lucy died? She could not wait until tomorrow to find out. Surely he would court her now.

Elizabeth rushed down the stairs and grabbed her cloak, fastening the silver frog and pulling up the hood. She checked her reflection in the mirror and adjusted the hood to frame her face, then pulled one curl forward and grinned. Perfect.

Taking one step toward the door, she paused and turned back to the mirror. She ripped the fichu from around her neck and adjusted her stays. The cloak was parted at the perfect angle to frame her assets. She ran out the door before she could rethink her boldness, or be seen by her father.

Samuel checked the horses while he waited for Lucy. He hadn't liked the one's gait on the way into town, but he wasn't familiar with the Marden's animals. He did not find an injury, but he decided he wasn't taking any chances. Next week he would use Old Brown. The horse would balk, as no doubt Old Brown considered being hitched to a sleigh beneath him, but Samuel would not have to worry about arriving safely at his wedding or home with the sure-footed animal.

Catching him by surprise, a woman rushed up behind him and grabbed his arm. Thinking it was Lucy, Samuel turned, a smile on his face and a kiss not far behind. His smile quickly faded as he jerked out of the vise grip on his arm. Elizabeth pressed herself closer, letting the cloak fall open more.

"Is it true? Are you rid of that insipid girl?"

Samuel stepped back, attempting to put distance between them. "Miss Garrett. I believe I made it perfectly clear last Sunday that I am a married man." Samuel continued backing around the front of the horses.

Elizabeth stalked him like a wildcat stalking its prey. "But, Samuel," she purred. "Don't you know we were meant for each other?"

Samuel reached the front of the sleigh and weighed his options. If he crossed behind the horses, would she be stupid enough to follow? He knew he could navigate the traces safely but doubted she could in that dress. The chances of her getting kicked and injured were too high. He held up his hands. "Stop! Miss Garrett, another step could get you kicked."

Elizabeth stopped. When the horse closest to her stomped his foot, she stepped back.

Lucy came around the side of the church in time to hear Samuel yell, "Stop!" She paused for a moment before realizing he was not talking to her but someone hidden from her view. She continued toward the sleigh, wondering what the problem was. Then she noticed Elizabeth stalking around the sleigh. Problem indeed. Jealousy flooded her for a moment until she recalled Samuel's description of Elizabeth throwing herself at him at church. She paused, not wanting to be too hasty in her reaction.

"Miss Garrett, I suggest you return home. I am waiting for my wife to come back and wish to have no further conversation with you." Samuel backed around the conveyance, putting more distance between them, but Elizabeth followed him.

"You expect me to believe that you want to be married to that frumpy thing?"

"What you believe is not my concern. I am happily married to Lucy and request that you cease demeaning my wife." Samuel's words had a hard edge to them. Lucy's heart soared at his defense of her. She hurried the last couple of strides to his side, then slipped her arm through his.

"Good afternoon, Elizabeth." Lucy took in Elizabeth's lack of proper attire before Elizabeth grasped at the open cloak and closed it.

"Miss Simms," she began.

"Mrs. Wilson. Mrs. Samuel Wilson," Samuel corrected as he turned to lift Lucy into the sleigh.

Elizabeth sputtered, and for one blessed moment, Lucy hoped she might have run out of things to say.

But Elizabeth tried one last time. "You can't be married to her. You don't even know who her father was. Her mother was nothing more than a tro—"

"Enough! Hold your tongue. I'd be very careful where you repeat your mother's gossip." Samuel settled into the sleigh and put his arm around Lucy. "As you are proving, Miss Garrett, one's parentage and one's character are two very different things. Lucy's character is above reproach. The same cannot be said for a woman who would repeatedly foists herself on a married man in a state of undress such as yours. Good day." Samuel flicked the reins, and the horses set off.

Elizabeth stood in the middle of the street, staring after them, her cloak flapping in the wind.

As they rounded the corner, a piercing scream caused the horses to prick their ears and speed up. "Whoa, there, steady now. It's not a panther."

Papa Marden had told Lucy that a panther's shriek sounded similar a woman's, but until now she'd never believed it.

"I am sorry you had to witness that, my love. I was as stupid as Pa's mule when I didn't run from her last fall. Forgive me?" Samuel peered at Lucy.

Lucy appraised him. "I think I shall, but it may cost you."

Samuel raised a brow. "Cost me what?"

"I shall think on it. A pirate such as ye is bound to have some treasure to share." Lucy's eyes sparkled with mischief belying the innocent face she tried to wear.

Samuel placed a hand just above her knee, sending a shiver up her spine that had nothing to do with the cold wind that had started to blow. "Aye, lass, I can think of something to share. Would a kiss be payment enough?"

Lucy's eyes grew wide. If she wasn't careful she would end up taking her vows in the snow as Emma had. She swallowed with difficulty before answering. "Yes, just one on the porch, when you drop me home." Any more than that and she would be much more like a wench than she had ever pretended to be.

Twenty-nine

THE WEEK WAS THE SHORTEST week of Lucy's life. It started well enough with the reverend using her scripture as the text for the sermon. Samuel had been embarrassed as he'd listened to her choice—1 Samuel 2, verse 26. "And the child Samuel grew on, and was in favour both with the Lord and also with men."

Snickers sounded from almost every pew. Emma pointed out that it was a good thing the twins had not been around to hear it. Daniel, Mark, and Sarah tried to make up for their absence, asking their brother if he was "in favor with woman too" so often that Emma threatened to send them to bed right after dinner.

Since Sunday, Lucy found that she didn't have enough time in the day to get everything done. There was so much cleaning and cooking and sewing. Each night she fell into bed exhausted, only to think of something she'd forgotten.

She sorted Papa Marden's clothes. Most things were too small for Samuel but about right for the twins. Emma had not needed Benjamin's clothing for her boys, so that had been donated to the church relief boxes. Lucy, though being almost the same size as her mother, found she was not yet equal to wearing her mother's clothing, and so she packed it carefully away for now, knowing that in time she might find wearing her mother's clothing comforting.

While cleaning the wardrobe, Lucy had come across a small chest carved with her mother's initials. Locked. So far her cleaning efforts had not revealed the existence of a key. She left the chest where she'd found it, knowing Sarah would be unlikely to discover it.

Old nightmares were replaced with new ones. On Tuesday night, she'd dreamed that she stood with Samuel, pledging her troth, only to have a sleeve fall off her dress because it was just basted together. Twice she dreamed that she wore her old shift without any covering. Thursday she'd dreamed all the food had spoiled and that Elizabeth had tried to wrestle her out of Samuel's arms.

Lucy and Emma worked at a feverish pace to sew a dress from the lengths of cloth Lucy had received for her birthday. At Emma's urging, Lucy had stitched the fanciest dress she'd ever owned. Feeling that it was not practical in the least, Lucy reasoned that the dark-blue petticoat could be used without the fancy overdress until Emma pointed out that it would wear out faster, leaving the overdress without a match.

"In the summer, it would be beautiful with a white petticoat trimmed in lace. You could retrim the sleeves and bodice to match," Emma suggested, her mouth full of pins during a final fitting. "That would give you another year of it not feeling old. Providing you still fit into it come summer."

"Emma!" Lucy reddened at the insinuation. Standing on a chair with Emma pinning the hem, Lucy stood trapped by her dress and a woman with a mouth full of pins.

"Can't blame an old lady for wanting more grandchildren, can you?" Emma continued without letting Lucy respond. She'd mastered the seamstress's closed-mouth way of talking with pins in one's mouth. "Even after you make Sarah a dress from the dark blue, there will be enough left of both fabrics to make a couple of smocks for my grandchildren."

The color on Lucy's face deepened. She knew her mother would be teasing about the same thing if she still lived, but it did not lessen her embarrassment.

"It is a fine thing to make a babe's first dresses from the mother's wedding clothes. It helps the father remember how things got this far.

Helps him love the babe too. Men are not too keen on them when they are crying."

Lucy found her voice. "Papa Marden was. Well, he was until they were soiled."

Emma laughed. "Even the best of fathers wants to hand the baby off then. Don't you worry. Daniel, Matt, and little Beth all gave Samuel plenty of training. He knows what to do with a wet wee one."

Samuel chose that moment to come in from the barn. Lucy leaped off the chair, scurried out of the room, then proceeded to listen to mother and son through the door.

"I told you, son, you need to knock. She doesn't want you seeing her dress before Sunday."

"Ma." Samuel dragged out the name.

"I see you rolling your eyes. It is important to her. Didn't your father explain things to you in the woodshop?"

"He told you?"

"Of course he did. You don't think the only thing he does is brush my hair at night, do you? That is our chance to talk without you and your brothers listening in. Best tradition your father ever started, brushing my hair. You might consider it too."

Lucy came back into the room in her brown work dress, her cheeks flushed and her mop cap slightly askew. If his mother had not been there, he would have crossed the room and planted a kiss on her slightly upturned lips until they'd bloomed into the full smile he craved.

It was the longest week of Samuel's life. He went to Lucy's each day, often bringing Emma, who complained that her house was too quiet with only Daniel and Mark around. He did not find it quiet with his youngest brothers dogging his steps all day. The hours he spent carving, cleaning stalls, and taking care of both farms seemed to drag by.

Samuel spent very little time alone with Lucy that week as either his mother or Sarah were usually nearby. His little brothers seemed to be underfoot more often than strictly necessary, giving him cause to wonder if they were under Ma's orders to "help him." He was smart enough not to inquire.

The result was that he had more than sufficient time to devote to creating gifts out of the maple burl. Replacing the broken mortar was more practical than frivolous, but he found the matching pestle he carved to be more a labor of love since it wasn't needed. He carved a band of flowers around the mortar bowl and caught himself humming "Lavender Blue." He couldn't wait for spring to see if the little vale was as perfect as he remembered.

The little trinket box was more precious to him, as was the cameo he hoped she would keep in it. He'd purchased the cameo in Boston. Carved from a shell reportedly from the West Indies, it reminded him a bit of piracy, and given their first kiss, was even more perfect than when he'd first spied it in the jeweler's window. Unlike the mortar and pestle, this gift would not be given on Christmas morning but on the morning of their wedding so that Lucy could wear the cameo with her new gown.

With Lucy's approval, he'd incorporated several pieces of his furniture into their home. The chest his father had built the day of the lectures found a place in their bedroom. For once he believed that one of his father's tangible reminders was a good thing. He wanted a dovetail marriage. He tucked the rocker he'd made four years ago up in the hayloft and out of sight. He planned to carve some flowers on the back. Samuel reasoned he had a few months to finish it before his wife would want a rocker of her own. Then he would start on a cradle.

Friday morning, Emma, Lucy, and Sarah ensconced themselves in the Wilson's kitchen baking a Great Cake. Emma preferred to bake the cake in Lucy's oven, but moving it would be too difficult. The recipe called for forty eggs, five pounds of flour, four pounds of sugar, four pounds of butter, and an equal amount of fruit. Since just family would be in attendance, Emma decided they could safely cut the recipe in half. It would still take over five hours to bake. They also prepared soups and suckets. The candied oranges were Sarah's favorite sweetmeat. Squashes were brought up from the cellar and boiled for pies.

The boys made general pests of themselves. Emma's broom threatened them more than once that morning. Mark found himself peeling potatoes after sticking his finger in the cake batter. Daniel pinched a sugarplum and found himself scrubbing the parlor floor. Samuel was wise enough to not get caught when he stole a few sugared almonds, along with a kiss. The kiss did earn him a stern look from his mother, so he retreated before she noticed the almonds in his hand. Samuel and his brothers vacated the house after being told that dinner would be nothing more than cheese and bread.

When Thomas and the twins returned home well after dinner, Emma rushed to tell her husband the news.

Thomas smiled ear to ear when he learned of Sunday's wedding.

Thirty

ELIZABETH GARRETT HAD NOT WORN such a dower dress to Church in her life. To be forced to wear it on Christmas Eve was almost more than she could bear. She'd played sick last week and was glad of it when she learned that Lucy had chosen the sermon text, as was her right as a new bride. This week her father had refused her pleas, and so Elizabeth found herself seated in the Garrett pew more than ten minutes before services. Even with her back to most of the congregation, she noticed the entry of the Wilsons—both families.

Just a peek at Samuel revealed that he was dressed as neatly as ever in his finest coat and new breaches. Was that a new waistcoat? She fumed at the sight of Lucy. The girl almost looked pretty. Her blue dress rivaled any in Elizabeth's wardrobe. The print was exquisite, the lace delectable. Mrs. Wilson did tat the finest laces in the area, so, of course, she would have given some to Lucy. And the hat! She hadn't seen finer this season. It must have come from Boston. The cameo—she had to get a closer look at it. If only her father would let her near. It had to be a wedding gift. She had not seen its equal.

Mr. Garrett chose that moment to enter the family pew. Seeing his daughter's gaze, he nudged her over and sat so that he blocked her view of both Wilson pews. For Elizabeth, the sermon was very long indeed.

I wonder if this is how Elizabeth feels each week. Lucy was aware of the many admiring eyes upon her. Samuel's possessive hand on her back added a thrill all of its own. Several women delivered compliments before taking their seats. Other's nodded as she passed. Sitting in the pew next to Samuel, she found she had no desire to look to the front of the church as she should. She kept peeking at him. He traced patterns upon her wrist for most of the service, the feelings his thumb evoked were very distracting. All too soon the service was over, and they stood for the final hymn.

Samuel thought Reverend Woods had deliberately preached an extended sermon this morning. Was it possible to recite Isaiah and Luke so slowly? However, when the services were over, the noon bell chimed just as it should. Samuel was glad Reverend Woods had refused the invitation to officiate the second wedding. He could not abide a second long-winded sermon today. Pa said he would like to say a few words but promised they would be short. Samuel gave Lucy's hand a squeeze, wondering if she were just as excited as he was.

The Wilson's large parlor overflowed with laughter and love. Thomas tried three times to quiet his brood. Finally, he sent Joe and John to opposite sides of the room as he had when they were little. His grandson shrieked in Junior's arms until he settled in the embrace of his grandmother, where he put his thumb in his mouth and promptly fell asleep.

Samuel adjusted his collar instead of rubbing the back of his head. Ma threatened him with the back of her wooden spoon if he rubbed it even once that afternoon. He doubted she would, but he didn't want to push his luck.

Before him stood Lucy, more beautiful than even an hour before. In her hands she held a bouquet of dried lavender and some other flowers Carrie had provided. Her maple-syrup hair had been twisted and turned and pinned into something he itched to undo. One tendril had been pulled over her left shoulder. He longed to wrap it around his fingers. Lucy blushed under his scrutiny.

Thomas cleared his throat. "I want to read a few words from the Bible before you vow your love to each other. From Ephesians: 'Husbands, love your wives, even as Christ also loved the church and gave himself for it.' And also this verse: 'So ought men to love their wives as their own bodies. He that loveth his wife loveth himself.' And lastly this one: 'Nevertheless let every one of you in particular so love his wife even as himself; and the wife see that she reverence her husband.'

"Your Ma and I have tried to live these words our whole lives. Even though they are addressed to the husbands, much guidance can be found in replacing the word *husband* with *wife*. You know I would be lying if I said we've never had our troubles. You children have eaten burned porridge enough to know when we don't always agree."

Emma blushed as her children turned to her. She had managed to "accidently" scorch meals from time to time when she was at odds with Thomas.

"But she always makes it up to all of us with a tasty cake." Everyone laughed.

Thomas continued. "I can't tell you how to run your marriage, so I will leave you with this thought. There is nothing better than waking my dear Emma each morning and knowing she is happy to see me. Samuel, when you wake up each morning, wake Lucy and let her know how happy you are to see her for another day that God has given you. Lucy, find it a blessing to wake up and smile at your husband each morn."

Though the room was full, Lucy found her heart was missing a few people. How she would love to have Papa Marden standing there, adding his advice. She was sure he would have advised them to pray together often and remember the Lord in all things. Mama would have given her last bits of advice when Lucy had dressed, as Emma had just minutes ago while pinning Lucy's hair.

"Now, take each other's hands." Lucy passed her bouquet to Sarah and placed her hands in Samuel's. When she looked into his eyes, the rest of the room faded from her view. She listened to Thomas speak and watched as Samuel said yes, his gaze never faltering. When it was her turn to respond, Samuel had to bring her out of her daydreaming with a light squeeze to her fingertips. Carrie and Emma both let tiny giggles escape at her blunder. Apparently Lucy was not much better at saying her vows when conscious.

When Thomas finished, Samuel first drew Lucy's fingers to his lips, earning him boos from his brothers. Then, stepping closer, he pressed his lips to hers, a cheer went up around the room.

As the sun hastened its descent toward the horizon, Samuel wrapped his arms around his new wife's waist and kissed her under the mistletoe the twins had hung in the doorway. The entire family laughed. Sarah jumped up and down, clapping and yelling, "Again! Again!" Her exuberance rained bits of dried lavender from her sister's bouquet around the room. The twins rolled their eyes. One of them hummed the refrain to "No, no, oh, so, no. Oh, oh, poor Samuel." Little did they know he wasn't feeling poor at all.

"Best get going, son. The snow is coming down pretty hard. Hate for you two to get stuck in a snowbank." Thomas winked at them.

Samuel settled Lucy's cloak over her shoulders, adjusting it to cover all of the new blue dress.

Then they hurried out to the sleigh as snowflakes danced about, covering them like tossed rice.

Tucking the blankets around Lucy, Samuel paused to kiss a snowflake off her nose. Lucy crinkled her nose and blushed to the shouts and whistles of his brothers.

"Go on!" The twins yelled in unison from the porch. Samuel grasped the reins and set them off with a flick of his wrist.

Sarah held Emma's hand and waved. Samuel would miss the chatterbox this next week. Or maybe not.

Lucy let out a sigh.

"Happy?"

"Yes, it was a perfect day. Do you think Elizabeth is still pouting?" she asked.

Samuel roared with laughter. "She may be recovered by now. I doubt she will repeat any more of her mother's gossip about you for a long time. It seems as if her father has taken her to task."

"Yes, I noticed her dress wasn't very fashionable."

"Did I mention how beautiful you are in your new dress?" Samuel gave his wife an appreciative look.

Peeking under her lashes, Lucy answered, "You may have mentioned it a time or two."

Samuel leaned in for a kiss, his lips not quite touching Lucy's when the sleigh stopped with a jolt, ripping them apart. Old Brown protested, snorting and stomping.

"It would seem we are stuck." Samuel completed the kiss, ignoring his horse's protests.

"I wonder if this is how your parents got stuck all those years ago."

"Hmmm. Maybe so." He kissed her again. "But since it is daylight and we are on the road, let me see if I can get us out of this." He leaped from the sleigh. A few pushes and maneuverings later, Samuel and Lucy were once again gliding over the snow and toward home.

Samuel put Old Brown in the barn, rewarding him with two carrots pilfered from Ma's cellar. All the animals received their nightly feed early. The sun had not yet set, but he had no intention of coming back to the barn tonight or reappearing at the crack of dawn. He gave the animals as much water as their troughs could hold. Nanny had dried up two days ago—a Christmas gift from the goat. Speaking of Christmas, Samuel realized he needed to retrieve a few gifts.

He reached inside of the tack room and pulled Lucy's gifts off the top shelf. She'd nearly discovered them yesterday. He could not believe it when she'd stepped into the room to inspect it. He had hidden her Christmas and wedding gifts in there just that morning. He'd joined her and blocked her view of the carved mortar and pestle with a kiss. Then, with his arms around her, he'd twirled her out of the little white room before she'd noticed the small jewelry box. He smiled.

The kisses had been full of promises from both of them. Lucy would dream different dreams of the tack room now.

Lucy smoothed the new yellow-and-blue star quilt Emma had given her on the day of their first wedding over the new linen sheets. She paced, wondering if she'd forgotten anything. A dinner of leftovers was tucked in the oven, kept warm if they decided to eat later. She wore a new shift made of fine muslin, one her husband had not seen, under her dress. She fiddled with her hair. Should she take it down?

She sat at the dressing table, her fingers hovering over the first hairpin, when she heard the door close. Samuel fastened the bolt with a thunk, closing out the world. Lucy's hand froze over her hair. Her husband was coming.

"I hope you are not going to deny me the privilege of removing those pins myself and brushing your hair."

Lucy let her hand drop to her lap. "Never."

Samuel dropped a kiss on the nape of her neck and pulled out the first pin. What he whispered in her ear, she never told. The mirror reflected her blush. He reached for the second pin.

As the golden fingers of dawn crept in the window that Christmas morning, Samuel woke Lucy with a kiss. Lucy opened her eyes, and a smile bloomed. To Samuel, it was more radiant than the sunrise beyond their window.

Reaching up, she stroked her husband's cheek, coaxing him to give her a second kiss. After several more, Lucy nestled into his side.

"This is how I always want to wake up."

With another kiss, Samuel promised her she always would.

The End

Historical Notes

MODERN READERS MAY BE CONFUSED at colonial meal times. The term *lunch* was not commonly used, though it first appeared in a London play in 1786. The 1810 edition of Webster's dictionary defined lunch as "a large piece of food." The noon meal was referred to as "dinner" and the evening meal as "supper." The larger meal was served at noon, and often leftovers were served for the evening and breakfast meals. Drinking water was considered unhealthy, and depending on the source, this was generally true. Germ theory was not yet known, and often the same water that provided drink for one family had been fouled upstream by another. Weak ale, beer, and hardened cider, along with boiled drinks such as tea, chocolate, and coffee made up the majority of colonial beverages.

Marriage laws and practices varied widely throughout New England both before and after the Revolutionary War. As colonists, the citizens were subject to British common law. For example, a woman could not be forced to wed without her consent or own property independent of her husband in most cases. However, each colony was run semi-independently, and common law was oftentimes ignored, giving women far greater freedoms than allowed in England.

Throughout all the colonies, common-law marriage, also know by the Latin *verba de praesenti*, was practiced by couples exchanging vows in front of witnesses and others not. This was particularly true in smaller settlements on the edges of the frontier. There are anecdotal stories of young women secreting friends in closets or other places so that the groom could not plead misunderstanding a few months later. Even Benjamin Franklin, who courted his wife for some time, never had an official ceremony and lived in a common-law marriage.[1]

Puritans in Massachusetts viewed marriage as a secular matter. They are credited with requiring the first marriage "licenses" in the Americas. The term *license* is perhaps a misnomer, as the local clerk was paid three pence, the 1644 price, per entry in the court register, making it a marriage registration rather than what we consider a license. This system of recordings did not follow that of England and seems to have been a new invention of the Colonists.[2] Massachusetts marriages during the early colonial period were most often carried out by a magistrate or justice of the peace, and usually at the bride's home.

By the time of the Revolution, Massachusetts lawmakers also required a fifteen-day waiting period when "intentions" were posted either over the pulpit or by written notice in a public place, such as the post office. The colony of New Hampshire offered same-day marriages for two shillings as a way to expand their prerevolutionary coffers. Meanwhile, New York, which included modern-day Vermont, recognized common-law marriages for some years after the war for independence.

I took the liberty of combining these traditions in the unconventional marriage of Emma and Thomas Wilson, which took place before America's independence. In Massachusetts, they could have been fined for fornication as well as for failure to register their wedding—thus their claim that they had been in New York.

The Massachusetts Justice, written in 1795 by Samuel Freeman, was an invaluable tool in determining laws not only for marriage but for swearing, nonattendance at church, and other misdemeanors that do not exist today. The section on marriage included the forms the clerk

---

1 Walter Isaacson, *Benjamin Franklin: An American Life* (New York: Simon & Schuster, 2003), 75.

2 Robert René Kuczynski, "The Registration Laws in the Colonies of Massachusetts Bay and New Plymouth," *Publications of the American Statistical Association*, vol. 7, no. 51 (September 1900), 1–9.

would have needed to use to post intentions and record marriages. Curiously, the bride and groom did not sign these documents. The Boston Library has digitized several "intention to marry" notices that have survived until today. I suppose some brides kept them as keepsakes.

People in Massachusetts were slow to give up their Puritan traditions. Rings, which had not been exchanged at Puritan weddings, slowly came into vogue. John Hancock did give his wife, Dorothy, a plain gold band on the occasion of their wedding in 1775. However, he was one of the richest merchants in Massachusetts, and it is unlikely that those not of the same class had rings to exchange.

The majority of weddings continued to be officiated by magistrates in homes well into the nineteenth century. Ministers of the various religions performed weddings depending mostly on the sect's views on marriage and were required to report these weddings to the courts. Since the parish ministers were funded in part by local taxes through the early 1830s, one could say most marriages were performed by public officials.

For the marriage of Samuel and Lucy, I chose a more traditional religious marriage but took the wording from *The Massachusetts Justice*, which stipulated that the bride and groom hold hands. It did not, however, stipulate a kiss.

Though weddings were quiet, home-based affairs, the celebrations spilled over into the public eye. Brides were allowed to choose the text for the first sermon given after their marriage, and they often used great ingenuity in choosing these texts. Abigail Smith, who married John Adams, decided upon the text: "John came neither eating bread nor drinking wine, and ye say he hath a devil." In some congregations, it was also tradition for the newlyweds to stand and display their wedding finery during the sermon.

The folk song "Lavender's Blue" first appeared in print in the 1600s and was a popular tavern song with several bawdy verses. By the early 1800s it was sanitized for a children's rhyme. In the last fifty years, the song has been modified by Burl Ives and the movie industry to be family friendly. Having been a bachelor at Harvard and having been to various local pubs, Samuel would have been familiar with the racier verses, which would never make the cut for a G-rated movie or this book.

Acknowledgments

THERE ARE NOT ENOUGH WAYS to thank those who helped me bring about this first book. I dedicated this book to my eleventh grade English/Humanities teacher, Marie Lindsley Rinard, because she had faith in me all those years ago and started me on a thirty-year journey. I will say no more here as curious readers will find that story on my blog.

Anita and Tammy have been there for years encouraging, alpha reading, beta reading and re-reading and then talking me into not giving up and assisting in photo shoots of daughters (Araceli and Amaya), Massachusetts blizzards and cabins. I know I would have quit without both of you cheering me on.

Huge thanks to my first beta readers; Michelle, Julie, Naomi, Nanette and Erin. I hope you recognize the book. The writer friends I picked up on the way especially Sally, Nicole and Cindy, whose critics and input have been invaluable. Thanks to all the writers in Cache Valley League of Utah writers, and iWriteNetwork, each of you have made me a better writer. Thank you for your part in my growth as a fledging writer.

Nancy, Stephani and Yvonne thanks for describing the taste of wine to this Mormon girl.

Kami H. thank you for your advice to rewrite sections in adherence with Commonwealth laws of 1795.

Thanks also to Michele at Eschler Editing for the edits and finding oh so many little things to fix, any mistakes left in this book are not her fault.

My family, especially my mother, Bonnie, who read and spell corrected all four hundred versions of the manuscript. To my children Kendon, Dallin, Katelyn, and Eileen for sharing their home with the fictional characters who often got fed better than they did. And my husband who encouraged me every crazy step of the way, and who is my example for every love story I dream up. The real one is better.

And to my Father in Heaven for putting these wonderful people, and any I may have forgotten to mention, in my life. I am grateful for every experience and blessing I have been granted to form my life.

Waking Lucy
is the recipient of the
2017 Recommended Read Award
in the League of Utah Writers
published book contest

About the Author

L ORIN GRACE WAS BORN IN Colorado and has been moving around the country ever since, living in eight states and several imaginary worlds. She holds a degree in graphic design which comes in handy with creating book covers. Currently, she lives with her husband, and a dog who is insanely jealous of her laptop.

When not writing, Lorin enjoys creating graphics, visiting historical sites, museums, painting furniture, and reading. Three of her books, her debut novel, *Waking Lucy* (2017), *Mending Fences* (2018), and *Not the Bodyguard's Baby* (2020) have won Recommend Read awards in the League of Utah Writers Published book contest.